OREGON AT LAST BOOK 2

CHRISTMAS IN OREGON

A.T. BUTLER

CHRISTMAS IN OREGON

Historical Women's Fiction

OREGON AT LAST
BOOK 2

A.T. BUTLER

CHAPTER ONE

While scrubbing the soil off the potatoes she would be using for supper, Annie Wheeler—formerly Annie Hudson—let her mind drift. She had been alone most of the day and was keeping herself occupied with memories of her wedding just a couple weeks earlier. Though unsure how long it would take her to feel like a wife, she hoped she would never forget the special details of the day she vowed to be one. The way the whole town, it seemed, had turned up to support her. The small bouquet, including pine boughs, collected by half a dozen little girls, all excited about the first wedding in their new little settlement. The way her betrothed had looked at her, promise and joy in his eyes.

Her whole life had changed before that, over the previous year, and the day she got married had been the end of a very long journey. And the start of another.

She set the cleaned potatoes to the side of the broad, rough wooden table. This had been one of the first pieces of furniture her husband had made when they moved to Eden Valley, their new home in the Oregon Territory. Annie and Isaac Wheeler had been married as soon as their home had been completed, on a homestead he had chosen a few miles outside of what would be the center of town. Now, alone in the one-room cabin, everywhere Annie looked she saw a project that needed to be finished —or, in the case of the empty corners waiting for more furniture, begun. Poring over her memories helped keep her from being too overwhelmed at her unending list of chores.

Annie carried the bowl of dirty water to the door and stepped outside. She noticed that the sun was low in the sky. Winter was coming and the days were ever shorter. As soon as she'd had the chance, Annie had planted a winter garden on their new homestead, around the side of the house where it would get the most sun, but time would tell if it would be a success. Nevertheless, she carried her bowl to her plot and watered what she could; she doubted any of the root vegetables she'd planted would make it this first winter, but she wanted to try. She needed to learn how to live in this brand-new wilderness, not just to survive as she had been doing all the long previous year.

As she returned to her front door, a broad swathe of orange sunlight cut through the clouds, through the trees near the horizon, and across the meadow that led to the front of Annie's cabin. She felt the warmth on her shoulders and turned to squint into what little light remained of the day. The Oregon Territory was far more overcast and rainy than her home in Virginia had been, and Annie had taken to seeking out every bit of sun she could get, even just this little final sunset.

There had been no ray of sunshine on her wedding day, no blush of spring flowers or warm afternoon in which to relax; it had not, by any stretch of the imagination, been what a person might call a beautiful day. Her wedding to Isaac Wheeler had taken place on a chilly day in early November. It had been a day of such cold and wet that no amount of significant progress would be made on the buildings going up around the settlement. And so, they figured they might as well get married instead.

The Sullivan-Mills wagon company had reached the Oregon

Territory in the middle of October, had chosen a site to develop, and had immediately set up a more long-term camp. Annie had been living out of one of the Hudson family's wagons with her sister, sister-in-law, and nephew. It was crowded, but no more so than over the ten months it had taken them to get all the way to Oregon from Virginia. Of the forty families that were settling this community together, most of them continued to live from wagons and tents while more permanent homes were built. The men of each family joined together and, under the direction of their new mayor, George Mills, cooperated to get proper structures up before the first snow fell. Now that they were expecting snow any day, the pace of work was even more frantic.

Returning to her kitchen—the table, fireplace, and couple shelves on one side of the room—Annie began chopping up the potatoes she had just washed. Her husband had trapped a rabbit in the meadow behind their home, collecting it just that morning but leaving before he could skin it for her. This was a task that Annie had never done before arriving in Oregon; in Virginia the Hudson sisters had only ever bought their meat from Mr. Healy, the butcher. Though Isaac still skinned their game when he had time, Annie was getting better at it. This time it only took her less than an hour, and with far less mess than previous attempts.

She smiled to herself as she cut up the potatoes; she couldn't wait to tell Isaac of her accomplishment.

The meat had been cooking slowly over a low heat, and she had since added onion, carrot, and a handful of dried peas; the potatoes would be the last to go in. But now that she'd seen how late it was, Annie was dismayed to realize she had run out of time to cook everything properly. She chopped them hastily, as small as she could, hoping they would be cooked and tender enough by the time Isaac returned.

The hearty aroma of the stew filled their home. Annie took a deep, appreciative sniff as she stirred in the potatoes and recovered the pot.

The last several weeks the wagon company had spent on the Oregon Trail had been fraught with hunger and scarcity. Many of the families had reached the end of their supplies long before they reached the end of the trail. Though the Hudsons had been luckier than most, Annie still hadn't grown used to the relative abundance that came simply from living in one spot. From having space to store what they could, not to mention the occasional access to the closest fort and its port. Even before she married, when she was still sleeping in a wagon, several of the young men had traveled to Fort Vancouver to bring back food, supplies, and even, in some cases, little treats. The onions, potatoes, peas, and carrots that made up tonight's supper had been grown by the families who had settled Oregon Territory the previous years.

Contributing to the general welfare in the territory would be part of her own job in the year to come, though Annie wasn't certain how she would manage it.

When she had lived in Virginia with her sisters, Annie had contributed to the household by teaching piano to the children of Norfolk. The money she'd earned had helped purchase much of their necessities. Yes, the Hudsons had a kitchen garden, but that had been mostly her sister Josie's responsibility. Annie, on the other hand, still felt uncertain about her skills.

At Annie and Isaac's wedding, Josie had tried to gift her the best chopping knife she had brought west from Virginia, but they'd managed to convince her to keep it. Isaac had enough to stock their home, as he had been in the Oregon Territory already for a couple years. Beyond that, though, was what had gone unsaid: Josie didn't have a man to provide for her; she would need to hang on to every resource she had until that day came.

While the vegetables cooked down and the stew simmered, Annie settled into one of their two chairs and tried to focus on her knitting. She had so far completed one sock for Isaac and hoped to finish the other today.

But now, she realized, looking around the room, she had run

out of light. The front door of the cabin was still propped open as it had been most of the day, but all the light that had poured in earlier was now gone. The room's only illumination now was the fire. She rose to close the door against the cold and light the lamp that sat in the middle of their table.

Isaac would be home at any time. She should have put the potatoes in earlier. Fretting, Annie crossed to the pot and stirred it. She looked hopefully at the vegetables, wondering if she should add more wood to the fire to make it hotter, to make sure the potatoes would be cooked all the way. But what if doing so would overcook the rabbit? Annie wasn't sure. She didn't know quite how to do all this. It smelled good, so far, but that was no guarantee of anything.

After their parents had died, her sister Josie hadn't just been in charge of the Hudsons' garden; she had been the family's homemaker. While their oldest sister Louisa had tended to her seamstress business and Annie to her piano, Josie had made sure that their home was clean and well-stocked. She had cooked every meal, repaired most things that needed doing, and kept track of what their home needed. Josie had never complained, and Annie had been grateful, but now she realized that all the skills and habits her mother had tried to train in her were rusty from disuse.

And so, she did things like add the potatoes to her stew too late for them to cook thoroughly before her husband returned home after a long day of work.

With a sigh, Annie decided she could make the fire a tiny bit bigger, let the stew cook a tiny bit longer. All she could do then was hope everything worked out. Isaac had so far been easy to be married to, but she didn't want to give him any reason to regret his choice.

It was just stew, she reminded herself.

She checked that there was water in the kettle before putting it too over the fire.

Annie had spent so long worrying about even making it to Oregon; she hadn't had time to worry about what was waiting for her when she got here. But the truth was, by answering the newspaper advertisement to be Isaac Wheeler's bride, Annie was walking into a marriage and a life from which she knew little what to expect.

The front door swung open, and a broad smile took over her entire expression when she saw her husband enter.

"Hello, wife," he said genially, as he hung his hat and coat on the hook installed just inside the door.

Though their one-room cabin had only just been completed a couple weeks earlier, Isaac had spent every spare minute improving and in general making it as cozy and comfortable of a home as he could. His strong work ethic was one of the first things Annie had noticed about him. She had at first protested his constant activity, insisting that he should rest after a long day of hauling logs to build walls, but only half-heartedly; in the end, her desire for a home of her own, after months in a wagon, had won out.

"Supper will be ready in maybe fifteen minutes or so," she announced, crossing the room to greet him.

Isaac kissed her cheek, squeezed her upper arm with one hand, and passed her to settle with a tired groan in the other chair.

"How was your day? I didn't expect you all to be working after dark."

"Well, it was a big day." He leaned forward to remove his boots, groaning again as each foot was freed. "We finished Daniel Mills's place. There was only a few more steps to take when the sun set, so about half a dozen of us lit a couple lamps and stayed to finish."

Annie gasped with delight. "Does that mean they'll be getting married soon? I know how much Caroline longs for that."

He nodded. "Think so," he said, massaging his feet. "Not that we talk a lot about wedding plans, you know. Me and Daniel." Isaac chuckled and leaned back in his chair.

Annie set a cup of hot tea in front of him. "Since that house is finished, does that mean you'll be moving on to another project tomorrow? Or will you get to stay home with me?"

He gave her a sad smile. "You know all I want is to stay home with you, but weather is coming and there are far too many women and children without a roof over their heads still. Including your sisters. The mayor even has a number of us diverted from finishing the church and general store, so folks like old Mrs. Norton can have a proper bed soon. No, I think tomorrow I'm to help put up the final walls for the Abbott family's place."

Annie stirred her stew as she listened. "And my sisters?"

"Soon, I think. I'll remind Mills again tomorrow."

"Thank you."

He gave a contented sigh. "Feels like we're really making this place our own, doesn't it?"

Annie smiled.

CHAPTER TWO

"Tell me all about your day," Annie had said, and Isaac had complied. As they waited the final minutes for the stew to finish, she listened while he brought her all the news of their new little community.

In addition to finishing the house for the younger Mills family, another team of men had finished the house for Frank and Hope Waters, and a third team was finishing up the church for Pastor Montgomery. Ben Findley was making a list for his next trip to Fort Vancouver. Young Amy Cole was constantly underfoot at the work sites, determinedly helping Dr. Martell—whether he wanted it or not. The burgeoning town of Eden Valley was gaining a foothold in the wilds of the Oregon Territory, and every day that Isaac set out to help fell trees, till soil, or build a wall, he became more and more connected to these folks he had only just met. Annie peppered him with questions, fascinated and impressed by all that was being accomplished every day.

"Seems like it took you only a few weeks to learn everyone's names," Annie said. She stirred the rabbit stew again, looking anxiously at the vegetables and trying to determine if they were cooked all the way through. One of the smaller potato pieces she was able to smash against the side of the pot, demonstrating it had been cooked thoroughly. That was probably enough, then. She didn't want to make Isaac wait any longer, so she served up a hearty helping. "I think it must have taken me months, and probably the only reason I made a friend at all was because she sought me out."

"Are you lonely out here all by yourself?"

"Not as much as I expected to be, I think. It's nice to have the quiet and the space after the chaos of traveling in the wagon company. Strange being away from my sisters, though. I'll probably get used to it eventually."

Annie set the bowl of steaming-hot stew in front of her husband, then placed a folded scrap of worn cotton next to it. Filling the second bowl for herself, Annie sat beside him in the small corner of the house that served as their kitchen. Besides the two chairs, the Wheelers had exactly two bowls, two plates, two mugs, and two sets of silverware—all of which Isaac had brought with him from his previous home in Dempsey. He had left most of the furniture, saving the space in his wagon with the confidence he could easily again build what he needed. Annie knew this was just the start of their life together, that one day she might again have such things as a serving platter used only for Christmas or even a separate room just for dining. But for right now, this stark fare was still better than the alternative of squatting in the dirt and eating over a campfire.

Isaac unfolded the napkin and placed it in his lap as he leaned over his bowl of stew with a pleased expression. "This the rabbit?" he asked, scooping up a bite.

"Yes, and skinning it earlier today was my quickest time yet. One of these days I might even do it as quickly as you can."

"So proud of you," he responded with a teasing grin. His chewing slowed as a confused look crossed his face. "Is this . . . what's in this?"

"Just the same thing I always put in stew. Why?"

But Annie knew without having to ask. She braced herself for his criticism.

He shook his head. "The, uh . . ." He swallowed, with seeming effort. "The potatoes. They're not quite—"

"Oh, I know, I'm sorry," Annie responded in a rush. "I added them too late. They didn't all have enough time to cook all the way through. I'm so sorry. I mean, they won't hurt you, but . . . I know. I'm sorry. It was stupid of me."

"It's fine," he reassured her, though Annie thought she could hear the disappointment in his voice. "Now you know for next time. I'd rather not be chewing my vegetables raw, you know."

Annie nodded and took her first spoonful of the stew herself. The potato in that bite was hot all the way through; at least there was that. But, yes, she should have added them much sooner. It seemed as though every day she came across some task or skill that she needed to learn, and every day she was disappointed in herself for getting to age twenty-six without knowing it yet.

She tucked the loose strand of blond hair behind her ear and watched his expression carefully, for clues of how upset he might be as he picked around the larger pieces of potatoes. A man who worked as hard as he did all day deserved the best she could give him, and the guilt from her error overwhelmed her, though she tried reminding herself that she had only really known Isaac for a month or so. Maybe she wouldn't be able to recognize his specific habits or tics just yet.

Isaac Wheeler had been living in the Oregon Territory for two years already, having originally come west with his first wife. When his wife, Gertie, had died on the journey out, Isaac wasted no time in placing an ad for a new bride in the newspaper in his hometown of Richmond, Virginia.

True, they had exchanged a handful of letters when she had responded to the newspaper listing, but all sense of his temperament and how he would be to actually live with had not been apparent until he had appeared on the Oregon Trail. It had happened one fateful day in October, when a group of men from the town of Dempsey had come looking for the Sullivan–Mills wagon company. The son of the captain of the wagon train had ridden on ahead looking for assistance, as the forty families that had almost made it to the territory didn't have enough food or energy to travel the final miles. They needed all the help they could get lest they become stuck in the mountains over the winter like previous companies had suffered.

And so, Annie's first meeting Isaac in person was at a time when he was there to veritably rescue her. The gratitude she felt for her future husband in that moment had been tremendous. He had taken care of her; he had taken care of her whole family and others besides, even teasing her a bit about her need to be rescued. In the weeks that followed, Isaac had worked ceaselessly to build them a new home, here in Eden Valley so Annie could stay near her family and friends. He was giving up the life that he had begun nearly ten miles away in Dempsey, yet never once did he complain.

Annie never wanted to give Isaac any reason to regret the things he had done and continued to do for her every day.

"I'm sorry," she said again. "I'll do it better next time. You don't have to eat that. I can . . . I can find something else for supper, maybe."

"It's all right," he insisted, with perhaps a bit of frustration in his tone. "It's fine. Really. Just remember for next time. But we can't waste any of this."

Annie nodded and took another bite. It really wasn't that bad, she admitted to herself. Whatever potatoes he ate around, she would return to the pot to be warmed up again in the morning. It could have been worse. And she truly meant it when she said she wouldn't make that mistake again.

Though it seemed as though there was always a new mistake

to make. Maybe one day she would reach the end of the mistakes she could make.

The pair ate in silence for several minutes while Annie worried over her new husband's reaction.

"How was your day?" he finally asked, as he scraped the last bits of gravy from the bottom of his bowl. "You skinned a rabbit. What else?"

"The stew," she said with a gesture. "And the loaf of sour-dough. Both took longer than I expected. I'm not quite used to being in charge of all the cooking."

"You'll get the hang of it. My wife always used to say just when she solved one problem, four more would crop up."

Annie froze at the mention of his wife. His *first* wife, he should have said. His wife who had passed. The wife of his youth, who Annie heard about more and more every day. She knew they had married young and had been very happy. There was no part of Annie that wished Isaac had been lonely and miserable before he married her; she did wish, though, that he wouldn't compare her to Gertie Wheeler as often as he did.

"And I, um," she stumbled on, trying to remember what she had been saying. "Oh! I knit a sock for you. I can finish the pair tomorrow, I think. I cleaned the floor . . . There must have been something more, but I can't recall."

Annie looked around their small home. There was so much still to do to make it a comfortable place for them to live that it was overwhelming. If they had all the goods and supplies needed, she could easily fill her days from morning till night with sewing and repairs and cleaning and cooking. Next fall she would be busy, hopefully, preserving all the crops they would be growing over the next year. Maybe a child would come along one of these years. Maybe they would build a bigger house, with even more rooms that needed to be kept clean.

The work was unending, and it was so much for her to get

used to. This was not how Annie was accustomed to spending her time.

"Although," she said with a hopeful smile, "if the piano was here I probably could have spent all day playing that."

Isaac sighed and leaned back in his chair. "I'm sorry. I don't know what the delay is. I know I told you the piano would be here by the time you got here, but I probably shouldn't have promised such a thing."

"It's all right," she assured him. "I didn't mean to make you feel bad. There must be all manner of things that can delay a ship coming all the way around Cape Horn. Maybe it's better I'm not so distracted by it."

"Hopefully we can get it before winter sets in. I've dreamed of evenings sitting by the fire, listening to you play. A little Christmas dram of whiskey, fresh cinnamon rolls, and my wife singing my favorite holiday hymn."

"Me too. Maybe with my sisters," she answered, relieved that any frustration over the potatoes seemed to have dissipated. "That sounds like exactly how I would like to spend Christmas. Our first Christmas in Oregon."

CHAPTER THREE

As the days grew colder and the end of the year drew closer, the people of Eden Valley became more and more frantic. Every hour that slipped by needed to see more progress, and each settler became more fixated and desperate to put sturdy wooden walls between themselves and the inevitable harsh winter. Sleeping in a covered wagon, with only a piece of heavy canvas to protect from the rain and cold, may have been fine in July, but by December it led mothers to fear for their children's fingers, or fathers to question their ability to take care of their family.

For the next several days, it seemed as though Isaac was only home long enough to sleep. Even without him saying so, Annie could feel the mounting pressure like an approaching storm. There were still so many families that didn't have the protection they needed from the winter that was nearly upon them. Annie wished she could help more, but it was all she could do to stay on top of her own cooking and cleaning.

Why had she never realized how much work keeping a house was?

Still, both Wheelers pressed on, daydreaming about resting

soon, grateful for what they had and what they were able to share with their neighbors.

Finally, they reached the big event that everyone in town had been waiting for—the church had been completed. It was the largest structure in Eden Valley, large enough to hold most of the town at once. Though time may bring a town hall or school, at the moment Pastor Luke Montgomery's church would be the central location for the folks of the town to gather.

On the last Thursday evening in November, the pastor invited all who wanted to pray over the finished building to join him an hour before sunset. Though it was right before suppertime for most families, nearly the entire population in Eden Valley streamed toward the small, rough building that day. Each and every person had been stretched so thinly in getting everything done that they all gladly seized this chance to come together as a community.

Isaac came home in the late afternoon and the Wheelers rode their wagon into town, along with some of the other families who had built their homesteads miles out. As she walked hand in hand with Isaac down the dirt path to the new church from where they had left the wagon, Annie watched the tired yet exhilarated faces of the other women who were present. They entered the new building, full of the fresh scent of cut lumber, and Annie let her eyes adjust to the dim light. There were no pews—those would have to come later—nor yet was there a pulpit. No windows; no art. Not even any paint to freshen up the walls. On the surface, the church was nothing more than a blank wooden box. But even walking through the door, Annie could feel the peace and sacredness of a house of worship.

The only thing actually inside the church was a long table at the front, near the altar, upon which stood maybe a dozen lit taper candles, each burned down to various heights.

"I need to go talk to John Pierce," Isaac told her. "You'll be all right alone?"

"Of course."

"I'll come find you again when I'm done."

Annie nodded, but she was already distracted listening to the conversations around her as more and more families squeezed into the space. Excited children, asking where the stained-glass windows would go. Pompous men, eager to impress whoever would listen with what they personally had contributed to the construction. Serene women, trying to manage all of it.

Annie aspired to be one of those women. Like Mrs. Sullivan: The woman had gone from wife of one of the company captains, with half a dozen children and all the responsibility that entailed, to widow, losing one child to death and gaining another surrogate daughter. She had been through so much yet still wore a smile.

"Hey there," Annie heard whispered in her ear. "Fancy meeting you here."

Her dear friend Rebecca Tenney stood just at her left shoulder and grinned when Annie turned to look at her. The two women gave each other a quick hug, leaning in to whisper while Pastor Montgomery moved to the front of the room.

"I've missed you," Annie said in a low voice. "Laundry is very different without you to chat with."

Rebecca tittered. While the wagon company was making their way west, she had always managed to find Annie on laundry days, always trying to cajole her into washing Rebecca's own clothes too. It had become a regular joke between them, and Annie missed the camaraderie.

"Well, it's probably nice for you to only have one other person's laundry to do, rather than four, huh? How's married life treating you?"

"Less laundry, as you said. More cooking, though. I can't believe I never noticed how much Josie must have been hunched over the campfire making all the meals for us. Do you know that that man wants to eat more than once a day?"

Rebecca nodded knowingly. "The gall of him. Seems never-ending."

"All right now, all right!"

Both women looked up to see Pastor Montgomery raising his hands for everyone's attention. Rebecca linked her arm through Annie's as they listened.

"I'm so pleased you all like it," the pastor said loudly over the milling crowd, which had just about filled the once-empty room from wall to wall. "I won't ask you to find a seat . . ." The sea of townspeople chuckled. "All we got is this one chair so far."

Isaac appeared beside Annie, having made his way through the crowd of people back to her. He took her hand and squeezed it, but turned his attention to the front of the room without saying anything.

Though from her vantage near the rear of the crowd Annie couldn't see much, Pastor Montgomery suddenly raised himself above the heads of the crowd and she realized he had stepped up onto a chair. He put both arms out to balance as the chair wobbled a bit below him. His wife, Olivia, stood nearby and put a steadying hand on the back of the chair, shaking her head at her husband's antics.

"There now," he said, a broad grin on his face as he looked out over his congregants. "Now I can see all your beautiful faces. I'll make this short. I know my wife would appreciate I not be perched up here any longer than I have to be."

Olivia Montgomery mouthed the word *please*. Low chuckles sounded throughout the room.

"You all were here only a few weeks earlier," he continued, "to watch us turn over the soil to mark the foundation of this house of worship. And now, through the dedicated work of so many of the men of Eden Valley, we have put the final nail in the last roof beam, and can gather now to dedicate this completed church. My prayers of the last year have all been toward this moment, and I thank the Lord that all of you are here with me, safely in the

Oregon Territory, directing our honest labor to God's glory with every day."

Applause broke out, punctuated with several audible calls of "Amen!" from the crowd.

"The next project, as you can probably tell, will be to build the benches to fill this place, so you're not all standing around listening to me yammer on. Hopefully by Sunday, just a few days' time, that will be started. But I don't want to keep you standing longer than necessary. Tonight, if you'll join me, I'd like to pray over this space, offer this house to God for his work and his glory, and then my wife and Mrs. Mills have organized something special for us."

Annie looked around, her heart soaring at all the nodding heads, the glistening eyes, all the grateful expressions of the emigrants who had given up so much to get so far. Though they had been settling into the Oregon Territory for more than a month now, this was the first time many of the families had felt a roof over their head. It was the first time many of them had finally felt at home.

Annie understood. The church her family had attended back in Virginia had been a second home of sorts. She'd played the organ there many mornings, sung in the choir with her sister too. All of her piano students had come from the other families that attended that same church in Virginia. Now, here in Oregon, she hoped that peace could be replicated.

Pastor Montgomery's prayer for the church and the body of Christ within was a balm to Annie's soul. She had spent so much of the previous week stretched thin and overwhelmed; she'd forgotten what it was like to have her spiritual welfare, at least, taken care of by someone else. This wasn't the first time she had been grateful that there was a pastor in their wagon company, and she knew it wouldn't be the last.

After his prayer ended, the blessing successfully given to the new church, the men and women of Eden Valley made their way outside again, talking over the exciting changes that were coming for the town and that had already arrived. The settling in of the previous month had been busy and a bit chaotic, but things were coming together.

As Isaac said hello to another friend, Annie and Rebecca walked out together arm in arm, and her friend filled Annie in on all the gossip she had missed since she'd moved out of the temporary campsite. Being with friends—being with people at all—made Annie realize how quiet and lonesome her home was becoming, way out at the edge of town. She wished they had closer neighbors.

"Ready to head back, wife?" Isaac asked, after speaking briefly to the pastor. In the interim Rebecca had been pulled away by her parents, and most of the crowd was breaking up, heading to their suppers and cozy night.

"We're coming back on Sunday, right?" Annie asked.

Isaac looked over her shoulder to the empty church building and the crowd of people who had spilled out onto the path that led up to it.

"Maybe I'll have time to build a bench before then," he responded. "Seeing as we have one of the only small wagons so far to bring it to church in."

"And I'll bring you coffee and biscuits as you work," Annie said. "Thank you. This is more important to me than I realized. Anything you need that I can help with, just let me know."

Isaac put his arm around his wife and led her back home. "I could get used to this."

CHAPTER FOUR

Early in the afternoon the following day, Annie brought her butter churn out to her front step where she could sit in the sunshine. The milk had come from the Sheldon family's cows; they were just starting to produce again regularly after the stress of traveling west along the Oregon Trail. Everyone in Eden Valley wanted the treat of fresh dairy, and the prospect of such had put a spring in her step. Isaac had negotiated two full buckets for their family, and Annie had anxiously awaited the cream separating.

The last time she had made butter had been at least ten years earlier, but she'd seen her sister Josie do it innumerable times, and her mother before that. There were only a handful of steps, though it would still take her all day. Annie was excited that they had reached such a point of settling in that this was even a choice. There was such a sense of accomplishment when after only an hour or so of work she could point to the thing she had just made. It was far from done, but the progress was clear.

It was a far different sense of accomplishment than that of doing laundry over and over again, or even teaching a child how to play the piano. Keeping her own home had become a daily balance of making progress she could see and maintaining their comfort in ways she could not easily notice.

And so, Annie sat on the low front step of her one-room home, patiently churning as she watched the meadow and hills that stretched out before her. The Oregon Territory promised to be a beautiful home. As her body moved with a steady rhythm, her mind wandered to thoughts of her sisters, miles away at the camp in town.

Her oldest sister, Louisa, had had such the plan for them, when she had undertaken to get all of the Hudsons west to the Oregon Territory. But then, heartbreakingly, Louisa had died on the trail, only a few months before they'd arrived, taken ill by one of the many diseases that spread throughout the wagon company. Annie had only just begun to truly appreciate Louisa's strength and compassion when she had lost her. Every day of that journey west was harrowing, allowing them only to think about putting one foot in front of the other. The day Louisa had passed had been unbearable.

But they had to keep going. They had to continue to the coast. They had to ration the food they had left and push themselves beyond what they'd dreamed possible. Until, one day, Annie had looked up and her future husband was there with her. The life she had been working toward was finally starting. Though she hadn't quite allowed herself to think about it during the six months on the Oregon Trail, now that they were settled, she found herself excited about plans and imagining the future.

With such beautiful dreams filling her mind, the afternoon seemed to pass in an instant.

Just as Annie finished churning, the butter creating a delight-fully pliant block, the sound of footsteps picking through the grass and brush seized her attention. She looked up to see her sister Josie and their sister-in-law Margaret walking along the narrow path that served as the road to the Wheelers' home.

Annie stood abruptly. "What are you doing here?" she asked in surprise. "Did you walk the whole way?"

"We missed you, of course," Josie said, opening her arms for a hug. "Haven't seen you in, what? At least two days. Unacceptable!"

Annie laughed and stepped into her sister's embrace.

"Come inside with me. I won't even put you to work. You must be exhausted."

"It's a beautiful day," Margaret insisted. "A handful of miles across mostly even ground is nothing. We walked this and more on the trail, didn't we? We're happy to be here with you."

"Here, I'll carry the churn," Josie volunteered.

"I didn't see you last night at the church," Annie said, as she collected the butter and led the way into her small home.

"We didn't stay long," Margaret responded, following Annie through the door. "We hadn't eaten supper yet before we went, and Lawrence was getting hungry."

"What is Lawrence up to today?"

Margaret sighed, but she couldn't hide the indulgent grin on her face. "He's been put to work like all the other men. Though I don't know how my precious little boy can be considered a man already."

"He's fourteen," Josie reminded her. "And taller than me. Not a baby. Would you want such a young man tied to your apron strings still? Shirking his duty?"

"Of course not. But that doesn't mean he's not still *my* baby," Margaret protested.

Annie laughed over their banter as she transferred her mound of butter to a clean piece of cheesecloth. She wrapped up the butter tightly and then carried it with her smallest pot over to the table, where her sisters were already sitting. As Josie and Margaret teased each other back and forth, Annie stood and set to work squeezing out any last bit of moisture from the butter that she could into the pot. The Wheelers would try to make this pound of butter last at least a month if they could, knowing how few dairy cows would be in Eden Valley over the winter.

"Did you know that Nora and Jasper are courting?" Annie asked. "Rebecca was just telling me last night."

Josie put her hand out to stop Annie from squeezing the butter more. "Wait, Annie. Did you rinse that?"

Annie frowned. "What? Rinse it? No. What do you mean?"

"Oh, well . . ." Josie stood and looked around the room briefly until her eyes fell on the bucket of water that had been boiled and set aside for the Wheelers' cooking. "You need to wash the butter first, to make sure there's no buttermilk still clinging to it. That will make the butter spoil faster."

"Oh, goodness," Annie said, dejected. She looked down at the pot and cloth-wrapped butter in her hands. "Oh, no. Did I ruin it?"

"Not at all. We can just rinse it now."

"So then I have to do this part all over again?"

"Yes, but at least we were here to help," Josie responded brightly. "How sad would it have been if all your work went to waste and the butter had spoiled? We can fix it. Easy."

Annie nodded and stepped aside to let Josie show her what needed to be done.

"Running a household is far more work than I expected. I don't know what I was thinking, assuming I could just step into this. I didn't realize how much of all this you did, Josie. I should have said 'thank you' constantly."

Josie waved a hand dismissively as she carefully spooned a dipper of clean water over the lump of butter. "You'll pick it up, little by little. And I'm always here if you have questions."

"Which actually brings us to why we're *actually* here," Margaret interjected, leaning forward at the table.

Annie looked at her curiously. "What do you mean?"

Margaret and Josie shared a quick look before Margaret continued.

"Now, mind you, we're just being precautious. But it's going to be December in just a couple days, and we know the first snow fall won't be long after that. We haven't really had a man to advocate for us. Lawrence does his best, but, as we just talked about, he's only a boy. It must be hard enough getting the older men to take him seriously, let alone listen when he asks for something."

"All that said," Josie added, as she continued with the butter, "we're not completely confident our home will be done when we need it to. So, we were hoping we could count on you to help, depending on what we need. You and Isaac."

Josie continued handling the lump of butter, but Annie was completely distracted by her sisters' words. Imagining her family, who she loved more than anything, huddled and shivering under just a piece of canvas as snow fell, spurred her into action.

"Well, of course I'll help! I'll nail boards together if I have to. As long as you all have a home."

"I'm not sure nailing boards together is how a house is built," Margaret said with a smile, "but the enthusiasm is appreciated."

"Well, I can take instruction, then. Whatever you need." Annie walked around the table to where Margaret was seated and hugged her from behind, talking quietly in her ear. "Please—*please* —don't hesitate to ask. And I'll talk to Isaac. I'm sure it won't be a problem."

"Thank you, dear." Margaret patted her arm before Annie stood again. "It might not even be a question. But we wanted to be prepared."

"The house is started, isn't it?" Annie asked. She crossed the room to sit on the edge of her bed, as both of the chairs were occupied. With Josie taking care of the butter, Annie relished the chance to relax, if even for a moment. "The spot you all picked out was pretty well cleared when I saw it."

"It's started," Josie confirmed, now wringing the liquid out of the butter. "Not big, of course, but bigger than a wagon, and frankly that's all I care about right now."

Margaret nodded. "The rest will come."

Josie asked Annie for a bowl. "Or however you want this to keep," she added. "I assume you don't have a fancy mold or something else you'd like me to put the butter in, do you?"

Annie stood, returning to the table. "Yes, I think I have something . . ." She brought Josie a small saucepan. It had belonged to Isaac's first wife and so was the only food container in the house that Annie didn't use regularly. "Will this do?"

"Better than nothing," Josie said. "Keep it covered as much as you can. And away from the fire, of course."

"We shouldn't stay. There's the whole walk back to consider before dark. But it was so nice to see you," Margaret said, standing again. "We'll let you talk to your husband privately. And, really, we might not need the help anyway." She put a hand lightly on Annie's arm and looked at her kindly. "Please don't fret. We just want to be prepared."

"Right. Yes, of course." Annie nodded vigorously. "Anything we can do, I'm sure Isaac will be happy to."

"And we'll see you at church on Sunday, won't we?" Josie asked.

"Absolutely. Isaac was going to try to build a bench before then, too, so maybe we'll even have a place to sit."

"Or old Mrs. Norton will have a place to sit, at least."

Annie walked them to the door of her home, and the other two women stepped outside into the late afternoon light.

"How long before this place starts to feel settled, do you think?" she asked.

"It feels settled to me," Josie said with a shrug. "But then I've never been as glamorous as you."

"Me?" Annie laughed. "Glamorous?"

"With your soft hands and piano and dozens of adoring students," Josie teased.

"I'm not sure my hands will ever be soft again."

"Maybe when your piano arrives, then," Josie responded. "One of these days, you'll wake up and feel as though you have always been here, and you have always been Mrs. Isaac Wheeler."

"One of these days," Annie repeated, and her sisters hugged her goodbye.

CHAPTER FIVE

Though she told herself her husband would surely not object, Annie was hesitant to actually talk to Isaac about what her sisters had asked of her. She didn't want to upset him; she wanted to present the request in a way that made him eager to agree. He always claimed he wished to give her whatever she desired. No matter how many times Annie told herself she was overthinking it, she couldn't stop herself. She owed her husband so much and didn't want to do anything to jeopardize their new life.

And so, that evening passed without her saying a word about her sisters. He returned in the late afternoon, just before sunset, and Annie was too pleased and flustered to have him home that she found innumerable other things to discuss. They talked about their neighbors, what was going on in town—everything but the actual topic that consumed Annie's mind.

Isaac spent the following day working at home with her instead of going off to help another family, and yet she still couldn't find a way to bring it up to him. No matter how many times she reminded herself that he wanted to help her family, taking that step was intimidating.

"This is silly," she whispered to herself, as she kneaded a loaf of sourdough bread. "He is your husband. What would Louisa say if she knew?"

She glanced out at Isaac through the front door, propped open as usual to let in light and crisp winter air. He had spent the morning splitting a long tree in order to make a bench for the church. Spread across the grass area in front of their home were wood chips, a bucket of drinking water, and the whetstone for his axe. Even with the late November weather, he had removed his shirt while he worked to let the bright afternoon sun warm his shoulders.

She watched as he straightened, standing upright and hoisting his axe to his shoulder as he looked over his work. She watched as her kind, hard-working husband gave up another entire day of labor to make something for the community instead of for himself. Pride was not a strong enough word for how Annie felt about the man she had married. All the doubt and worry she had felt in accepting a proposal by mail from someone she had never met were completely washed away. Isaac Wheeler was a gift.

The Wheelers toiled along, side by side, he outdoors and her within, throughout the day. The sounds of birds and the wind in the trees were Annie's orchestra as she hummed to herself and put the bread over the coals to bake. She had been without a piano for a whole year by now—the longest she could remember —but the songs still lived in her heart. Her hands still remembered the chords, and as she finished kneading the bread and put it in the fire to bake, she found herself lightly tapping out the chord progression of one of her favorite hymns along the edge of the table.

Laughing at herself, Annie looked around her small kitchen space to remind herself what chores still needing doing. Next would be the quail that she would roast for their supper, and then she would have to start peeling the potatoes.

There was always so much to do, she thought with a sigh as she started plucking the bird.

The sourdough was baking nicely, and would come out of the dutch oven about the time she would need to put the quail in. It would pair perfectly with the butter Josie had helped her with the day before.

"Annie, can you come out here, please?" Isaac called to her.

She wiped her hands on her apron and went out to meet him. "Everything all right?"

"Do you think you could lift that?" He used his discarded shirt to wipe the sweat from his brow, then nodded to indicate a roughly hewn bench, about six feet long but several inches thick.

"Lift it? Me?"

"Just one side. I'm wondering if you and me can get these in the wagon or if I need to find other help."

Annie crossed to the bench, eyeing it warily. "I don't know . . . It seems pretty solid."

Gamely, she squatted and wrapped her fingers around the end of the thick beam of wood, lifting slowly. The end of the bench rose as she stood, but she couldn't move it more than a few inches after that.

"Hmm," Isaac said, watching with his brow furrowed. "Probably can't get it high enough for the wagon, then, huh? All right. I might ride over to the Waters camp after supper to get one of those boys to help. If we can get these in the wagon tonight, we can take them to the church for service tomorrow morning."

Annie lowered the bench, trying to be careful, though it seemed so sturdy that she wasn't sure she could hurt it if she tried.

"These are amazing," she told her husband. "I can't believe you made all this in one day."

He shrugged. "You should have seen the first time I tried to make something like this, a couple years ago. Took me, I think, six tries to split the log cleanly without breaking. That was a mess."

"Well, I'm sure Mrs. Montgomery will be so grateful."

He grinned at her before turning his attention back to sanding down some of the sharper corners. Annie, watching him, realized this might be her best chance to mention her sisters, that he might be in the best mood now, at the end of his hard labor.

"Actually, I was wondering if you could do something for me," she began timidly. "Please."

"Gladly, wife. You don't even have to look so worried about it," he said with a wink. "It gives me pleasure to give you what you want."

"Well, my sisters were here yesterday, and they told me that their house doesn't seem like it's going to be ready before winter is here . . . and I was just wondering—"

"If I could say something to Mills?" he finished for her. "Of course I will. You Hudsons have already gone through so much without having a man to lean on. This is the least I can do." He walked the few steps between them and kissed her cheek. "I'm happy to."

"Thank you."

Annie didn't add that they had asked to stay with the Wheelers if the house wasn't completed. That would be a confrontation for another day, and only if absolutely necessary. She preferred to hope everything would work out instead, not risking the peace.

"I need to go in and finish supper," she said. "Unless there's something else you needed my help with."

"Nope." He waved her away and gave her a teasing grin. "Get those potatoes in before it's too late."

Annie turned away before he could see the flash of hurt on her face. He didn't mean it. She knew that. He wasn't trying to be cruel; he was just teasing, she told herself. Nevertheless, the first thing she did upon entering her kitchen was start peeling the potatoes, even with the quail half plucked on the table.

The Wheelers were up just after dawn for coffee, breakfast, and to make their way to church. Angus Waters had come by the previous night to help lift the benches into the wagon. With the extra weight to haul to church, as well as the need to unload the wagon before the service started, they would need to leave early. They kept their front door closed tightly as they got ready, the fireplace warming their one room. Eden Valley's first Sunday morning service with a completed church building was also the first morning with frost on the ground. Annie had not seen such cold weather since she had been in Virginia, and it would only get colder.

It wasn't until they were about to leave home that Annie realized her heavy coat must still be packed with the rest of the Hudsons' things in the wagons. So she wrapped one shawl over her head and neck, and another around her shoulders, grateful that her gloves and thickest stockings had made it in the move.

"Will you be warm enough?" her husband asked with a frown. "Why didn't you make sure you had packed everything to move here?"

"I—I'm sorry. I didn't do it on purpose. This is enough to keep me warm for now, and then we'll be inside. I'll just have to collect my coat from their wagon after church. And the frost should melt off in a few hours, don't you think?"

Isaac looked up at the sky, dark and overcast. "Hopefully."

He helped her into the wagon, their horse, Rocky, already hitched up, before climbing in himself. She huddled close to her husband on the wagon seat and managed to stay warm enough.

When they reached the church, Annie was excited to see that theirs were not the only benches that had been built in the previous couple days. There were more than enough seats for the old and infirm of the congregation.

Nearly everyone had come to the church for that very first service, even if it meant standing in the back of the room. The sermon was on Psalm 127:1, and the pastor announced he would be holding a special Christmas Day service. Annie's heart felt full, grateful for this community.

After Pastor Montgomery had prayed to close the service, the families in attendance spilled out of the church onto the grass around it. Annie had been right, and the frost was long gone, though the slight crisp chill in the air remained in the early afternoon. Margaret had sent Lawrence running back to their camp to find Annie's coat. He ran back soon after, slightly panting but victorious. When Isaac went to hitch their horse back up, Annie stood with coat draped over her arms, face basking in the sunlight, eyes closed, and almost didn't hear the approaching footsteps.

"There you are!"

Annie turned to see her dear friend Rebecca Tenney opening her arms for a hug.

"I am still not used to not seeing you every day," she said. "It must be so quiet out at your homestead by yourself."

Annie nodded. "I sing to myself a lot. I miss having folks nearby far more than I expected."

"So . . . Mrs. Wheeler. It's been a month now, hasn't it?"

"Close, yes." A blush crept up Annie's neck. "A month married."

"You don't regret it yet?"

"Rebecca!" The other woman laughed, and Annie continued. "No, I don't regret it. Isaac is wonderful so far. He's a good man. It's difficult to get used to living with a man, and not one I know very well just yet, but he really does try to do everything he can for me."

"Well, you probably wouldn't have come to Oregon without his offer, right?"

"Of course, but—" Annie blinked in confusion. "Yes, but I'm still grateful to him. Not every mail-order bride manages to be so lucky."

"That's probably true. I still can't imagine marrying someone without knowing them very well. My husband and I were friends since we were kids. No one knew me better than Andrew, even before we were married."

"Yes, I'm sure I still have a lot to learn, but, so far—"

"Ready, wife?" Isaac called to her, as Rocky and the wagon pulled up the road just next to where the women were talking.

Annie stuttered, cutting herself off as her husband interrupted. "I—I'm so sorry, I should go."

Rebecca frowned lightly, but then smiled her acquiescence. "Hopefully I'll see you soon. Our home should be finished any day. Or that's what Jasper keeps saying."

"I would love that," Annie said, waving goodbye as she hurried to Isaac and their wagon.

CHAPTER SIX

All of Sunday afternoon and into Monday, Annie was quiet, thinking, trying to put a finger on what caused the melancholy that seemed to be overtaking her. Cooking and cleaning kept her hands busy as she thought it over. Isaac talked to her about their next steps, winter garden plans, and what furniture he should make next. He didn't seem to notice if she was quieter than usual.

But she wasn't only quiet. Annie had never felt the same shrinking into herself as she had in the last couple weeks. Her elation at seeing a friend for a few minutes seemed all out of proportion, and her subsequent moroseness when arriving home again felt debilitating. Where she had hoped her husband could be a support to her in this new life, she more often felt as though she was letting him down or was even wary of him.

It wasn't until Isaac came home on Monday night with stories about his day—Mrs. Larson had shown up at her home site with her two oldest daughters and insisted on helping—that she finally identified precisely what she was feeling.

Annie was lonely.

This new responsibility as a wife and homemaker was hard

enough, but to do it without friends nearby seemed to be breaking her spirit.

The solitary way in which she spent her days was draining her. On that particular day, she would have given anything to have been with Isaac and the rest, there to help in the construction along with the Larsons, or even just to talk to Mrs. Larson; that would have been far better than how she had spent her day, desolate and distracted. Annie hadn't realized how deeply she missed that social connection until she heard about someone else getting that very thing.

Rebecca may have expected it, but Annie hadn't seen the truth.

As Isaac continued his story—Hattie Larson had to be taught how to hold a hammer—Annie turned over this epiphany in her mind. No wonder these new emotions felt so confusing. She had never been lonely before, she realized. She had never had an opportunity to be.

Through all the years she was growing up, Annie had never thought of herself as a particularly social person. She enjoyed being home with her family, and having three siblings meant there was always someone in the house. She enjoyed practicing piano and knitting in the few hours she had that she wasn't at school or at church or doing some chore around the house. Annie had always been perfectly happy being alone back when she had lived in Virginia. Being content by herself had been an important skill she'd had to learn after her fiancé had died several years earlier. That had been difficult to get used to, but once she did, she thought no more of it.

It wasn't until she married Isaac that Annie found herself truly, fully pulled out of the life she knew best. She had moved into a house away from her sisters, away from the town, and was alone most of the day. It was only in this brand-new environment that she had recognized just how often she saw other people in her previous life in Virginia. There, she would have a quiet hour after seeing her students and before joining her sisters for supper. Here, she could go days without seeing anyone other than her husband, and even he was often only home to sleep.

And so, after another full day by herself, trying to keep busy with cleaning and cooking and not thinking too much about how quiet it was, Annie sat down to supper with Isaac and felt a wave of relief at his smile. At his voice. At the mere fact of his presence at the table across from her.

"I'm so glad you're home," she said, after he had said grace over the supper.

"Me too," Isaac replied. "Believe me. Nice to be safe and sound. There was another injury today. Before the Larsons got there, in fact, so maybe it was good they came. Seems like it might be a bad one. There was a lot of blood."

Annie paled. "What happened?"

"I didn't see it, mind you. This is all just secondhand. But I hear that a saw slipped and Judah Kirk might have lost a finger, maybe two."

Annie gasped. "A finger? No! Oh, goodness, is there anything that can be done?"

Isaac shook his head. "We were able to get the bleeding stopped and his pa took him to the doc to get sewn up. I'm sure we'll hear for sure. But imagine trying to hold a nail in place without all the fingers to grip it."

"Oh, that poor family. What will they do now?"

He shook his head. "I don't know. He'll figure it out. It might not be that bad."

"Not that bad?" She looked at him, aghast.

"People adapt. It may take a bit, but he'll figure out how to hold things again without one of his fingers. Plenty of other men have made do with worse, losing a whole arm or leg. And other people will step up to help. That's what neighbors are for, why we all came west in a big company instead of on our own, right?"

"I suppose . . ."

"Don't you worry about Judah, wife," he said, cutting into his supper. "We've got plenty of troubles of our own without borrowing any."

Annie smiled in self-deprecation. He wasn't wrong. Half the reason she kept holding off on asking for something from him now, or confronting her sister Louisa about how they were spending money in the past, had been because she was borrowing trouble. She would procrastinate and imagine the worst thing that could happen. It was too easy for Annie to think up all the ways something could go wrong and just stay quiet to avoid that bother.

"How's your supper?" she asked.

She had spent much of the day letting the rabbit roast over a low heat, adding vegetables, gravy, and a little bacon at the very end. She was afraid it might be too salty, but Isaac seemed to enjoy it.

He nodded vigorously while he chewed, not wanting to answer with his mouth full. "Potatoes are cooked through, so that's good."

Annie felt a flash of shame, though she knew he was teasing. "Good. That's good."

"It's wonderful, wife. Really. Thank you."

"You're welcome—"

"I wish you could have tasted the way my wife cooked rabbit, though," he continued. "There was some herb she always added . . . I don't remember . . . or maybe some other secret ingredient she took to the grave, because I've never tasted anything like what she was able to make." He took another bite, chewing thoughtfully, as though trying to figure out what was missing.

"Oh." She cleared her throat, trying to figure out how to respond. "Um, yes, I . . . I'm sorry I can't, um . . . Maybe the next time I see Josie I'll ask her for tips. She was always the cook in our house."

"That's a great idea." He beamed at her before turning his

attention back to his meal, cutting into the tender meat with the side of his fork.

They ate in silence for several more minutes. Only the sounds of wood crackling in the fireplace and knives scratching against the tin plates filled the air. Annie thought longingly of the boisterous meals she'd had with her family back in Virginia, with half a dozen people, family and neighbors. When her nephew Lawrence was around ten years old, he had gone through a stage where he insisted on singing instead of speaking, making up the melody and trying his best to rhyme with every statement. Louisa had always been domineering and often held court from the head of the table, talking loudly about the latest politics of their little town and bemoaning the fact that women had no say in their local affairs.

The contrast with Annie's small, quiet, nearly empty supper table now was striking.

She didn't know if she could ignore that ache much longer.

"Isaac?" she began, watching his expression carefully.

"Hm?" He raised his eyebrows in question, but continued eating. "Is this bacon?"

"Yes, do you like it?"

He looked at the small slice speared on the end of his fork, shrugged, and put it in his mouth.

"Well, um . . ." Annie was flustered. She wanted his focused attention so badly. "I was thinking . . . today, when I was by myself, I did a lot of thinking. I really miss my sisters. And nephew. Do you think we could . . ." She hesitated, not knowing quite how to word her request.

"You want me to take you into town with me tomorrow?"

She blinked in surprise. "Yes," she gasped out. "That would be exactly what I need. Thank you."

"Of course." He grinned. "I live to serve, you know. You can visit with family, and I think Daniel Mills should be back with another load of supplies from the fort. We can see what we can trade for and put in an order for next time. Maybe see about some kind of holiday treat."

"Thank you. I would love that so much. I'm sorry if I've been down. I didn't realize I was so lonely out here by myself until the last couple days."

He nodded knowingly. "I figured. I should have guessed. I don't know why you didn't say anything. My wife had the same problem when we very first left Missouri."

Annie cast her eyes down at the table at the mention of his late wife again.

"Even with all the folks in our wagon company," he continued, oblivious, "the trail to Oregon was a little lonely for her, missing her family. She had been used to five sisters all within a mile's walk when we lived in Richmond, and not having them around was a shock to her."

Annie bit her tongue to keep from pointing out that *she* was Isaac's wife. But how could she gracefully ask him to stop referring to Gertie Wheeler as such? He wasn't trying to hurt her; she just had to keep reminding herself of that.

"Right. Yes." She nodded. "Then you understand."

"Of course. Goodness, the number of times I had to cheer up Gertie." He grinned at her. "And I'm happy to do the same for you. But I think going into town is a good first step. There's nothing around the house that you need to do tomorrow?"

Annie looked around the small space and shook her head. "Just the same things as can be done any other day. I imagine in the summer, when the garden is in full bloom, it will be harder to leave for a day. But right now it can all wait."

"Then we'll do that. And you'll get that spring back in your step."

He took another big bite of the supper she had made him—the supper that probably wasn't as tasty as whatever his first wife had made. But the expression on his face was so full of expectation that Annie wasn't about to ruin it. It was only natural that he reference his first wife, especially since that other woman's death was the entire reason Annie was now here in Oregon in the first place.

Even though Annie had also lost a young love, she had not been married to John Sherman. She supposed it must be different.

Maybe tomorrow she would also go find Rebecca Tenney, who had lost her husband less than a year earlier. Yes, Rebecca would be able to tell Annie what Isaac must be feeling after losing a spouse; Rebecca would reassure her.

She took her own bite of the rabbit and offered a smile back to Isaac.

CHAPTER SEVEN

The door to the Wheelers' home stood open to the morning air. Isaac was in the yard out front tending to the horses, already bundled up to leave. Annie drained the last of her coffee and immediately put the tin cup in the pan of dishwater.

"Will you be ready to go soon?" Isaac called to her, as she bustled around their small house cleaning up after breakfast.

Most mornings, her husband left to go work at another site before she finished washing the dishes and putting away the food after breakfast. She wasn't used to having to complete her chores under his impatient eye; she found herself rushing to not make him wait.

"Coming!" she called back.

She scrubbed the cup quickly, rinsed it in clean water, and set it to the side. The dishes weren't quite dry, but they could finish drying in the cupboard just as well, couldn't they? As she stacked the plates on top of each other and the tin mugs on top of that, with the utensils shoved haphazardly inside, Annie felt certain she was forgetting something. She looked around her small space for something that might seem out of place.

But she realized, as she dried her hands on her apron, that she didn't much care. Whatever it might be, she could worry about it tomorrow. She was far too excited to see her family, to see her friends. To be around people again instead of cooped up inside by herself.

Pulling on the coat Lawrence had found for her, Annie rushed outside.

Isaac was already waiting on the wagon seat when she emerged from the house. "I thought we could go to the store together, and then I'd take you to your sisters' for the day while I go back home," he said when he saw her.

Carefully closing the front door behind her, Annie thanked him again for taking her with him. "I already feel lighter," she said.

"I'm glad. Just wait till you have a full day there."

Isaac lightly flicked the reins, urging Rocky forward as the Wheelers headed into town for the day. It wasn't quite as cold as it had been a couple mornings earlier, but Annie was grateful for her coat and gloves. Maybe they could ask Daniel Mills about bringing back wool the next time they went to the fort so she could knit herself some warm stockings for the winter.

It was a short trip into town, feeling far shorter than Annie had anticipated, given how far out and alone she had felt on their homestead. But it seemed as though she had just gotten through telling her husband what she would like to see about trading for when their wagon pulled up alongside the site of the general store in the center of town.

Though the general store of Eden Valley had not yet been finished being built, the mayor, George Mills, had decided that any public trading of goods and supplies should be done in the general vicinity of the store. So when his son, Daniel, or Ben Findley returned from trips to Fort Vancouver, they always brought their supply-laden wagons to the cleared patch of ground in front of where the building was going up. Neither young man was in sight this morning, but Tom Jameson, the storekeep, stood leaning against his wagon, which remained half full of the goods that had been brought back on the last trip.

"Morning, Tom," Isaac called out.

Mr. Jameson tipped his hat to the Wheelers as Isaac helped his wife down out of the wagon.

Fort Vancouver sat about thirty-five miles to the northwest of Eden Valley, right on the Columbia River and almost a hundred miles inland. It was by far the largest of the forts the wagon company had come across on their journey from Missouri, and would easily be the largest port destination near Eden Valley, even as the Oregon Territory grew and filled up with settlers. Situated near the coast as it was, Fort Vancouver was the best place for the new settlers to acquire anything they could not make or grow themselves.

"Is there anything you would like, wife?" Isaac murmured, as they looked over the selection from a distance.

Even this early in the morning, at least six other women and couples were gathered around the wagon. Of course, Annie reminded herself, there was so much to do to get settled in the territory; shopping, such as it was, would surely evolve and change over the coming years. For now, though, the families of the former Sullivan–Mills wagon company were so strapped for necessities and so desperate for what they needed to survive the winter that there was already a haggling going on over the little they had managed to bring back.

"I'm so glad you already had a wagon," Annie whispered to Isaac as they walked toward the crowd. "And some dishes and things. Imagine having to start from scratch like so many of these other families. I think the Davises left all their tools out on the prairie somewhere because they were too heavy."

"It's hard. It was even harder for me and Gertie when we arrived, since our wagon company was so much smaller."

"Mm-hmm," Annie said noncommittally, as they approached Tom.

In the weeks since the company had settled, Daniel Mills and Ben Findley had come up with an ingenious system for bringing back as many supplies to Eden Valley as they could. One of the young men would ride his horse the several hours to Fort Vancouver, where he would first purchase a finished wagon. Then he would fill said wagon with the food, clothes, tools, and anything else his neighbors had expressed a desire for—whatever they could afford with the little money and goods they had to trade, though much of the town's building thus far was the result of kind generosity and extensive lines of credit. Once the young man returned to town, there was no shortage of families who would gladly purchase the new wagon from him rather than spend the time breaking down their Conestoga to reconfigure to something more accessible—especially since many of the families were still living out of their enormous covered wagons and couldn't give up that protection just yet.

This most recent trip, Daniel seemed to have loaded up on hearty food that would keep for months—barrels of potatoes, sides of bacon, and more. There were a few higher-priced items; Annie spotted three pairs of men's leather gloves that most of the settlement would never be able to afford, no matter how badly they were needed. And just to one side of the wagon of goods from the fort, Mr. Sheldon stood with half a dozen buckets of milk on the ground around him.

He was busy negotiating with Matty Jones, but Annie was quick to nudge her husband and point. Isaac's face lit up, and he immediately went to claim what he could.

While he did so, Annie looked over the food again. She only knew so many recipes, only some of which could be made from the dry and canned goods of the winter months, but they could always use potatoes or rice. Making a mental list as she glanced over the wagon, Annie waited for her husband and tried to stay out of the way of the other couples collecting their own food for the coming week.

"More milk!" Isaac said triumphantly, returning to her side carefully holding a full bucket. "We can use this, right?"

"Of course. Yes! I'm so excited." Annie was delighted at this unlooked-for bounty. "But I thought the Sheldon milk was all spoken for. It usually goes so quickly."

"So did I. But David says the settling in and having plenty of grass has made his girls all bounce back faster than he had expected. It's still a fraction of what they would have produced back east, or will indeed next spring, but I am happy to take whatever he has to sell. Did you decide what else you wanted?"

She pointed out a few selections, reiterating more than once that whatever he decided they could afford or had room for, she could make work. With the holiday approaching, she needed to start thinking about how to make the day special for them—their first Christmas together—but at the same time, Annie didn't know their finances. The last thing she wanted was for this generous man to feel bad for what he couldn't give her.

"But really," she concluded, "I'm just grateful for what we have."

"Leave it to me. I'll pick out the perfect surprise for our first Christmas together." He wrapped an arm around her shoulder, pulling her to his side as they looked over their options. "In fact, you can walk to your sisters' camp from here, can't you? Why don't you let me take care of all this, take it home, and I'll come back for you in a few hours."

"Oh, no, I don't know—"

"Wife," he said, his voice low in her ear. "Please let me take care of you. That's what I'm here for."

A contented feeling of security coursed through her at his words. "Thank you."

"You stay through supper, in fact," he continued, "and I'll come get you not long after it gets dark, if that's not too late."

Her mouth fell open in surprise. "If you're sure. Won't traveling after dark be particularly difficult? None of the roads around here are anything close to finished."

"I'll bring a lantern and we'll go slow. We can make it work. It's more important to me that you get as much time with your sisters as we can manage. I don't like the listlessness I've been seeing from you the last few days."

"Thank you." She kissed his cheek. "Thank you so much."

"Now get going. Maybe if you get there soon enough you can see your nephew before he's called off to put in someone's floorboards."

Annie left Isaac to his haggling, wondering idly what kind of food and supplies might be waiting for her when she got home that night. But she didn't linger in those thoughts for long. Her steps quickened and she felt a broad smile across her face as she drew closer to the spread-out camp where her sisters were living. As she wove between the other wagons, families eating breakfast and getting ready for their days, all Annie could think of was the love and welcoming ahead of her.

She all but stumbled into the Hudson camp just as Josie was pouring a mug full of coffee.

"Why! Annie Wheeler, what are you doing here?" Josie exclaimed.

"I missed you," was all Annie could get out before her voice broke and she was enveloped by a hug from two different directions.

CHAPTER EIGHT

"No, but, Annie, dear . . ." Margaret pulled away from their hug, holding Annie by the shoulders, and looked at her with concern. "Honestly, though, what are you doing here?"

"I missed you," she said again, as Josie handed her the fresh cup of coffee and returned to the campfire. "Honestly, that's all it is. Isaac has sensed I've been feeling a little down lately, and then after seeing you even just that short amount of time a few days ago, I realized what it was I was missing. It's hard being on my own day after day. So . . ." She shrugged, embarrassed to finally admit to it. "I guess I'm taking a day off? So I can see my sisters?"

"You sound like you're not sure," Josie teased, as she finished the family's breakfast.

"No, I'm sure, I just . . . it's a little embarrassing, isn't it?"

"To admit that you like your family?" Margaret laughed.

"No." Annie grinned sheepishly. "To shun my responsibilities because I'm lonely. I can't help thinking about the look on Louisa's face if she were here. Sarcastically asking who would be scrubbing my front steps while I sit here sipping coffee."

"You really think Louisa would care about that?" Josie asked seriously. "Maybe if you word it poorly. 'Oh, yes, sister, I am being lazy today because I wanted to gossip.' But that's not what you're doing, is it?"

Annie shook her head and sat on an overturned bucket by the fire.

"I think," Margaret said as she joined them, "and you'll forgive me if I am making assumptions. I know you all knew Louisa better than I did. But I think what she cared about most was that her family was happy and taken care of."

"Which is why we all ended up in Oregon, don't forget," Josie interjected.

"Precisely," Margaret said, pointing at Josie in emphasis. "And part of being happy is not being alone all the time. Right?"

Annie nodded.

Margaret softened at the hopeful expression on Annie's face. "Louisa loved you so much. She would have loved Isaac, too. And I promise if you deny yourself any kind of happiness—"

"Especially something as essential as visiting your sisters," Josie interjected again.

"Especially that," Margaret agreed. "You'd only be discarding the blessing that she gave to all of us. Think of everything Louisa went through to get us all here, because this is what she believed would make you happy. Your job is to appreciate that."

"Taking a day off from baking bread and doing laundry is nothing to have a crisis over," Josie said. "And if you're really feeling that poorly over it, I will gladly put you to work."

"Oh, but I wish you would." Annie leaned forward, her hands clasped together. "I realized in the last week or so that I only know a couple recipes, and you saw what I did with the butter . . . I cannot believe how much of managing the house I let you take care of without even bothering to help or even learn what you were doing. I'm so overwhelmed most days."

"Well, then! Let's get to work."

For the next several hours, Annie was as good as her word,

eagerly taking on everything thrown at her. When Josie repeatedly asked her if she was sure she wanted to fetch water or form biscuits, she reminded her sister that she wasn't taking a day off from her own home because she was tired. Learning all the tricks and skills of an accomplished homemaker would make future days easier for her, especially if she could continue to visit with her family.

"It's too bad I missed Lawrence," she said, hours later when Josie had given her a break.

"He'll be back for supper."

"What time is it now?"

Margaret looked up at the sky. "Our pocket watch is hanging on the inside of the wagon, but if I had to guess . . ." She squinted. "Maybe two o'clock or so?"

"That late . . . If I go visit Rebecca, will you be okay?"

"You mean, will I finish the chores I had intended to do anyway? Yes, Annie. You go have fun."

"I'm sorry, I just thought she might—"

"You don't have to explain yourself," Margaret said gently. "Tell Mrs. Tenney we said hello."

Annie washed her hands, tucked her loose hair behind her ear, and set off to find the campsite where Rebecca lived with her parents and brother. Now, a full month after Annie had been married and living on her homestead, the spread-out camp of wagons had thinned by at least half. So many of the families were getting roofs and walls every day. As she walked across the packed earth, she didn't think the Stephens family had yet moved into a homestead elsewhere, but lamented to herself that she did not know for sure. How many other details and updates about her friends was Annie missing while she was out alone in her own home at what felt like the edge of town?

As she passed between campsites, around the outside of the Alden family's wagon, Annie's eyes fell on Jasper Stephens, Rebecca's brother, checking the shoe on the Stephenses' horse just next to a parked covered wagon. He looked up when he heard her footsteps.

"Mrs. Wheeler, what can I help you with?" He wiped his hands on the legs of his trousers and came toward her. "I would have thought that you'd still be getting as much out of your finished home as you could. There are dozens of women who would gladly take your place, even if it meant leaving their own families." Jasper chuckled.

"It is nice," Annie admitted. "And warmer than you have here. I almost feel guilty thinking about all the children still sleeping in wagons like this."

"You could always fill your floor with mats and pillows for them." He grinned.

"Can you imagine? A temporary boarding school in my kitchen? I'd never sleep again."

"Ah, well. There are far worse places they could be sleeping. Imagine if we hadn't gotten over the mountains in time."

Annie shook her head. They had all heard the stories of the emigrants who had tried to take a short-cut and gotten stuck; the mothers who had watched their children perish one by one because they hadn't gotten to the territories before their food had completely given out. No, Jasper was right: Annie was lucky compared to the rest of town, but the entire company was fortunate as well. Their wagon company had lost people on the way—including Annie's own sister—but at least they were all settling in now.

"I don't think I want to imagine that," she said softly.

Jasper looked stricken. "No, of course . . . I'm sorry. Very callous of me." He looked over his shoulder, as though hoping someone could rescue him from his own foolishness. "You looking for Rebecca? I think she's in the wagon, sorting through our warm clothing. I'll get her for you."

"Thank you."

He ducked under the canvas flap and Annie heard the

murmuring of conversation. Trying not to eavesdrop, Annie looked away, and her eyes fell on the campsite just next to the Stephens family. Little Jack Keegan, only six years old, sat shivering in a large tub by the campfire, while his mother poured warm water over his head. Steam came off him in billows as the warm water hit the cold early December air. That poor child. Annie averted her eyes again. She may have only been married for a month, but that was long enough to have mostly forgotten about some of the drawbacks of living out of a wagon. Being reminded of the lack of privacy made Annie resolve to enjoy her alone time more when she got back to her home later that night, even if she also felt guilty about it.

Rebecca and her brother emerged from the wagon and the former hurried to greet their visitor.

"Annie Wheeler, what are you doing here?" She opened her arms to hug Annie, still talking into her hair. "I can't imagine coming to see me would be tempting enough to lure you from your cozy fireside."

"Such vanity! Not just you," Annie retorted. "I just came from my sisters' camp."

Rebecca laughed. "All right then, but I still don't think I would have left the warmth of a cabin to risk the outdoors of the Oregon Territory in December unless I absolutely had to. Is everything all right?"

Annie opened her mouth to respond—to pour out her hurt at Isaac bringing up his first wife, to be comforted and reassured—but at the last moment she realized she did not want to be seen complaining. Jasper was right—the whole town was comparatively lucky to be there at all, to not have lost more of their members. Rebecca was right—Annie was one of the few women in the entire town with a roof and a proper bed and a fireplace to cook her meals over. What kind of person would she be if she brought her troubles to Rebecca's feet?

"Yes," she answered resolutely. "Yes, everything is really

wonderful. But Isaac and I came into town to see what Daniel had brought back from the fort, and I thought, of course, since I was here anyway, I might check in and see how you're doing. Still sleeping in a narrow cot in a wooden box and all?"

"God willing, not for much longer. It will still be a narrow cot, but at least it will be in a proper home with walls more sturdy than fabric. Pa keeps saying any day now, and he's been saying it long enough it must be true eventually, don't you think? Come sit in the wagon with me. I was in the middle of sorting through things and need to get it all put away before we can sleep tonight."

So Annie followed her friend into their wagon, sitting on one of the beds and allowing Rebecca's cheerful chatter to wash over her. Maybe this, she thought, was all she needed. Maybe just a little social visit every few weeks would be enough for Annie, to remind her of the connections she had all around her.

"And, anyway," Rebecca was saying, with a laugh, "when I heard that Caroline had insisted that her friend's little brother teach her how to hunt, that's when I realized that I was born to be a woman of leisure."

"Wait, what happened? She did what?"

"You didn't hear? I suppose not, living out on the edge like you have been. It became a much bigger mess than it needed to be because June Mills didn't approve, and this was before Daniel and Caroline were married, mind you, and she just stormed over to the Sullivan camp and— Well, trust me. It was quite dramatic. Unnecessarily so, but it made for good gossip for a couple days."

"But . . ." Annie frowned. "Why did she want to hunt? I thought she was some New York heiress or something?"

"You know she was living with the Sullivans, of course, and just waiting for her house to be finished so she could marry Daniel. I suppose it's just that she has more energy than she knows what to do with. Both Hannah and her mother are plenty to keep that household going, so Caroline was just looking for a way to help. I can't imagine ever doing that myself. I'd much rather lay in the grass and watch the clouds, but it's likely opportunities for that will be few and far between in Eden Valley."

"Hmm," Annie murmured. She had always been able to find ways to fill her time—especially when she had a piano—but maybe Caroline was more like Louisa Hudson. It takes all kinds to make a world, Annie supposed. And since she wasn't completely happy with what she had been doing so far, maybe she could take a leaf out of Caroline's book.

CHAPTER NINE

Rebecca Tenney never failed to lift Annie's spirits, and so it was later than she had intended when she finally returned to the Hudsons' camp that evening. Though Annie had meant to get back early enough for Josie to teach her some things about the soup recipe she was making, she'd had no idea when her sister was starting. Annie strolled back through the bustling camp, the men and boys having arrived back after their day of work and the women deep in preparation of supper. The hum of conversations around every corner made Annie feel more comfortable than she had been in her own home. She even stopped to watch the little Jones boys playing some version of tag, reminiscing about her own childhood with siblings filling the house.

By the time she finally reached the Hudson camp, she found Josie already stirring a pot that had been simmering over the campfire.

"No," Annie said, hurrying to her side. "That smells amazing, but you were supposed to wait for me. Weren't you going to put me to work?"

"You weren't here, and I needed to get started if we were

going to eat before midnight." Josie waved her off. "It's nothing, took very little effort. I can tell you right now—the biggest tip is to put the salt in early in the cooking to make sure it flavors all bits of the soup instead of just the final bites."

"I'm sure there's more to it than that."

"Not much. And anyway, I know you haven't spent time with Rebecca hardly at all since you were married. You deserve to take as much time as you need."

"I'm sorry. I really meant to be here."

"Well, yes, but also, when you make soup you need to start the broth hours and hours before, so if you wanted to be here the whole time you couldn't have seen Rebecca."

Annie's jaw hung slack, before she laughed awkwardly. "But . . . why didn't you tell me that?"

"I'm telling you now. If I had known you were coming for the day and known you wanted a cooking lesson, I could have made other plans. But we will have plenty of time for all of that in the future. For now, just sit down and relax. You may not get another day off from chores for goodness knows how long."

"Who got a day off from chores?" Lawrence asked, approaching the camp with the fingers of each hand wrapped around the handle of a full bucket of water. "How do I get one?"

"Lawrence Hudson, have you grown in the few days since I've seen you?" Annie asked.

He shrugged. "Maybe. I do keep bumping my head on the ribs of the wagon."

"Would you fill this pot with water, please?" Josie asked him.

"Let me do that," Annie said, cutting in to help. "I have been completely useless all day. I can pour a bucket of water, at least."

She took both buckets from her tall nephew, set them in the dirt, and then—while his hands were free—hugged him fiercely. "I've missed you so much."

"Okay, Aunt Annie," he said with an awkward grin.

"That will be drinking water," Josie instructed, grabbing their attention again, "so once the pot is just about full, find a spot over the fire for it."

"What did you do today?" Annie asked her nephew, as she carefully poured the water into the pot as instructed.

He collapsed in the dirt next to the campfire and rubbed his face in exhaustion. "I don't remember all of it. There are so many homes so close to being done that, in just the few hours of daylight we had today, me and a couple of the boys were at three different sites. Everyone is in such a hurry. I feel like I could sleep for a month."

"I'm sure part of that is because you're growing too," Margaret said softly. "I promise, once we're all settled in for the winter, we'll find chances to make you rest. Eat a bunch. Fatten up like the bears do. Even if that means I have to split firewood."

"I'm not *that* lazy," Lawrence protested with a laugh.

"We'll see," his mother said. "Remember how hard it was to get you out of bed this morning?"

He groaned.

"Supper's ready," Josie announced.

The Hudsons gathered around the campfire, and Josie spooned ladles full of soup into their bowls and handed each person a thick slice of fresh, crusty bread. When they had been living on the Oregon Trail, trying to make so many miles of progress each day, there hadn't been time for a long, involved supper like this more than once or twice over the six months. Annie settled in next to her sisters and took her first tentative bite of the hot soup. Venison they had traded the Sullivans for, with onion, potatoes, carrots, and some kind of herb that Annie couldn't place but imagined Josie had gathered from any one of the meadows surrounding their camp—herbs that Annie wouldn't recognize if pressed. It was delicious. Warm and hearty. It reminded her of what her home had been like when someone else was in charge.

Now, she would have to figure out how to do all this on her own, for Isaac and any children that came along.

Annie had no idea how she could possibly accomplish that.

She spooned more soup into her mouth and put such challenges from her mind.

As they settled in to eat, Margaret asked Annie how her day had been. "How is Mrs. Tenney?"

"She's good, as far as I can tell. For as much as she has been through, she doesn't complain at all."

Josie nodded. "There are quite a few women like that in this town. Imagine being Mrs. Sullivan and losing both a husband and a son. Or the young Mrs. Mills, before they got married, and finding yourself completely alone on the other side of the continent."

"It's amazing what folks can do," Annie agreed. "In fact, Rebecca mentioned something about Caroline learning how to hunt. Do you think I could do that?"

Josie looked at her carefully. "But . . . why? Don't misunderstand, dear. I'm sure you could figure out how to do anything you wanted to. But what would Isaac say? You have a husband who enjoys caring for you, and plenty of tasks of your own to do at home, and you just talked about wanting to learn better cooking skills, so I guess I'm just confused about what the purpose of you pursuing this whole new skill would be."

"More than one skill, really," Margaret added. "I know you girls mostly got meat from the butcher, but my father hunted most everything we ate when I was growing up. You barely know how to shoot, Annie, so there's that, not to mention learning about the local terrain, the animals, tracking skills, trapping, and then dressing the game once you've managed to bag it. It's not like learning to play a piano, where you just sit down and practice your hand movements over and over."

"I suppose that's true," Annie said. "I was just thinking about what you said earlier about Lawrence needing to rest. I bet Isaac would favor my giving him a chance to do the same, don't you think?"

Josie looked thoughtful. "I'm not sure. He was the one who encouraged you to come into town today, wasn't he? Seems like you're always telling us other tasks he's taking up."

"Well, yes, but doesn't that mean I should return the favor?"

"There are some men—women, too—who take it as an insult if you imply they need to stop working. Think it means they're considered weak or some nonsense," Margaret said knowingly. "Now, I don't know if Isaac is that kind of man, but it's worth paying attention to. Not worth a fight to just let him spend his evening building a whole new smokehouse instead of sleeping."

Annie laughed, then lowered her voice to a whisper. "I think Mrs. Mills might be like that, from what I've heard."

"Oh, absolutely she is," Margaret declared with conviction. "No doubt about that."

Annie laughed again, but it quickly turned into a sigh. "I don't know what I need. I certainly don't know what Isaac needs. I thought everything would be easier once we were finally in Oregon, but it seems like it's just a different set of problems instead."

"We'll get settled," Josie assured her. "You're a step ahead of most folks, even, with that roof over your head."

"You're right. I should be grateful. I *am* grateful. I'm just trying to find my place. This doesn't feel like home yet, and I don't know how to make it one."

"At least you have Isaac," Josie reminded her.

"Did I hear my name?"

Just outside the circle of firelight stood Annie's husband. She rose to meet him.

"How was your day, wife?" he asked as he hugged her.

"Perfect."

"Was it? I'm glad. You'll have to tell me about it on the ride back."

"Have you eaten?" Josie asked him. "The soup is still plenty hot."

"I munched on some of yesterday's bread at home, with a bit of the smoked fish. We should get on the road, but I thank you."

Annie turned back to her sisters and nephew, far happier and at peace than she had been the night before. "Thank you so much," she said as she hugged Lawrence, Margaret, and Josie in turn. "Today was exactly what I needed. I've been missing you all so much, and this has helped. Even if you didn't let me make the soup."

"Any time," Josie said. "You know that."

"And we may descend on you in turn," Margaret said. "Especially as the weather gets colder and you have those snug log walls."

"Any time," Annie replied.

Isaac had given her privacy for her goodbyes, and was waiting for her with Rocky and the wagon just on the edge of the campsite. A small lit lantern hung next to Isaac's seat, lighting up the ground a couple yards all around.

"Do you need help climbing up?"

In response, Annie planted one foot on the outer rim of the wheel, gripped the sides of the wagon as tightly as she could, and hauled herself awkwardly into the wagon seat next to him.

"Easier than I expected," she said with a grin.

He flicked the reins, and Rocky started on down the road to the Wheelers' homestead. Isaac kept him going slower than usual, watching for dips in the road in the dark.

"Good day?" he asked, keeping his eyes on the drive.

"Great day," she responded, and she slid closer to her husband on the wagon bench, slipping her arm through his. In spite of all her worries, she was grateful for what she had, for the home she was returning to, for the man by her side.

CHAPTER TEN

Even though Annie had spent less than a day with Rebecca and her family, getting used to the isolation and responsibility of being in her own home again was surprisingly difficult. It was as though her heart had seen what else was possible and so rebelled against reality. She would rise with Isaac, make coffee and breakfast, wrap up a cold lunch for him, and kiss him goodbye all before dawn.

And then there came the long stretch of hours she had to fill by herself.

There was, of course, the putting away of the food and other supplies that Isaac had purchased when they went into Eden Valley. There was also the never-ending cycle of cooking enough for each meal and then cleaning up after it. There was water to gather—the closest source was about half a mile away—and the floor to sweep.

But the Wheelers didn't have many belongings that needed repair—not yet, at least. They didn't have a surplus of harvest that needed to be preserved. There were no children, and barely any animals on their farm that needed tending to. They were still so close to the scarcity of what life had been like when traveling on the Oregon Trail that many of the maintenance tasks and small luxuries that kept most women busy back east were simply not available to her here.

All of the ways Annie would be filling her winter days in the years to come did not yet apply to their life now.

And so, by early afternoon, she felt bereft and stuck, like a young animal in mud.

She churned the butter from the new milk they had acquired. She started knitting another pair of socks. And then she cast about for something to distract her from the quiet of her empty home.

In her distraction and her melancholy, Annie found herself going out to the front of her home repeatedly, looking down the trail for signs of her husband or a neighbor or really anything at all. She tried to tell herself that the town would grow, that more people would settle throughout the countryside, but right now all she felt was alone and incapable.

After a couple days like this, Annie found she could not simply suffer in silence. Though she couldn't make herself pretend that everything was fine, neither could she make herself come out and tell Isaac exactly how lonely she felt. Instead, when he came home one evening later that week, she peppered him with questions, using every trick she could think of to bask in his attention.

"Come! Sit!" she exclaimed as he walked through the door.

Annie had barely given him time to take off his coat and hat before she had ushered him into his usual chair at the table and put a cup of coffee in front of him.

"How is Mrs. Montgomery? Did you all get the Larsons' home finished? What's next? Oh, I'm sure the women in that campsite are starting to get anxious over the idea of not having a warm place for their children to sleep soon."

Isaac chuckled at Annie's exuberance. "Are you all right?"

"Wonderful. Yes, great." She manufactured a smile for him

before turning back to finishing up their supper. "Just wondering about town and all. I haven't talked to anyone since you left this morning, and I thought . . . well, anyway. Supper is ready. Fresh bread, and the soup recipe Josie told me about the other day."

She carefully carried a bowl of steaming soup to where he sat, returning with the soft bread.

"Smells wonderful, wife. Thank you."

As Annie settled in across the table from him, she gestured. "Go on. Please. Tell me all about the goings-on."

"Days with fresh sourdough are my favorite days," Isaac said, picking up a piece. "And fresh butter to go with it, right?"

"Oh! Yes!"

Annie popped up out of her chair again to get the mixing bowl that held the lump of butter she had made earlier in the week. She pulled off the towel that had been resting over the top, then paused.

Something was wrong.

She sniffed. Her heart dropped.

"Oh," Annie said under her breath.

She blinked hard and looked again, hoping she was mistaken. But no, there was no mistaking that color, that slightly sour smell that wafted up from the bowl.

"Oh, no . . ."

"What's wrong?"

She turned to him, dejected, holding out the bowl for him to see.

"The butter . . . it spoiled."

"What do you mean, the butter spoiled?" Isaac asked. "How could that have happened?"

"We have other butter. The batch my sister made last week. But this newer—"

"Having other butter doesn't help us, Annie. Now we have to throw out all of that"—he pointed at the bowl in her hands—"and we cannot afford to waste food at all, but especially in the winter, and especially something as precious as milk. You know those cows won't be producing much when it gets too cold. I can't believe you let this happen."

"I didn't—I mean, I don't know, I must have . . ."

Annie thought back to a few days earlier when she had set aside time to churn the milk into butter. But she had been so distracted that day, she could barely remember. She couldn't sort out her actions of that day from those of before, when Josie had helped her.

Then, suddenly, in searching her memories, Annie realized her mistake.

"I messed up. I didn't . . . I skipped a step. This is my fault."

"Is it?" He stared at her for a long, hard moment. His expression was inscrutable, and Annie had to look away. She gazed down at the bowl in her hands, tears smarting her eyes as the shame of her failure overwhelmed her.

If only Isaac hadn't been home when she discovered her error. She could have hidden it away. She could have avoided his anger, avoided this shame.

Isaac got out of his chair with such deliberate care that it was clear he was trying to hold his temper. She had never seen him this angry—frustrated at a dull axe or when she didn't cook the potatoes all the way, yes, but nothing like the fury shining in his eyes now.

"I'm sorry," she said softly.

"Sorry doesn't fix it," he said coldly. He paced away from the table, as though trying to put distance between them, and turned back around to face her. "And it's not just the butter, is it? You are in way over your head here, and I am the one who has to suffer for it."

"What? No—"

"Yes, Annie. When I asked you to come out here, I made the assumption that you were capable of taking care of yourself, let alone a house. But now you want to spend days with your friends and spoil an entire bucket of milk and expect me to just pick up the pieces."

Tears spilled down her cheeks at that, but she couldn't speak. There was nothing she could say to defend herself.

He was exactly right.

"When you responded to my advertisement, you told me you had been engaged. That you were already twenty-four years old. I thought, Wonderful—a mature, competent woman who can be a support to me out here in the wilderness."

He took a step closer to her, and she shrank back.

"Isaac, please . . ." Annie took a deep breath, trying to slow her pounding heart, but kept her eyes cast down.

"But that's not anywhere close to true, is it?" Isaac continued, his voice now low.

The cold fury she had heard in his words had turned to sorrow, but still Annie could not look at her husband. She was mortified. Because of course he was right. She had been moping over a lack of friends in this new life, when really she should have been concerning herself with learning the skills she needed. And it had taken his very real anger for her to see the truth of her imagined problems. She had spent the afternoon gossiping with Rebecca instead of making supper with her sister. She had let her mind wander to thoughts of her nonexistent piano instead of paying attention to all the steps needed for the butter.

Annie had never been one to seek out an argument, and now, when she knew she was in the wrong, all she could do was sink into herself and absorb every word of his criticism.

"Say something."

Finally, at that prompt, she looked up. Isaac had walked back to the far side of the room, as though to put space between them again, but she saw a pleading in his face now, an entreaty for her to have a reasonable explanation or make a believable promise that nothing like this would ever happen again.

Annie could not give that to him. She wasn't certain of anything.

She shook her head in apology and looked down again.

"Annie," he said softly. "We have to be in this together. When me and Gertie—"

"All right, I'll say something." She looked at him directly, steeling her courage.

He gestured as though to tell her to go ahead.

"I'm not Gertie."

He frowned. "I know that."

"I'm sure you know, but you seem to be hoping otherwise all the same."

His frown deepened, the lines in his forehead becoming pronounced, even despite the low light. "You mean I am hoping my wife hadn't died? Of course I am. What kind of thing is that to say to a person?"

"Well, yes—but . . ." she spluttered. "I wish my fiancé hadn't died either, of course. I wish a lot of things were different, but I'm not casting them up to you as though it were a failure of yours."

"You think I'm blaming you for Gertie's death?" He smirked, taunting her to admit how ridiculous that sounded.

"No. Of course not." She was growing frustrated. Her complete avoidance of arguments for most of her life meant that she was ill-prepared for the tricks and turns that he could employ. "I mean that . . . well, you bring her up constantly. It's always 'My wife would have done that differently,' and even though *I* am clearly your wife—the only one you have at the moment—what you're really saying is that I'm not good enough. I'm not smart enough. I'm not . . ." She threw up her hands in anger. "I'm not what you hoped for. That is apparent. And we're both sorry about that. I'm so sorry to be a disappointment, but I'm what you have now. I'm all you get."

"Annie—"

"I'm sorry," she said again, taking a backward step away from him. "I'm sorry I ruined the butter, and I'm sorry I forget how to make soup broth and put the potatoes in. I'm sorry I'm scared of wielding the axe to cut firewood, and I'm sorry that you have to manage all the animals. And I'm—" Her voice cracked. "I'm sorry that I'm *lonely* and that everything feels harder than it needs to be and you have to take care of me."

"Come now. You are overreacting. I didn't mean—"

"You meant all of it." Her shoulders slumped as the truth consumed her. "You mean it every time you tell me what a better homemaker Gertie was. And you're right. And it hurts every time."

"Well—but . . . I—" He looked helpless, unwilling to lie to her but unsure how to salvage the situation. "Annie, please."

Isaac took two more steps toward her, until he stood directly behind his chair at the table. He held one hand out to her, but with the furniture between them, she would need to come around to his side of it if she was going to take his hand.

Because of course he expected that. In all of this, even with all her faults and failures she could recognize, the fact was that Isaac expected more of her than he was willing to give himself. He held her to a standard without examining to see if he was meeting it himself.

Annie looked at her husband—the man who she was going to spend the rest of her life with—and felt defeated.

Without a word, she spun on her heel and ran outdoors.

CHAPTER ELEVEN

Throwing open the front door to her home, Annie stumbled down her front step and plunged into the darkness of the night. All she wanted was air. She needed to breathe. She couldn't be in that small house anymore, that crowded space with Isaac. She needed room to think, to disconnect from the torrent of emotions that her husband had brought up in her—the shame, the disappointment, the confusion and hurt.

It wasn't until Annie had to divert her path around a tree that she fully shook off her fog of pain and realized where she was. She stopped short and looked around. The early sunsets of December meant that it was now long after dark. Though the moonlight cast a tiny sheen of visibility on the forest around her, she was effectively in complete darkness.

"Annie!"

She turned to see Isaac standing in their doorway, holding a lantern up to light the surrounding area, and scanning for her. But she had already run far enough into the nearby grove of trees that she was hidden from him. From this vantage, with Isaac all lit up, she could observe him without him seeing her.

He called her name a couple more times, but didn't venture off the front step. As he shook his head and went back in the house, Annie realized she was being left alone.

This was what she wanted, yes. But it still hurt. That he would just let her go. That he would abandon her in the woods.

Wrapping her arms around herself, she rubbed her body and shoulders, trying to stay warm. It was cold and it was dark, and she was outdoors without even a bonnet or shawl. She couldn't stay out here, though as she took a deep breath that helped her chest relax, she knew she had done the right thing in that moment, but it was apparent that Annie had not thought past getting away from her argument with Isaac.

She knew she needed to go back, but the cold invigorated her. She couldn't let this fight with her husband fester, but neither could she have stayed in that close room with his criticism and disappointment all around her. She had run away, like a child, but when the alternative was listening to more criticism, Annie didn't know what else she could have done. The sharp, dry air clarified her mind as she thought back over what she had said to Isaac.

Maybe she would stay out here a little bit longer.

Under her feet, the dried pine needles crunched. Years—hundreds, at least—of growth and decay covered the forest floor. Scattered among the ponderosas were firs and cedars, each stretching up above her head, dozens of feet in the air. These were the trees that had been cut down to make her own home, as well as those of her neighbors; these were the trees that would protect and provide for her over the next decades as she made her home here in the Oregon Territory.

It was too dark to walk any farther into the wood. Annie stopped and leaned her back against the trunk of a cedar that must be at least a foot and a half in diameter. Even though it was nighttime, even though it was winter, all around her Annie heard the buzz, twitch, shuffle, and other noises of wild creatures. She did not feel unsafe—her front door was right there—but neither did she feel at home.

In fact, Annie couldn't remember the last time she had felt at home. Certainly part of her motivation for answering Isaac's advertisement for a bride was because she didn't feel as though she belonged where she had been living anymore. After making that decision, she had spent nearly a year living on the road, in wagons and boarding houses, crowded into too-small spaces with her family. And now she had her own home, in theory, but her seemingly constant failures within its walls kept her from feeling as though she truly belonged there. How could she claim it as her own when she couldn't even manage to make supper without some mistake or another?

The cold was beginning to set in, but Annie's adrenaline from her argument with Isaac kept her from noticing too much. She knew she really should go back inside, should submit again to whatever Isaac had to say to her. But not yet. She was in the forest, in the dark, in the cold, without a weapon or even a shawl to protect her, and yet she could not bring herself to go back.

A memory of her oldest sister sprang to her mind.

Louisa Hudson had been a seamstress in their town of Norfolk, Virginia; she was not the only one, but she was the best, in large part because of the standards of perfection that she held herself to. Those standards kept her at her shop late, determined to finish dresses ahead of her clients' deadlines or repair just one more shirt for one of the sailors getting ready to ship out in a couple days. There were many nights, in Annie's recollection, that Louisa didn't return home until well after supper, sometimes after Annie and Josie had gone to bed.

One of these such nights, Louisa didn't come home at all, and it was not until Josie was serving up breakfast the next morning that they even noticed. Annie volunteered to go check on her, wrapping up bread and fruit to take to her shop in town. Though she was petrified that she might find some tragedy, what she actually found was Louisa still hunched over the waist of a dress, her candle burned down to a nub.

Through a series of concerned questions and distracted answers, Annie finally realized that Louisa had chosen to stay awake, working all night to perfect attaching the delicate lace to her client's gown, rather than do the job haphazardly or miss her deadline. In her mind, any choice that did not involve Louisa doing her absolute best was no choice at all.

And now, Annie thought, here she was letting missing her sisters keep her from making butter correctly. That was no excuse, and she did not want to be that person any longer.

Annie didn't want to let the memory of her sister down, not after everything Louisa had sacrificed to help get Annie where she was today. Her ineptness and her loneliness would have to be conquered, though Annie didn't have any idea how she was going to do that. Especially if she had to do it all under the judgment and disappointment of the man she had married. Not that Isaac was particularly terrible; in fact, his frustration at her ruining the butter was completely understandable.

But that didn't mean that Annie had to just stand there and take it.

They couldn't go on like this. She couldn't handle more fights like this. She would have to formulate a plan. There had to be a way that she could perfect the skills she lacked without further upsetting Isaac or ruining anything that he purchased for them. And, she told herself, with a town full of people, there had to be some way that Annie could be more involved. Some small routine she could take part in or group she could join.

The Wheelers had two horses—Rocky, that Isaac rode out every day as he helped build the homes Eden Valley needed, and Pansy, that was left with Annie in the small shelter that served as the stable. She was far from an expert horsewoman, but so too was she far from completely isolated out here on her homestead.

Annie stood again, slowly making her way back to her small cabin.

She just needed to take action.

What action, though, she had no idea. But thinking about Louisa watching her, shaking her head in disappointment, was enough to spur Annie on. She could do this—if not for Isaac and herself, then at least for the memory of Louisa Hudson.

And then, maybe from there she could feel more comfortable making this new life her own, making this home her own.

She made a fist, forcing her numb fingers into movement. Though Annie's heart raced at the thought of what she was returning to, she was too cold to put it off any longer. She put her hand on the door and pushed it open.

The only light in the place came from the low flames in the fireplace. The fire was dying down; she was surprised Isaac had not put another log or two on the embers. It would surely be out by the morning.

But as her eyes adjusted, she realized the dying fire was the only light in the room. She had not been gone that long, but in that time, Isaac had snuffed out the two candles that had been burning earlier, as well as the lantern he'd held in the doorway as he called after her. Annie didn't know exactly how long she had been outside thinking, but in whatever time had elapsed, her husband had gone to bed instead of looking for her, or even waiting up for her.

Still standing just inside the front door, Annie froze. Her husband's behavior hurt her, but maybe she deserved it.

What she wouldn't give to be able to just walk back out that door and stay overnight with her sisters again. More than anything else, more than any other obstacle or conflict, what hurt Annie the most every day was how much she missed her sisters.

Maybe it was running away, but it was also running to something she loved.

But that was not something she could do anything about. She

had made her choices, married Isaac Wheeler, and now she had to build this life with him.

And so, after putting a couple logs on the fire to burn down overnight, Annie quietly undressed in the dark room. She tucked her boots under the bed and hung her dress on its designated hook.

After pulling her simple cotton nightgown—a wedding gift from Isaac—over her head, Annie hesitated. Isaac lay on his side of the bed, with his back to the middle. From where she stood, Annie couldn't tell if he was actually asleep or if he was simply avoiding her.

Was this what it was going to be like being married to him?

Annie bit her lip as she carefully pulled back the quilt and slid down into bed. She was only a few inches from Isaac and so moved slowly to keep from disturbing him. Whether he was truly asleep or not, it seemed clear he wanted nothing to do with her at that moment.

Lying on her back, staring up into the dark, Annie ran through all the friends she had in Eden Valley, all the people she could ask for help or turn to for advice. Telling herself to come up with a plan was one thing, but actually figuring out what that plan would be was something else entirely.

She turned over, her back to her husband, and closed her eyes.

Sleep did not find her for a long time.

CHAPTER TWELVE

It took a long time for her to fall asleep, and when Annie woke the next morning, she immediately felt something wrong. She opened her eyes, looking at the ceiling of her little home, and realized what felt off.

It was too quiet.

Reaching an arm out across the bed, Annie realized Isaac was gone. The bed was cold.

Across the room, the fire was lit and burning cheerily, but a quick assessment of what else had been disturbed told Annie that her husband had left for the day, and not merely outside.

He had left their home without saying goodbye. Without even waking her. He must have tiptoed around the place to keep from disturbing her. To keep from having to speak to her. She was now a problem in his life that he had to manage, instead of the helpmate and comfort that she so wanted to be.

She sat up in bed, turning to put her bare foot on the cold wood of the floor. Whether her husband was there or not, she needed to start her day. The cooking, the cleaning, the shoring up for the months ahead—it all still needed to be done, even if her mind was distracted thinking of Isaac the whole time.

Her heart swelled a little when she saw that he had left her a bucket of water, had even set it near enough the fire to warm up a little. It was a bit of a distance to their closest water source; that would have taken a chunk out of his morning. So, then, she wasn't being completely shunned, which was a small relief.

Annie quickly got dressed and performed her toilets, which included washing her face and combing out her hair in the small mirror that hung above their washstand.

Without the distraction of Isaac in the house as she went through her morning routine, Annie realized all over again just how much time she had to fill in a day.

In the bright light of morning, Annie felt her problems were both more insignificant and more insurmountable than they had been the night before. What she needed for herself and what Isaac needed from her seemed incompatible, and Annie had not the slightest idea how to move forward.

She went through the motions of making herself breakfast: coffee and johnnycakes, without butter. This small morning meal was one of the few tasks that Annie felt she had learned how to do well, likely through the daily repetition. As she thought through how to make up her failures to Isaac, she thought hungrily of the whirligig her sister had made only a few months ago, even over the campfire. Her birthday meal just over a year ago, when the Hudsons had decided to come to Oregon, had been full of the hearty, flavorful food that Annie most missed. They had fresh seafood from the bay near Norfolk, and Louisa had even found the funds for fruit out of season.

Now, here in Oregon, Annie couldn't even manage butter.

On the ever-expanding list of responsibilities Annie needed to take on was learning how to properly preserve meat now that they no longer had a local butcher to rely on. Isaac had built them a smokehouse in the early days of their marriage, but he hadn't yet taught her how to use it. She would need to ask him, certainly, and then perhaps have to submit herself to a series of conversations in which she disappointed him.

That reminded her, suddenly, of the Fowlers, the Hudsons' neighbors when they had lived in Virginia. The homes in Norfolk had been far closer together than the homesteads out here in the territories; the town had grown up rapidly, and living closer together, closer to the center of town, had been necessary in the early days of the settlement. As near the other homes as they had been, there were times when Annie or one of her sisters would be in their garden or feeding their chickens and overhear snippets of conversation from the Fowlers' garden.

At first, the sisters had not paid it any mind. The Fowlers' discussions of their budget or their plans for the dairy cow seemed so ordinary as to not warrant attention. But slowly, over the years, the conversations became more and more heated. Annie had heard everything from despondence to pointed criticism float over the fence between the houses. The arguments grew more frequent for a time, until one day Annie realized she hadn't heard either of the Fowlers in a few weeks.

After a while, Annie realized the conversations seemed to have stopped altogether. When Annie saw Mrs. Fowler in town she never spoke of her husband, though she would chatter on about her children or her animals. When she saw them in church on Sundays, Mrs. Fowler focused all her attention on the children, even putting the four of them between her husband and herself in the pew.

Annie shuddered to think of living next to someone day after day—years of watching their children grow, of making decisions about the home and the future—all while being married to a person she despised.

She could not imagine ever feeling that way about Isaac, but Annie had seen enough of marriage in the community where she grew up to know that the road to contempt could begin with something as seemingly little as a silence.

Once she had finished her breakfast, cleaned the dishes, and put everything away, Annie stood in the middle of her home, hands on hips, and looked around her expectantly, hoping for some spark of inspiration. Last night she had promised herself that she would do something to make a change. Now what would it be?

Nothing inside was inspiring her or pointing to options, so Annie grabbed her bonnet from the hook near the door and headed out.

The smokehouse Isaac had insisted on building as soon as possible was about fifty feet from their front door, and not far beyond that was the stand of trees that stood between the Wheelers' homestead and that of their closest neighbors—the Abbott family. In the other direction lay their minimal stable, and beyond that the creek.

Though Annie wished her own sisters could have been as close, because they wouldn't have a man of age until Lawrence turned eighteen, there were other considerations about where they could live until they were able to officially claim a homestead.

Annie kept walking, into the trees, slowly, listening to the woods around her while her mind gnawed on the problem ahead of her. Above, birds called to each other, trilling through the morning light as they too began their days.

Soon, Annie found herself humming along, though she didn't realize it immediately. Music had been so deeply engrained in her life when she lived in Virginia that losing it as they set off across the continent had been one of the more difficult things to get used to.

That's it, she realized.

That was what had been missing all this time, and that was

what she could do now to both spend time with other people and help create the community in which she was building her life. And who knew, maybe focusing on something she was already good at could even help Annie's confidence in other areas. Goodness knew she would be hesitant to try making butter again anytime soon.

The solution seemed completely clear now—Annie would lean into her expertise as a musician. She would start a choir. The church could have a choir, even if they had no instruments just yet, and Annie herself could help make that happen.

The rest of her day went by in a blur as Annie turned over plans and ideas in her mind. She didn't have any of her music with her, but she remembered plenty, and could slowly build out Eden Valley's repertoire of songs. Though it seemed like an enormous project, it was the idea of building something big—of making her home where she was—that most appealed to her.

That afternoon, as she was checking on her biscuits, her husband returned. Annie almost didn't hear the door open; Isaac was so quiet and far more subdued than she had ever seen him. With the thud of his boots on the floor, Annie spun around, taking in the contrite and cautious expression.

They stared at each other for a long moment, neither willing to begin the conversation.

Annie warred internally. She wanted to be brave and not begin this marriage with a wall between them. She didn't want to be like the Fowlers, with their bitterness and silence as their marriage went on.

One of them would need to say the first thing.

Annie stood a little straighter and said, "Hello."

At just that word, Isaac seemed to relax. "Hello. How was your day?"

"Oh . . ." She shrugged. "It was a day. Much like all the rest of my days, though I took a lovely walk outside for a bit. How was yours?"

He smiled, almost shyly. "Much like all the rest of my days, though I missed saying goodbye to my wife this morning."

She felt a smile creeping over her face. "I missed that too."

They held each other's gaze for a long moment before Isaac took the few steps to close the distance between them. At that simple gesture, Annie was relieved to step into his waiting embrace.

"I'm sorry," he whispered. "I never meant to . . ." He pulled away from their hug and looked Annie in the eye. "I really should not get so angry. It's not something I'm proud of. I probably wouldn't remember all the steps if I tried to make butter, either. I shouldn't have said anything about it. I was disappointed and tired from the day, but I should have tried to be kinder."

"Thank you. I'm sorry I am just not . . ." She shrugged. "I'm not the housekeeper you thought you were getting, I suppose. But I'm going to do better."

"I know you will." Isaac smiled at her with satisfaction as he moved to take his seat at the table. "Because otherwise we'll starve."

He laughed, but Annie couldn't quite see what the joke was. Was that really how he saw the situation? That the life and death of the Wheelers was in her hands, based solely on her ability to quickly learn these new skills?

It probably was close to the truth, and not something Annie was prepared to joke about yet. There was far too much pressure on her already.

"You know," he continued, "I didn't do much of the cooking, but I think I watched Gertie make soup enough times that I could maybe help you figure out the recipe. If you want. Maybe someday later this winter, when I'm through putting up walls and things for the neighbors. Could be fun."

She paused before responding, trying to remind herself that he meant well. Isaac was only ever kind to her, even if it wasn't precisely in the way that she needed.

"Thank you. Maybe that's a good idea."

Isaac seemed satisfied with that answer, enough that he launched into a story about his day, detailing the way Mrs. Waters insisted that they move the front door of her house when it was almost too late to do so.

As he talked, Annie resolved to spend the next day in Eden Valley. She could saddle Pansy herself; she didn't have to tell Isaac she was going. And she could talk to Rebecca about all of this, maybe ask her advice. Yes, Annie was alone out here in her home most of the time, but she didn't always have to be.

CHAPTER THIRTEEN

The next morning, Annie tried to be as pleasant as she could to Isaac until he left. He meant well, she told herself over and over again, even while he again wished aloud that he had asked Gertie the exact steps that she used to roast a hen precisely as he liked so he could share them with Annie. Eventually, Isaac left for the day, off to finish the Valentine family's house, and Annie had hours ahead of her to put her plan into action.

Rather than try to hitch up her horse to their wagon on her own, Annie saddled the mare and braved the ride. Though she wasn't a novice, horse riding had never been something she spent a lot of time doing, especially astride. Where they lived in Virginia, most parts of town she had been able to walk to, and when coming west she had walked alongside the trail more often than not. Here, though, in the wild of the Oregon Territory, everything was so spread out. Town was a couple miles away from home, so riding was something she would need to get used to. With every step, she felt as though her entire body was tense, gripping with every muscle to the horse, saddle, and reins.

And so, Annie and Pansy rode the couple miles into Eden

Valley, to the campsite where those families still waited for a finished home.

When she reached the edge of the campsite, she noticed that it was more empty and more spread out from when she had visited only a few days earlier. So many homes and more permanent structures were being completed every day, and so more and more families were pulling up their temporary homes of tents and covered wagons to finally live somewhere permanent. Some of these families—like the Hudsons—had left their homes back east as much as a year earlier. It was no wonder that they were getting impatient.

Annie dismounted and led her horse between the campsites that remained. It didn't occur to her until that moment that who she sought might not even be there anymore. But she had come so far; she needed to at least check. It was a minor relief when she saw that the Stephens family's wagons were still in place, just as they had been the last time.

Wrapping Pansy's reins loosely around the spokes of one of the wagon wheels, Annie called out to the seemingly empty camp. Even the fire had burned down to ashes.

"Hello? Rebecca?"

There was a rustling sound from within the wagon, and then Mrs. Stephens—Rebecca's mother—poked out her head.

"Annie Wheeler, is that you? To what do we owe the pleasure?"

"Is your daughter around anywhere? I just . . . well, you know, it gets lonesome out there by myself. I thought I'd come talk to my friend."

"She's down by the water, child. Dawdling, no doubt, but that's no matter. She knows when she gets back I'm going to make her get down to business." Mrs. Stephens winked at Annie and shooed her away.

Annie left Pansy where she was and went to find her friend. The river where everyone in the camp got their water was a short walk away, and as the weather was warming to midday it turned out to be a nice stroll. As she got closer to the river, she spotted a half dozen other women and older girls, all fetching water for whatever chore they were in the middle of.

She hadn't seen Rebecca, though, until she went a bit farther downstream, where the shrubs on either bank thinned. Peeking through the branches, she noticed her friend sitting right on the edge of the water. As she drew closer, Annie realized that Rebecca had taken off her shoes and stockings, and was sitting with her feet soaking in the river up to her ankles.

"Rebecca Tenney, what under the canopy are you doing? It must be freezing in there!"

Rebecca turned in surprise at the sound of her name, but relaxed when she saw who it was. "Well, goodness, Annie Wheeler, I didn't expect to see you today," she said. "It's not even laundry day."

"Very funny," Annie responded. "Really, though, what are you doing?" She sat in the dead grass next to her friend, but kept her own feet safely tucked underneath her.

"Shocking my system, I suppose. I haven't been here long, but when your feet get numb and then you need to walk on them? It's positively invigorating. I imagine it must be like what it feels to be struck by lightning." Her eyes lit up excitedly at the thought.

Annie's mouth fell open in surprise. "You are crazy."

"Yes, well." She shrugged. "There's only so many places I can find entertainment in my situation. Not like you with your handsome husband and glorious house and no mother telling you she needs you to darn your brother's three pairs of socks. Honestly, does he keep nails in his shoes? How can all his socks have holes?"

Annie laughed. "Your mother did tell me when you get back she's going to make you do something productive."

Rebecca's eyes widened and she gestured mutely, as though to say *I told you so*. "Did you come by yourself?" She looked over Annie's shoulder as if to confirm.

"Yes, and actually, Isaac doesn't know I'm here. I just wanted to talk to you and the pastor's wife quickly, and then head back home."

"And see your sisters?"

"And see my sisters. Yes. Goodness. That's a lot." Annie laughed awkwardly and played with the cuff of her sleeve. "I don't know what I was thinking. Especially if I am going to have time to make supper."

Rebecca peered at her. "What is going on, Annie?" she asked softly, serious now.

And that small kindness, that gift of being seen by her friend and having her pain be taken seriously, brought tears to Annie's eyes. She had been so alone at home, for so long, she had forgotten what it felt like to be cared about like this.

"We don't have to talk about it if you don't want to," Rebecca added.

"No. I do. That's, um . . . that is actually why I came. But . . ."

"Take your time. You know what I have waiting for me when I go back."

That made Annie laugh, jolting her from the despair that had been threatening to overtake her.

"Can I ask you something?"

"Of course."

Annie paused. There were so many versions of the question she wanted to ask, she had to be careful not to offend her friend or sound ignorant. "Do you think about your husband a lot?"

Rebecca looked away with a soft smile on her face. "Every day. Coming to Oregon was his idea in the first place, so I can't get through a new idea for our home or even a conversation with Daniel about what he can get me at the fort without wishing Andrew was around to experience all this with me. This was supposed to be *our* adventure."

"But . . . do you feel like, um . . . do you talk about him a lot to other people?"

She frowned, thinking. "I don't know, to be truthful. I imagine I probably talk about him more than I realize I do. You might need to ask my mother or Jasper about that."

"I don't think I've heard you talk about him much," Annie said, "so I wondered if there was a reason for that."

"Not anything I've made a specific decision about. I think maybe . . . I think the memory of Andrew is still so raw and precious that maybe I'm just not ready exposing it to God and everyone. The little time we had together is still just mine, and I don't have to share it."

"I understand." Annie's own young love had died before they had married, but she remembered actively avoiding any conversation about him in the months that immediately followed John's death.

"Why do you ask?" Rebecca prodded gently.

"It's Isaac. From the way he talks sometimes, I wonder just how perfect his first wife was."

"Nobody is perfect."

"Of course, I know that, but . . ." Annie's shoulders slumped. "He compares me to her. Maybe not a lot by someone else's standards, but a lot more than I expected. Maybe that's my own fault, and I deluded myself into thinking both of us were putting our past behind us."

"Or maybe he doesn't realize he's doing it?"

"Maybe. It is generally when he's trying to be helpful, to suggest that I do something the way she did. I don't think he's trying to be deliberately critical, but also maybe I just don't know him well enough to know."

They sat in silence for a moment before Rebecca finally asked, "Are you going to talk to him about it?"

"I should."

"Yes, you should."

"But . . . it's hard. The things that he's complaining about— No, not complaining. As I said, he's only trying to help. I guess the things he's trying to be helpful about are things I see as my own failings. How can I complain about the way he is trying to help?"

"Right, yes, I can understand that. But also, Annie, how can he actually help you if you don't share with him how to do that?"

"What do you mean?"

"Let me tell you a story. A few years ago, before we got married, Andrew started bringing me flowers every Sunday after church. It was a complete surprise, and I was so flattered that he would spend the time and thought to do that for me. And it continued every week, for an entire summer. Every Sunday, I would walk home with my family, and within half an hour Andrew was on our front porch with a bouquet of beautiful purple asters."

"That sounds lovely."

"Oh, it would have been—if I wasn't allergic to flower pollen." Rebecca gave her a wry smile. "And asters are some of the very worst. You should have seen the hives I broke out in that first Sunday! I had to miss two days of school. After that, I learned to have my mother discard the bouquets right away before I could be too affected, but then the next Sunday he would be there again."

"What did you do?"

"I was young, I wanted to please him, so I just kept saying 'thank you' until finally my mother made me say something to him. She was tired of having to take care of my mess every week. But more than that, she wanted me to learn how to . . ." Rebecca searched for how to describe it. "She wanted me to learn how to let a man love me, I think. She told me exactly what I'm saying to you now—that man cannot read your mind, and he will only be able to give you what you need if you tell him what you need."

"But what if I hurt his feelings? He means well."

"You might. But the alternative is the rest of your life pretending."

Annie nodded. If there was one thing she had learned over the last year, it was that staying quiet to keep the peace—especially with people she loved—was more trouble than it was worth. Rebecca was right, of course; Annie had to say something.

"Thank you. You're right, and I'm sorry, but I need to go. Thank you for always talking to me."

Annie climbed to her feet, quickly calculating how much time she could spend with her sisters before she stopped near the church and still had time enough to go home and make supper for Isaac.

"I am always happy to see you," Rebecca replied. "And I should get back, too, if Mama is going to be able to rest her feet while I do all the chores, or whatever she has planned for me."

"Let me walk you back," Annie said, offering a hand to help Rebecca stand. "Especially if your feet are numb."

"I can do it. Probably." She laughed. "But I'd love company, thank you."

As they walked back, Rebecca made Annie laugh with stories about the Valentine girls at the camp near her. Annie said her goodbyes, collected Pansy from where she had left her at the Stephens camp, and guided her horse on foot to her sisters.

CHAPTER FOURTEEN

Annie dawdled with her sisters at their campsite for more than an hour before she realized the day was getting away from her. It was far too easy to settle in for a chat, to get comfortable and let everything keep on the way it was. But, she reminded herself, she came all the way into town for a reason: because there was something in her life she wanted to change. And so, finally, Annie tore herself away. Without telling her sisters her plans—just in case she failed—Annie again said her goodbyes and bravely set off.

As she finally left the campsite—fully aware that she had procrastinated so long that her conversation with the pastor's wife would almost certainly have to be rushed—Annie realized that she only had guesses for where to find the other woman. The general camp where the remaining families and their covered wagons were situated was on the north side of Eden Valley. Annie led Pansy into what would soon be the central, main street of town, and over the narrow, temporary bridge to the south side of the river where the church had been built.

The parsonage had been built in the open meadow not far behind the church itself. And, like the church structure, the mayor and other men had prioritized finishing the home for Pastor and Mrs. Montgomery, letting her move in long before many other members of the community. This meant that they'd had at least a couple weeks to settle in and make their home their own.

Such a cozy home seemed to be the best place to look for the pastor's wife, and as Annie directed Pansy around the back of the church, she saw she had guessed correctly. Mrs. Montgomery was at home, and Annie forced herself through her uncertainty to talk to her.

The other woman, about Annie's own age, had her dark hair pulled back in a tight knot and was kneeling in the dirt in front of the parsonage. A space approximately a dozen feet in length had been cleared of grass and large stones; to Annie's eye it looked as though the ground had even been tilled. Whatever the pastor's wife was working on had been afforded time and attention; making this new building a home was clearly a priority.

Mrs. Montgomery didn't seem to hear her approach. Annie dismounted and led Pansy a few steps closer, still without any notice from the pastor's wife. Finally, Annie spoke up.

"Mrs. Montgomery?"

The other woman started, putting a palm to her chest as though to calm her breathing, then turned around. "Goodness! I'm so sorry, I wasn't expecting anyone."

"No, of course. I'm sorry. I didn't mean to scare you."

"It's nothing." Mrs. Montgomery stood, brushed dirt off her knees, and crossed through the open land to Annie, a welcoming smile on her face. "It's my fault. I was miles away, thinking about springtime and everything that needs to be done over the next few months."

"I can imagine," Annie responded. "But you're gardening already?"

She nodded. "I put in onions and potatoes as soon as this plot was laid out. Back in October. I'm sure the men were irritated having to build around my little garden, but starting that early is the only way I could hope for any kind of harvest before a frost. Though I fear it was still too late. Time will tell."

"Did you garden a lot back in . . . I'm sorry, I don't know where you came from."

"Virginia. Like you, I believe, but farther inland. I lived with my aunt and uncle after my parents passed, and the kitchen garden was always my specific project."

A small expression of regret crossed her face, but she was beaming at Annie in the next second, leaving Annie to wonder if she had imagined it.

"I'm sure you didn't come here to talk about my weeding, did you? What can I help you with? I'm afraid the pastor won't be back for a few hours yet, but I'm happy to pray with you if you would like."

"Oh! No. I mean, thank you, but actually I came to talk to you."

"Oh? Would you like to . . . ?" She looked around. "I don't have anywhere for you to sit," she finally said in a carrying whisper. "I am not the model housekeeper one would expect of a pastor's wife, I suppose."

"I won't tell anyone," Annie teased.

"How about the front step here?"

Mrs. Montgomery gestured to the wide stone step that some man had built for her at the entry to her small parsonage. When Annie sat, the cold of the stone leaked up through her underthings and dress, but somehow she didn't mind. The step was narrow enough that the two women had to sit close together, shoulder to shoulder, looking out from their perch. The view from this step was, of course, mostly the church building, but beyond that was the river, the beginnings of the general store, and a couple roofs farther in the distance.

"The town seems to be coming together," Annie said. "When

we were trudging through mud and eating cold biscuits every day it seemed as though we would never get here."

"I know exactly what you mean." Mrs. Montgomery followed Annie's gaze, looking over the developing frontier town. "My husband had such a clear vision of his congregation and the future we would build here, but all I could see was the fifteen chores I still needed to do that day."

The Montgomerys had come west just the two of them, and not long after they had married. Annie realized it must have been a very different experience than her own, as she had multiple family members to help shoulder the burden, but the pastor's wife had been almost entirely alone.

"I've been thinking about that," Annie began uncertainly. "About what we all were expecting when we were finally in Oregon at last, and what we can do to bridge the gap between what we have now and what maybe we had hoped for."

"Is that why you wanted to talk to me?"

Annie nodded, steeling herself for the uncomfortable moment when she had to ask for something. "I was wondering if maybe— if it's all right with you and the pastor . . ." She cleared her throat. The pastor's wife watched her, not rushing or pressuring. "I thought it would be nice for folks if I start a choir?"

Mrs. Montgomery blinked at her in surprise. "A choir? Already?"

"Just a small one," Annie continued hurriedly. "And I know there's no piano, and I don't know how the pastor would feel about Martin's fiddle on a Sunday morning, but I used to teach piano back in Virginia, you see, and I was in our church choir back there, and we could even sing a cappella, we don't need much and . . ." Annie had run out of breath. In her excitement and worry, she had tried to head off every possible objection the pastor's wife might have and assure her in every way she could that she was serious. "But, of course, if you maybe already had plans yourself, or I suppose if the pastor doesn't think music is—"

"It's a wonderful idea," Mrs. Montgomery said, cutting her off. "I will have to speak to my husband, of course, but that seems more like a conversation where I will be informing him this is happening, rather than asking him for permission. He is unlikely to object. When would you like to start?"

Annie felt a wave of relief completely out of proportion to the reasonable question she had asked. But the promise it offered her was far larger, far more satisfying, than she could rightly express. This outlet was not the solution to everything she had been struggling with, but it would help.

"Thank you. Yes, goodness. Thank you so much," she gushed. "I confess I hadn't thought much beyond just this first step. I suppose I should speak to my husband, too, and I imagine with the sun setting earlier and earlier most folks won't want to be out after dark, and there's so much to do otherwise with the daylight." She frowned. "I'm sorry, I don't know."

Mrs. Montgomery nudged her gently with her shoulder.

"It's a lot to think about, let alone manage. If there's one thing I've learned lately when feeling overwhelmed, it's that it's okay to ask for help."

Annie nodded. "Thank you."

"So I will talk to my husband, and you talk to yours, and sometime in the future our little Eden Valley church will have a choir. I'm grateful to you for bringing this to me, Mrs. Wheeler. It speaks well of your generous heart."

"Oh!" Annie laughed awkwardly. "Please don't say that. I merely missed music in my own life and thought others probably did too."

"Whatever the reason, you are nonetheless making a big commitment. So, thank you."

Annie offered her a tight smile, wondering—not for the first time—if she was taking on more than she could handle. She had only just spoiled their butter, after all. She had a lot to learn.

That thought made Annie realize how late it was getting.

Though it was still midafternoon, there was not much daylight left, and she wanted to be home in time to make supper for Isaac.

"Thank you," she said again as she stood. "This means more than I can tell you."

Mrs. Montgomery looked at her curiously, but didn't press. "Then I'm even more happy that we could have this talk."

As Annie made her way home that afternoon, riding Pansy the few miles to her homestead, she felt a mix of peace and anticipation. Somehow this step she had taken was both exactly what she needed and far scarier than she felt ready for.

But, she reminded herself, it was nothing compared to what she had already been through in her life. Maybe things would be easier for her now going forward.

CHAPTER FIFTEEN

Annie had stayed in town longer than she'd intended, and the sun was setting by the time she had returned to her own homestead. She removed Pansy's saddle, brushing her down and making sure the mare was settled with fresh water, before entering her home to start supper. It all took longer than she'd hoped, and that was when Annie realized that the labors of the day had more of an impact on her than she expected.

The ride—likely the saddle or her tense clinging to it—had bruised her, making every step she took ache, worsening when she sat. Muscles she'd forgotten she even had were tender, causing Annie to move more slowly than usual. The sun had just about set, which meant that her husband could be home any minute; whatever they were going to eat that night would have to be something she could cook easily and quickly.

She started a fire in the fireplace, set water to boiling, and crossed gingerly to where her food supply was stored. Looking through her larder, desperate for some inspiration, Annie felt a low wave of fear, wondering exactly how upset Isaac would be at her failure to make the home welcoming and ready the moment he walked back through the door.

What praise for his dead wife would be mentioned, at Annie's expense?

Shaking her head at her own foolishness, Annie pushed the thought from her mind. There was no need for such overreaction. He was usually kind, and rarely as frustrated as she expected him to be. But *rarely* was not *never*. Still, she elected to prepare the same kind of fast meal that Josie had perfected while they traveled on the Oregon Trail. No time to soak beans or bake bread, but Annie could whip up some johnnycakes and bacon. That would have to be enough.

Though it would be enough, she still wished for eggs or fried potatoes or something more. Maybe in the spring they would have the fresh food she so missed.

Maybe in the spring was becoming a recurring thought, she realized.

No sooner had Annie assembled her ingredients and begun mixing the cornmeal than the door opened and Isaac entered.

"Good evening, wife," he said, hanging up his hat and coat. "How was your day?"

"Very full," she admitted, trying to focus on the meal in front of her and not forget an important step. "And I'm sorry I'm only just starting supper. It won't be long, though, if you want to sit. I just need a few minutes."

"Why isn't it ready?" Isaac asked as he sat—not with any disappointment but with genuine concern. "Did something happen? Is everything okay?"

"Yes, of course! I'm just trying to do too much and ran out of time."

As he pulled off his boots, he watched her another few moments, frowning as she gingerly walked from the fire to the table and brought him a cup of coffee.

"Are you sure you're all right?" he asked, his head tilted in concern. "You're not . . . Are you hurt?"

Annie flushed, but she couldn't meet his eye. "I didn't want to tell you. It's kind of embarrassing."

"Well, there's no one here but me."

"I think I bruised my . . . um . . . my seat."

Isaac stared at her blankly for a long moment—a long moment in which Annie wondered if she would have to find the words to be more explicit. But before she could open her mouth again, Isaac let forth an unexpected guffaw.

"And how exactly did you do that, wife-of-mine?" Isaac leaned forward on his elbows, eyeing her appreciatively. "Get up to something tricksy while your husband wasn't around, did you?"

"No. It's not like that at all." She blushed again, turning away to start the bacon sizzling in her frying pan. "But, if you must know . . . I rode Pansy into town, and it's been so long since I sat astride in a saddle that I had trouble with my balance, and . . . oh, never mind. It's silly."

"It's not silly." He crossed to her and put his arms around her, holding her tight against his chest. "I just didn't realize you would be going out at all. You know, if you want to go into town when I'm not here, I can always hitch up the wagon before I leave. That way you're not at the mercy of a saddle."

"I know. But I didn't think about it until you had gone, and . . ." She paused, strangely afraid to say the next part out loud. Why did asking for what she needed only ever feel scary? "Do you think you could show me how to hitch up the wagon? I'm sure I could figure it out, probably, since I did something similar with the oxen, after all, on that long trip from Missouri. But I don't want to hurt Pansy, and—"

"Yes, Annie. Yes." Isaac had grown serious, even perhaps concerned again at seeing Annie's own worry. "I am happy to help if you need it."

"Thank you." She shrugged him off. "Now sit, please, and I'll finish up supper. Tell me about your day."

The bacon and jonnycakes were just as quick to cook as Annie remembered, and soon she was sitting across from her husband, eating the warm and filling meal. She was hungrier than she'd realized. After so much riding and being out all day, Annie thought, even such a simple pairing of food was exactly what she needed.

"But tell me," Isaac concluded, after he had described Mrs. Valentine's joyful reaction when she finally saw her finished home. "What were you doing in town? Are we running low on something that I can get for you? I don't want you traipsing all over the territory if you don't have to."

"Oh, no, nothing like that. I visited my sisters, of course, and Rebecca." Annie hesitated before deciding that she would tell Isaac what she and Rebecca had discussed, but it could wait till later. "And Mrs. Montgomery."

"Really? The pastor's wife? I didn't realize you two were such friends."

"I went to ask her about— Actually, this is something I need to talk to you about, too, but I thought it best that I check with her first, in case there is some objection. I didn't want to bother you unnecessarily."

"Annie." He leaned forward, concerned. "You're being very mysterious. What is it?"

"I, um . . ." She looked down at her plate. She had cut her last piece of bacon into a dozen small pieces without eating a single one. Steeling herself—though she knew her hesitation was probably unwarranted—Annie finally said, "I asked her if it would be all right if I start a church choir."

Isaac's reaction was immediate, demanding. All his jovial nature was dropped in the face of his concern. "Why? Don't you think you have plenty to be getting on with here without taking on something additional? I confess I don't see how this makes any sense for you to be doing. Supper wasn't even ready when I got home, Annie. I'm sorry, but how will you be able to fit this into your life when you can't even find the time to do what you've already committed to?"

She blinked and sat back in her chair, surprised at the force of his objection. Her mouth fell open.

"I . . . but . . ."

Even though Annie had told herself that Isaac might not like the idea—even though she had prepared herself for a negative response—she was nonetheless hurt by the force of his doubt.

"Oh—yes, um . . . I see why you would worry. All right. I don't have to."

Annie kept her eyes down at her plate, unsure she could hide the hurt from her expression. Goading him into another argument was the last thing she wanted to do. They sat in silence for what seemed like minutes, her still unable to meet his eyes, before Isaac finally sighed.

"Annie, I'm sorry. It's fine. I don't know why I . . . I'm sorry. I didn't mean it. I'm sure it will be fine if you want to do that. But I need you to consider how you are needed here. I don't want you to take on too much and leave important things unattended to. We are meant to be building this home together, and we cannot do that if you're off singing every day."

Annie stayed quiet, focusing finally on eating the food that she had previously only been pushing around her plate. Was Isaac right? Was she fooling herself thinking she could learn the intricate balance of running a household while also traveling all the way into town regularly?

"Thank you," she finally whispered. "I don't have to, though—"

"No. You do," he interrupted with frustration. "We don't want the pastor thinking we're not invested. I just . . . I trust that you will figure out a better schedule than what happened today. There needs to be time for all your responsibilities now."

"I know."

She felt like a scolded child. Where was her supportive, loving husband who had taken so much joy in buying her a new dress as a wedding gift? She tried to reason that Isaac was under a lot of stress, too, and perhaps he had simply run out of patience that day. This vehement objection seemed unlike him.

"I'll do my best," she said, more confidence in her tone now. "And I understand my responsibilities. I'm sorry if this bothers you, but it's something I really want to do. I need to do. For me and for the town."

He sighed again. "All right. I can see your mind is made up. But, can you just explain to me why? It seems like such a big project to take on."

"This is all new to me, and if I'm honest I am not completely certain this is the right choice. But I'm trying to . . ."

He nodded. "Go on."

After all she had gone through to get to this point, Annie knew she could not discard it all by hiding from her husband what she truly needed. Rebecca was right: he could not read her mind. She held his gaze as she let herself be vulnerable, confessing her secret needs.

"I'm . . . lonely." Annie's voice cracked on that last word, and she shrugged apologetically. "I've never spent so much time alone in my entire life, and I don't . . . It's really hard for me. I can't do this every day by myself."

He frowned. "I *have* to do my part for the other families of this town. You know that. I can't just stay here with you all day."

"Of course. I'm not suggesting that. I would never ask that, and it's why I needed to find another solution. Maybe, as time goes on and we get closer neighbors—or when the children come along—it will be different, but right now I just . . . I can't keep my head down, working here day after day, by myself. Starting a church choir gives me a reason to spend time with other people while also providing a service to the community."

He looked thoughtful, taking this all in. "Well . . ." He heaved a deep sigh. "As I said, as long as you are not missing your responsibilities here, I suppose I can't object. But you have to be home when I need you." He waved a hand around, gesturing at their home at random. "The laundry and cooking and all of it. You know that."

"I know. I do, Isaac. I promise I'll do my best. Thank you."

In the back of her mind, Annie wondered how Isaac had made it through the year between when Gertie had died and Annie had gotten there. But she put that from her mind, resolving that he would never have occasion to regret his support.

CHAPTER SIXTEEN

Although she wished for more enthusiastic support from her husband, Annie took what she could get and dove headfirst into her new plans. Such resolution was new for her, but she wasn't willing to let the opportunity slip away. At so many other points in her life she had simply waited—for someone else to make the decision, for the right moment to arrive, for some unnamed factor or something outside herself. Her older sister, Louisa, had been such a strong force of action in the family's life that Annie didn't have near the practice of assertiveness that she needed to make such a substantial change. Even getting to the Oregon Territory at all had been much the result of Louisa's initiative.

But she needed to try. Nothing that she wanted would happen if she did not make it happen herself.

In almost every similar situation she had been in through her life, she realized in hindsight that in her waiting she had missed the most opportune moment. When her parents had died, for example, she had waited to even consider how their absence would change her life. In her grief and numbness, Annie had pretended nothing was different for weeks. She had refused to look at what was right in front of her, until it was too late and Louisa had already taken over the primary bedroom of their family's house, relegating their parents' belongings to the attic. When she was considering offering piano lessons to the children of the neighborhood, it was because one of the largest families in Norfolk had given her the idea; but by the time she had finally decided it was the right choice for her, the family had moved away and with it all of Annie's potential first clients.

Now, settled in Oregon and seeking out connection from the community around her, she didn't want to waste any time. She had permission from both Isaac and Mrs. Montgomery, and Annie was not going to let herself dawdle. She knew herself; if she let too much time pass, the opportune moment would be lost. But beyond that, of course, was her deep hunger to be around other people. She was always happiest when contributing to a friend's project or supporting a loved one in their goal. Annie was at her best when she was helping. Being out on her homestead, all alone for most of the time, made Annie feel unmoored. She wasn't sure how long she could take it.

Though leadership was never her strength, she was willing to try. Starting the choir at Eden Valley's church could provide exactly what she needed.

Now, how this new big project could work with her equally important goal of learning to be the homemaker Isaac wished her to be, Annie had no idea. But beyond dragging Josie out to the homestead to teach her something every day, there was no easy way to make that happen. She would just have to do her best.

So Annie focused first on the choir, trusting that everything else would fall into place.

The first Sunday morning after she had spoken to Mrs. Montgomery, Annie was far more nervous than she had expected. She tried to steel her courage, reminding herself how many times she had offered herself as a piano teacher in the past and been turned down. Small rejections couldn't hurt her; she knew that. But the larger risk of not being able to organize a choir at all loomed over her, consuming her thoughts. Uncertainty reigned, and the only way to get the certainty she needed was to take action.

As Isaac drove the two of them and their wagon into town for church, he chatted away happily about what he had learned the day before about progress on the Eden Valley general store.

"And Jameson says by this time next year he'll either have stocked or be able to order anything we could want," Isaac was saying. "I'm not sure I would be as confident as he is, but it's something to look forward to. Not that many folks will have the funds for wallpaper or crystal chandeliers at first, but it's a start." He chuckled.

Annie focused on what her husband was saying, distracting herself from her own worries.

"I don't know what it is," he continued, "but somehow, having a well-stocked general store just makes the whole settlement feel . . . well, settled, I suppose. It'll probably still take a couple years for Jameson to get into the rhythm, what with the different seasons here and difficulty getting supplies shipped from the east, but the moment he installs a bell on that front door, Eden Valley will feel like home to me."

"I can hardly believe how quickly this town is growing," Annie said. "You men are getting the houses put up even faster than I imagined. Just think what it will be like next fall, when we've had a full summer to grow crops and all."

On the narrow trail leading into Eden Valley, their wagon passed another completed small cabin, about fifty yards off the trail. From this distance, Annie could spot Mrs. Abbott helping her daughter, Marigold, tie on her bonnet, while Mr. Abbott helped their son into their own wagon. The Abbott family seemed to be on their way to church as well. Annie smiled to herself, thinking about the community settling in, watching these children grow and build homes of their own.

"I remember the way I felt the first time I realized Dempsey was an established town," Isaac went on, "and not just one more collection of tents. We had done much like Daniel Mills does now, going to the fort regularly for supplies and news. But one day, the man who had volunteered to go returned with a letter for me. Addressed to me at 'Dempsey General Delivery,' and it found me with hardly any delay. I knew then that this was where I well and truly lived.

"And can you guess who that letter was from?" he asked her with a wink.

She only smiled. Thinking ahead to the next big project that would help Eden Valley feel more like an established town, Annie realized that the companionship of these folks alongside whom she'd lived for so many months was far more homemaking for her than the idea of being able to buy new combs when she wanted them.

But she was happy if her husband was happy. And he certainly seemed pleased with his choice to settle in the west, away from the encroaching civilization.

Pastor Montgomery's sermon that morning was about the upcoming season and divine timing, as he urged his congregants to make what preparations they needed before the first snow fell. While Annie tried her best to pay attention, her mind kept wandering to what she planned to do once the service was over. Like most other churches back east, the congregation of the small Eden Valley church did not go home immediately afterward. The women in particular were starved for company and news, having been left behind at home every day while their men went off to help build the town.

And so, Annie found that she had the perfect opportunity to make it known that soon the church would have a choir.

She exited the church on Isaac's arm, walking with him to where the oldest of the Waters and Cole families stood talking. Listening with one ear to their conversation—again about finishing the general store—Annie looked around at the community gathered, trying to decide where to start.

She heard the familiar lilt of her friend's laughter, and her eyes were immediately drawn to Rebecca Tenney, who seemed to be teasing her brother about something. That was the perfect place to start. For one thing, Annie already knew Rebecca had sung in her church choir at home in Indiana. But for another, her friend always seemed to be on the lookout for something fun to occupy herself. Annie was confident Rebecca would readily agree.

She made a quiet excuse to Isaac and wove through the folks still gathered until she reached the small knot of people around Rebecca. Her brother, Jasper, and his sweetheart, Nora, were laughing over something, and all turned expectantly to Annie when she approached.

"Can I talk to you?"

With a couple quick sentences, Annie explained what she wanted, and sure enough, Rebecca jumped at the chance.

After that, gathering more interested choir members was easy. It was Rebecca's charm and magnetism that attracted several others; Annie was in awe watching her. Far from the timid, reticent widow that folks might expect, Rebecca walked right up to Mrs. Muriel Findley and insisted that the church needed her rich alto in the choir.

Mrs. Findley blushed. "Oh, I don't sing . . ."

"You do," Rebecca insisted. "I've heard you singing to yourself while you scrub clothes. And it's beautiful! Please join us. We won't have any instruments for a while, of course, so we need voices like yours to give the songs a full, rich sound."

"I'll have to see." Mrs. Findley smiled as she looked over her shoulder to where her husband was speaking to the mayor. "I'll have to talk to Samuel, of course."

"Of course," Annie said, cutting in with understanding before Rebecca's good-natured bullying could make anyone uncomfortable. "Talk to him. Let us know. We're looking forward to it, and hoping to have at least one song ready in time for the Christmas service."

Rebecca linked her arm through Annie's and pulled her off to talk to Mr. Benedict, who they had heard more than once belting out a rich baritone while walking westward to Oregon. Each step fortified Annie's courage. With Rebecca by her side, Annie felt far more confident about asking for such a thing from her neighbors. And asking was the first step.

When the Wheelers finally left church to return home, Annie felt elated. Between the two of them, she and Rebecca had secured the tentative commitment of almost a dozen men and women. She climbed into the wagon next to Isaac and felt like she must be beaming.

"How did it go?" he asked, his tone carefully light.

"So much better than I expected. I'm so grateful." Annie let out a happy little laugh. "I'm so relieved!"

"Did you really think that folks would be cranky or cruel about it?"

"A little. It does seem a bit frivolous when compared to all the real needs of the community."

He was thoughtful for a moment before saying, "Some folks need some frivolity in their life. It's what reminds them that we are civilized, why we all are putting so much work into building this town in the first place."

"Is that why you bought us a piano?" she teased him. "To remind yourself that we're civilized?"

"Why, yes it is, wife." He grinned and flicked the reins, urging the horse home. "Yes, it is."

CHAPTER SEVENTEEN

"How many houses are you all going to finish today?" Annie asked the next morning as she poured her husband a cup of coffee. "You must be so close."

The Monday after she had first started to ask neighbors to join the nascent church choir, Annie was all but bursting with plans and ideas and hopes for the future. Nothing was going to stop her. She was proud of herself for having taken the first step, though everything else seemed overwhelming at the moment. Rebecca had promised to talk to the folks still living in the makeshift campsite, and anyone else she ran into while in town that day, and they would meet again the next day. Annie was thrilled and grateful that her charming friend was willing to help, and lamented the fact that she herself had to worry about laundry instead. There were nearly a dozen men and women who seemed interested, which Annie thought was enough to be starting with.

She just needed to start.

"None today," Isaac answered, "but I think maybe three of the cabins are close enough that we can finish them this week. We're getting close, wife. Finally. I have to admit, when you all rolled into the territory in October, I couldn't see how all these families were going to be housed before it got too cold. I thought Mills had certainly taken too much on, with that big caravan."

Annie nodded. "It certainly is a lot of people. I didn't realize how big the wagon company was until we ran into other folks at the forts along the way."

"Fifty families—some of them with four or more children—is a lot of people to take care of. But, as our illustrious mayor must have foreseen, it's also a lot of men to help do the taking care of. I still think we might be cutting it close with some of these structures, but no one will be left out in the cold. It will be rough, but we'll make it."

"And then, in the spring, more work begins."

"That's right. Wells, stables, extra bedrooms. Bill Abbott wants a smokehouse like ours, and I told him I'd give him tips. That was one thing I somehow wasn't prepared for when Gertie and me came west. The constant labor just to make this place worth living in."

"Growing up in a town that had been settled more than a hundred years previously means all the wells have been dug, I guess," she said with a smile.

Isaac laughed. "That and other things."

"Teaching piano certainly didn't prepare me for all of this, either. The other day when I visited, Mrs. Montgomery was talking about the vegetables she wanted to plant in the spring. And I just . . . it seems so far away, but I know there's plenty to keep us busy. Spring will be here before we know it."

"And then we'll want to get the schoolhouse finished in time for fall."

"And all the planting. Barns for more livestock. Cows for milk."

Isaac nodded and sipped his coffee. "It's a lot."

"I cannot wait." She grinned. "I wish we could just go to sleep and wake up a few months from now with all those things done and the flowers blooming. This is . . ." She sighed. "This is all exactly the fresh start I had been hoping for when I decided to come west."

"I'm glad. Both that this is what you wanted and that you came at all. I know it was a difficult decision."

"But it was a good one. Thank you. I'm so grateful."

"You getting sentimental on me, wife?" he teased.

"Oh, you . . ." She laughed, embarrassed. "I miss you," she said, shyly. "I can't tell you how much I am looking forward to the day when all of your work for the town is completed and you can stick closer to home."

"Soon." He shoved a piece of bacon in his mouth, chewing quickly. "Very soon. But what about you? You're making plans for the church choir, aren't you?"

"I am. Did you want to join?"

Isaac laughed as he shrugged on his coat and patted the pockets to find his gloves. "I am happy to support you from my seat in the pew. Believe me, you don't want my voice."

Annie crossed to the door and kissed his cheek. "Be safe. Supper will be ready when you get home."

Tipping his hat, Isaac left her alone.

Her plan was to spend this day getting done as many of her chores as she could so she could spend the following day in town with Rebecca. Taking on this new project—especially living as far as she did from the church—was going to be more of a time commitment than she had initially realized. But at the same time, Annie was thrilled for the chance to do it at all. She would work from dawn till dusk and then some if it meant she would be able to see friends again regularly.

Annie fairly sailed through her chores that day, primarily because her mind was elsewhere. As she gathered water from the nearby stream, she was dreaming about her favorite Christmas hymn and if she would need to sing the alto part. While she fed more fuel to the fire so she could heat the water, Annie was caught up imagining the crowd of aspiring singers, all pleading to be included. There was most of the laundry and several loaves of bread that needed to be finished today, and Annie kept having to stop herself from singing and remember the next step of whatever task she was on.

Her thoughts were anywhere but where her body was. As she scrubbed at a stubborn stain on one of Isaac's shirts, Annie was thinking about if there was enough time to teach four-part harmony before Christmas. She was just trying to remember the tenor part when her hand slipped, plunging into the water past the washboard. The sound of tearing fabric dragged her attention back to the moment in front of her.

"No!" she gasped, pulling the shirt out of the soapy water to look at more closely.

For a split second she thought maybe the seam had just come apart—it would be an easy fix. But a closer look told her the fabric itself had ripped, close to the seam but still a wide, jagged hole. Any attempt at repair would be noticeable and ugly.

There wasn't any way that Annie could fix this without Isaac finding out. And she knew, with all the other purchases he had made recently, there were no extra funds for an unexpected shirt.

Annie slumped back, soapy water from the shirt dripping on her lap, soaking through the layers. What was wrong with her? She should have been paying better attention. That's what Isaac would say, for certain. Maybe he was right: maybe taking on this extra responsibility was too much for her.

But what choice did she have?

The rest of the day, Annie fretted, wishing she had just paid better attention, hoping Isaac wouldn't be as mad when he had been when she ruined the butter.

When her husband returned late that afternoon, she did not feel ready to admit what had happened. All through greeting him, hanging up his coat, and getting him settled for supper, Annie had on a bright, carefree expression, trying not to worry him.

Finally, when she served him supper, Annie knew she couldn't put it off any longer. She sat across the table from Isaac, distracted as he said grace over the food, and then, when he moved to take his first bite, she blurted out her confession.

"I have to tell you something."

Isaac put down his spoon, giving her his full attention.

"It was an accident," she continued, "but I still could have . . . Anyway, before you get mad, I just want to tell you that I'm sorry and it won't happen again."

"What is it?"

"I tore a hole in your shirt. The brown one." She winced. "I'm sorry."

"Can you repair it?"

"Maybe, but it won't be pretty. And you won't want to wear it to church anymore. I'm so sorry," she repeated.

"It was an accident?" he asked, searching her face.

Annie nodded.

"Like ruining the butter was an accident," he added coldly.

"I—"

"Annie, you know we can't afford many more accidents like this, right? I can't wear my blue shirt to church—it's far too stained. And I don't know when I will be able to get another one. This might have been an accident, but it has significant consequences. I don't know what else to say to make it clear to you. What on earth have you been doing?"

"You don't have to say anything," she insisted. "I know. I do. I'm trying to do better. It's a lot, but every day I'm trying."

He sighed and shook his head. Finally, Isaac picked up his spoon and began to eat without responding to her any further.

Annie supposed that meant the conversation was over, and he wouldn't be scolding her any more. But she couldn't help but feel his disappointment.

The Wheelers ate in silence across from each other for several more minutes before Annie could not stand it any longer. She came out with the second thing she needed to tell him. If he was going to get really angry, he would have done so when he learned about the shirt, she thought.

"I was going to go into town tomorrow," she said. "Rebecca and I made plans to talk over next steps for the choir, and . . ." She trailed off when she saw him huff. "Is that all right? I know you're not happy about . . . really, any of this."

Isaac sighed deeply. "I know I said this was all fine, but . . . Annie, you know the agreement we made. That you wouldn't let this distraction keep you from your responsibilities here. Your responsibilities to me. To our home. Taking better care of our clothes when you wash them, for example."

The scolding pricked like a needle. "Isaac, it was a mistake . . . I'm sorry."

He looked at her silently for a moment before asking, "Do you think you've been making more mistakes like that since you decided to start a whole choir?"

"No." Annie frowned; she wasn't about to point this out to him, but she had been making mistakes well before the thought of a choir had occurred to her. "People make mistakes. And I'm sorry that in my case it means . . . ruined shirts or butter. But . . . I don't have an excuse. I'm just sorry."

"I don't know what else to say. I am incredibly frustrated, but I shouldn't have to tell you what you can and cannot do. I'm not going to ask you to stop. I want to believe you when you tell me it's under control."

"It is under control," she insisted. "I promise. There won't be any other problems. I am completely on top of all of it, and I won't ask anything else of you."

He nodded. "All right, then. There's no need to be that dramatic." He offered her a teasing smile. "But I'm glad to hear that you are taking this all seriously."

She wanted to tell him she was doing her best, but she was even starting to doubt that. Maybe, hopefully, Rebecca would have good news for her tomorrow.

CHAPTER EIGHTEEN

The next morning, Annie woke up before the sun. She started the coffee before Isaac had woken and finished making their breakfast as the sun was just cutting up over the top of the mountain range in the east. Even if she had to go without sleep to do it, she would prove to her husband that she could manage the church choir and her household responsibilities. She couldn't bear the loneliness if she didn't.

"Did you want me to hitch up the wagon for you?" Isaac asked as they ate. "It's no trouble."

She felt his attempt at an olive branch, the careful way he was trying to show his support even in the face of his real feelings. Though she was grateful that he seemed to be trying to put his objections aside, she couldn't help but think of the Fowlers again, and the way their disagreements had faded away to not speaking at all.

"I thought about that," Annie responded. "Thank you, but no. With as muddy as the path has been these last few days, I would worry about getting stuck. It's better if I just get used to riding, I think."

He nodded. "And you'll be gone all day?"

"I don't think so. It shouldn't take all that long. But I'm . . . I'm not sure. I'll try not to be, and I'll certainly be back for supper."

"Thank you." He took his last bite of buttered biscuit and stood. "I hope you're able to . . . get what you need. I look forward to hearing about it tonight."

"Thank you."

Once Isaac had left her alone, Annie looked around her small home, mentally noting all the things she needed to complete that morning before she ran off to town. Isaac was being more than understanding about her need to get out of the house, but she didn't want another fight about any domestic responsibilities. He was trying; she would, too.

After she cleaned up their breakfast, swept the floor, brought in more firewood, and made the bed, Annie thought she could reasonably leave for a few hours. Telling herself she had gotten plenty done the previous day and would have time to do plenty the next day, once everything with the choir was settled today, Annie saddled Pansy and rode off toward Eden Valley midmorning.

As she rode, she passed half a dozen more of the settlers' homesteads, both near to the narrow trail and far in the distance. With only a few weeks left until the end of the year, the town was expecting the first snow to hit them any day, and workers were frantic. She would have to ask Isaac who their closest neighbors would be, and lamented that it couldn't be her family or Rebecca.

But the church choir would help that. Even if Annie never saw or spoke to the folks who lived closest to her, she would have a regular interaction with the other men and women who volunteered to sing on Sunday mornings. Satisfied with this dream of her future, Annie rode until she reached the campsite with the last of the covered wagons.

When they had spoken on Sunday, Rebecca promised to try

to feel out some other potential singers who were still living in the campsite just north of town. Every day that crowd of settlers dwindled down; even Rebecca's own family should be moving into their home for the winter within a few days. But now, with still almost ten families living there, Annie dismounted and led Pansy between the camps until she reached Rebecca's.

"Good morning!" she called when she was close enough. Rebecca and her mother were putting away clean dishes, packing them back into the trunk where they had been stored since the family left Indiana a year earlier. "How did you do? Tell me all about who else will be joining the choir."

"Good morning," Rebecca responded. She came forward to meet Annie, taking the horse's reins and helping them both get settled. "You're here earlier than I expected."

"I just couldn't wait. I've been awake for several hours already, making sure I finished everything, so Isaac doesn't have cause to regret his approval."

Rebecca offered her a small smile. "Well, it's so early that I haven't had a chance to really talk to anyone yet today, though there were a few yesterday."

Mrs. Stephens cut in. "And I've been keeping her busy with questions. Blame me for her negligence."

"Oh, no, I would never," Annie responded with a laugh.

"Ma did have some good questions though," Rebecca said. "Things I couldn't answer and we should maybe talk about?"

"Like what?"

"Come, honey. Sit." Rebecca tugged Annie gently, directing her into the lone chair that stood by the campfire. "You know it was Ma's idea to put together that bathing day for the ladies on the trail, remember? I just want you to know that all our questions and concerns come from wanting to help you make this successful, not because we're afraid of big projects."

Annie frowned. "All right . . ."

Mrs. Stephens poured Annie a cup of tea without being asked, and handed it to her as she settled in.

"Well, first, we were wondering how precisely this is all going to work," Rebecca began. "Will you ask everyone to come into town through the snow and cold?"

"Well, yes, that was my plan. But . . . do you think I shouldn't?"

Rebecca looked at her, concerned. "I don't know, Annie. It seems like a lot to ask of people on top of everything else they need to worry about right now."

"But they'll come into town for church."

"That's different. I wish it wasn't, but . . . the folks I got to talking to yesterday, not one of them wanted to commit to anything right now. You already got almost a dozen yeses, didn't you? And are other people we can ask, but maybe you should put off all this until the spring. Fresh start, easier roads, and all."

Annie slumped down in her seat. "But . . . really?"

Rebecca leaned forward and said softly, "Maybe."

Sitting quietly for a few moments, Annie thought about what her friend had said, what she was suggesting. She looked up at Rebecca. "You couldn't get anyone else to agree?"

Rebecca grimaced. "I'm sorry. Nothing certain. There seemed to be interest, generally, and there are still more folks to ask—"

"But they'll likely all have the same questions and objections, too."

"Likely, yes."

Annie sighed, before a sob escaped her lips. "I'm sorry," she said, wiping away tears angrily. "I don't know why I'm crying. This is so silly."

"Because you're disappointed. It's okay to be sad about it. I won't tell anyone." Rebecca nudged Annie teasingly. "And if we put off anything more substantial until this spring, that will give everyone a chance to look forward to it, right? Instead of a frantic, last-minute half-hearted commitment now."

"I suppose."

They sat quietly; Annie could feel Rebecca's eyes on her. After a long moment, she asked plaintively, "Why am I failing at everything?"

"Oh, honey, you're not! Remember how you learned to drive the team of oxen and did so much after your sister died? This is just . . . it's temporary. Winter is limiting, and God's timing is perfect. Didn't the pastor just talk about the divine timing of the seasons? It will all work out and none of it is your fault."

"It sure seems like *some* of it is my fault."

Rebecca reached over and clutched Annie's hand, squeezing it even as it sat in her lap. "How can I help?"

"I don't know. I thought I had this brilliant solution, and . . . I was wrong. Did I tell you I accidentally ripped one of Isaac's shirts yesterday?" She shook her head, exasperated at herself. "What am I even doing? I never should have come west."

"Oh, Annie," Rebecca breathed. "I'm so sorry. You must feel . . . I'm sorry."

"It's all right, I suppose. I know I'm probably being silly, so disappointed about something that is admittedly unnecessary. I just feel a bit hopeless right now is all. There doesn't seem to be an end to this."

"I'm sorry," Rebecca whispered. "I don't know that there's anything we can do about the choir now. Maybe instead you turn your focus on learning the skills Josie knows that Isaac wishes you had."

"Maybe."

"Or maybe, with the houses finishing, Isaac will have time to be around the house more and you won't feel so alone?"

"Maybe."

"Maybe we'll all get snowed in and he can't leave."

Annie let out a half-hearted chuckle and stood. "Thank you," she said. "I need to think about this a bit more. I'm just sad. I appreciate all your help, but I feel a bit too lost to figure out what my next step is just yet."

"Of course. I understand. I'm here when you need me."

"Thank you."

"Or, rather, I might be in our finished home when you need me." Rebecca grinned. "And then you'll have to visit me there."

"I'm so excited for you! I would hate to think about you living out here when the first snow falls."

The two women said their goodbyes as Annie led her mare to the other side of the camp, where her sisters were still living in their own wagon. As worried as she was for Rebecca to be caught out in the cold, she was even more so for her family. Maybe she would need to ask Isaac again about making room for them.

She didn't stay with her sisters long; Annie didn't want to give them a chance to suss out her frustration. She didn't feel equipped to handle anyone else's good wishes. Even so, seeing Josie and Margaret was a balm, and Annie stayed as long as she could.

But not too long; returning home in time to get Isaac's supper ready was the one thing she could do right.

CHAPTER NINETEEN

Annie was feeling quite defeated. Over supper that night, Isaac asked her a few questions about her day and about her plans for the church choir, but he didn't pry; when she was reticent to give him anything but the bare minimum, he graciously changed the subject, telling Annie about all that his work crew had finished that day.

Later that night, as they changed for bed and tucked themselves under the quilt together, Isaac reached for her, wrapping Annie tightly in his arms and cuddling against her back.

"Do you want to tell me what's wrong, wife?" he asked quietly. "You don't have to, but I'm here to listen if you need me."

Somehow the darkness, and not having to look Isaac directly in the face, made her disappointment easier to put into words. Tears pricked her eyes, but still she answered in a shaky voice, "I'm a fool."

"You're not. But do you want to tell me why you feel that way?"

"I told you I saw Rebecca today, but what I didn't tell you . . . she and her mother helped me see that right now, as winter is starting and some folks still don't have homes, is a terrible time to be asking people to start a choir."

Isaac waited a moment before asking gently, "So . . . are you giving up on that, then?"

Annie had expected to hear hope in his voice, but more than anything Isaac sounded concerned. Maybe worried for her. She rolled over, turning in bed until she was facing him, still with his arms around her. Their faces were mere inches apart.

"For now. But Rebecca and I thought we would try again in the spring. When all the other work starts up, I suppose. Do you think that's a bad idea?"

Isaac smiled and kissed her nose before answering. "I think that I'm sorry you're disappointed. And I think that, whenever it works out, a church choir would be a great addition to this community."

"I'm sorry I'm being silly about it."

"You're not being silly. I just hate to see you so consumed by problems you can't do anything about. Everything will work out, you know that, right?"

She nodded. "Yes." Annie rolled back over, facing away from Isaac but snuggling back into his arms. "Thank you."

He hugged her gently, and within the safety and support of his embrace Annie was able to forget her disappointment and fall asleep.

When they rose the following morning, Annie felt somewhat better about her failure, but the problem of feeling lonely weighed on her. That was just as much a problem now as it was before her idea of the choir, perhaps more so now after her hopes had risen and fallen so quickly.

As she prepared their coffee and breakfast, she thought over what she needed, what was the bare minimum she thought she could get by with, until spring brought with it all the changes she hoped for.

"And whose homes will be finished today?" she asked, echoing the question that had been on her mind every morning for the last couple weeks.

"Oh, I'm actually not going to build today. I told Mills I needed to go hunting before all the animals are hibernating for months. I'm a bit worried about our stores keeping long enough."

An impulse bubbled up in Annie, and she spoke the thought aloud before she let herself think about it too much. "Can I come with you?"

"With me? Hunting? Are you serious?"

His expression of utter confusion, rather than derision or ridicule, made Annie feel even more tender toward him.

"You're away so much, and I know that will change and things will settle, but right now . . . I just miss you. I don't want to be alone. I'm sorry if that's silly."

"I miss you too, but . . . have you ever been hunting? Do you even know what you're in for?"

"Not exactly, but did you know Caroline Harper—Mills, sorry, I keep forgetting—Caroline Mills got Junior Sullivan to teach her how to hunt. Because she wanted to help out, and that let Junior lend his hand to building. And, well, I don't have to actually do any hunting. I'm not much of a shot. But I can keep quiet, and I can watch, and we could spend the day together. Please?"

Isaac paused, frowning, then opened his mouth without saying anything, as though he was second-guessing the thoughts in his head.

"There's not some other pressing task that needs to be done? You're sure? Remember what happened when you went into town to talk to the pastor's wife? And you weren't even home most of yesterday."

"Just making supper. Nothing else that can't wait. And if you want to bring me back early so I can do that, I understand, oh, but, Isaac, please!"

"This is . . ." He chuckled. "This is not what I expected when I proposed to you, Annie Wheeler."

She blushed.

"But yes. Let's spend the day out in the woods together. Mind you, I *am* going to put you to work."

"Good. Yes. Please do," she said eagerly. "I am happy to help any way I can."

He shook his head. "I've never been hunting with a woman— never even knew one who knew how. This will be an adventure."

Over the next twenty minutes, he talked her through every-thing that he generally brought with him when he was going out to hunt, all the things he looked for and kept in mind.

"This is a little late to be starting out," he explained with a small frown, "but there's no help for that now."

Soon both the Wheelers had packed canteens, saddlebags, warm clothing, and—in Isaac's case—a rifle and ammunition, and had mounted their horses to ride out into the woods.

"What would you be doing today if you had stayed home?" Isaac asked as they followed the narrow slip of a trail farther away from the town center.

"Cook supper, obviously," she said. "I was planning on making a loaf of sourdough today, but that can wait. And I always have knitting to do. I want to use up all the yarn we have. I'm petrified of having to deal with snow without enough warm socks."

"All things that will be waiting for you tomorrow, then."

"Yes."

As they rode in silence, Annie let the gratitude and joy of this new adventure wash over her. Everything was hard, it seemed, but there were moments like this, moments when she and her husband could find a quiet connection, moments when she felt like Louisa would be proud of her for just *doing* something instead of waiting passively.

Annie didn't know anything about hunting, but she knew enough to stay quiet and to follow whatever instructions Isaac gave her. They stopped a couple times to rest and eat; Annie always marveled at how much better water tasted when she had been outside all day. Over the course of several hours, Isaac managed to bag a white-tailed deer and three pheasants, far more than Annie could have hoped for. She was giddy thinking about the savory meals that would come of this day.

Later in the afternoon, when they were stalking a second deer on foot, Annie accidentally stepped into a mud puddle and splashed dirty water all over the hem of her dress.

"Oh!" she gasped in surprise.

Isaac looked at her.

I'm sorry, she mouthed, not wanting to make noise and startle the deer.

"Never mind," he said. "It seems to have already smelled us. I could use a drink of water anyway."

They walked back to where the horses were tied, and Isaac grabbed the canteen, offering it to Annie first. As she took a sip, he said, "It's getting cold, don't you think? There's bound to be snow any day."

"You think any day?" Annie handed the canteen back to him. "I worry for those poor folks whose homes aren't done yet. My sisters. The Emerson family, and the few others."

"They'll be taken care of," Isaac assured her. "You know Mayor Mills didn't get all these folks all the way to the Oregon Territory only to let them freeze their first winter here."

"That's true."

"You know, I don't think I'll hunt any more today. We should head back," Isaac continued. "I'd love to get these skinned and processed before dark if I can. Maybe we'll have time to roast one for supper tonight too." He climbed up into his saddle, resting his rifle across the back of his horse.

Annie moved to mount her own horse but had trouble stepping up that high. "I'm sorry—I've been using the front step to get up on her before. Let me find something else I can use . . ."

She looked around at the small corner of forest they had found themselves in.

"Do you want help?"

"No, I can do it. Look, I can use that as a step up."

Nearby there was a thick log, a tree that had long ago fallen across the forest floor and was now grown over with fungi, moss, and other greenery. But it was still sturdy enough to help Annie easily reach her horse.

"I can use this and climb up without a problem."

Isaac eyed the log warily. "If you're sure . . . but be careful," he said in a low voice. "With as damp as it's been, that log is bound to be slippery."

Annie nodded, leading her mare to stand alongside the log. It was so high that Annie thought she might even have trouble climbing up onto it, but with Pansy as her balance it shouldn't be too difficult.

"There you go, girl," she whispered to Pansy.

She put one boot on the top of the log and pulled herself up, soothing the horse the whole time.

"Careful," Isaac warned.

But just as Annie moved to step off the slippery log and into the stirrup, Pansy moved a few steps. Annie lost her balance; one boot snagged firmly in the loop of the stirrup, the other shooting out from under her and bringing Annie down in the process. Her rear end hit the log before Pansy moved again, surprised, dragging Annie off the log into the dirt. Her head hit the log at the same time that her ankle was wrenched at an unnatural angle.

Pain crashed over her like a wave.

"Annie!" Isaac exclaimed.

CHAPTER TWENTY

Annie was in a daze, slowly coming to on the cold, damp forest floor. The last thing she remembered was Isaac calling her name from atop his own horse, but now, as she blinked rapidly, she saw her husband kneeling in front of her in the decaying leaves and mud, gently slapping her cheeks.

"Annie. Annie, please. Open your eyes."

She tried to sit up and groaned in pain.

"No, don't move. Not yet. We need to check you for injuries. Just lay still, wife."

She closed her eyes and lay back. Even with all the branches and pine needles overhead blocking out sunlight, the sky still felt bright to her. The longer she lay there, the more she noticed pain emanating from various parts of her body. She felt Isaac's hands testing her fingers, the length of her arms, her ribs. There were bruises all over her, but nothing hurt worse than her right foot—the one that had gotten stuck in the stirrup when she had fallen to the ground; the ache seemed to pulse up her leg.

"All right, let's take a look at this," Isaac said finally, moving to that injury.

The ankle was already swelling up; Isaac had to completely unlace the boot in order to pry it off her. She groaned when he tugged at it.

"I'm sorry, I'm so sorry."

Annie looked away, into the ferns and trees to her left. The sight of her bruised foot, combined with the pain, was more than she could bear. She tried to distract herself while Isaac gently prodded at her injury. Searching her memory, Annie returned to happier days playing the piano and mentally rehearsed the chord progressions for some of her favorite songs. She wondered if her hands would remember the movements when she finally got her piano after a full year without one.

"We're going to need to call the doctor," Isaac said. "There's no question. This is . . . well, let's just get you home. Into bed, get your feet up, and we'll see what he has to say. You poor thing. I'm so sorry, I should never have let you do that."

Annie allowed herself to be lifted, Isaac carefully letting her test her weight on her left foot. It didn't hurt nearly as much as her right, but Annie could still feel the bruises. Isaac did everything he could to help her into the saddle without putting weight on her injured foot, but even moving about at all caused pain to shoot up through her body. She gritted her teeth and tried to bear it. Just a little bit of effort now until she was safe at home again.

"Hold on," he said over his shoulder, leading her horse while also riding his own. "Not much farther."

The ride back home seemed a lot longer than the ride out had been that morning; Annie attributed that to the absolute hold the pain in her body had on her mind. Every step, every jostle, found a new bruise to jar. The sharp ache of her ankle was a constant, but all the other injuries seemed to be competing for her attention as well.

When they reached their small homestead, she held her breath, bearing up against the pain. Again, Annie gritted her teeth through the pain of being moved. She all but fell off the saddle into Isaac's arms, and he whisked her into their home and got her settled into bed.

"You'll be all right? I'll be back as quickly as I can."

Once he was gone, Annie tried to stay alert, but she didn't know how much time passed. She seemed to be dozing in and out of sleep, as though her body was trying to protect her from the low thrum of pain that overwhelmed her.

When Annie woke again, the door to her home was opening. Isaac and Dr. Martell entered, the former breathless and the latter serene. Though Annie had not had much reason to interact with the doctor since meeting him, she had heard that he was kind. If nothing else, the very fact that their community had a doctor at all was a boon.

He dragged one of their simple wooden chairs from the table to the side of the bed and took a seat.

"Well, now, young lady, let's see what we're dealing with."

Dr. Martell bent over to carefully lift Annie's foot up to his lap. She winced at the stab of pain that came just from moving the foot. Tears sprang to her eyes, but she kept her focus on the doctor, noticing what he was doing and how he was assessing her injury. It was clear he was trying to move her foot and ankle as little as possible.

"Other than the ankle, do you want to show me where else you've been hurt?"

Between the two of them, Isaac and Annie pointed out all the scrapes and bruises she had suffered in her fall. The doctor paid special attention to the lump that was forming on the back of Annie's head, but otherwise did not seem particularly alarmed.

"Well, Mrs. Wheeler. I have good news and bad news," he said as he sat back in the chair. "The good news is nothing appears to be broken, and other than some pain and discomfort for a while, you should heal as good as new. Nothing to worry about."

"And what's the bad news, doctor?" Isaac asked. He had been

pacing behind the doctor's chair nearly his entire visit, and Annie's heart broke at the look of panic on her husband's face.

"The bad news is this ankle is quite injured."

Annie felt tears run down her face. She was exhausted and in pain, and this was all more than she could handle. She closed her eyes while her husband and the doctor conferred.

"You need to stay off this," the older man continued. "I'm so sorry, Mrs. Wheeler. I know that's not what you wanted to hear, but it's very important that we don't make the injury worse."

"How long?" Annie asked, desperately.

"With all this swelling, it's hard to say. I'm fairly certain it's not broken, but even so it will be longer than you want. Fewer if you can stay off it, but it could be several weeks."

Annie gasped. "That's impossible! If it's not broken, shouldn't it be far less? I remember my sister hurting her ankle, and she was up and around after less than a week!"

"I'm sorry, Mrs. Wheeler, I can't speak to that. What we have here is a very bad sprain, one of the worst I've seen. Which means you need to take extra good care of it. I'll give your husband some suggestions for managing your pain and making you more comfortable, but the most important thing you can do is to stay in bed."

"Thank you, doctor," Isaac said, sounding more defeated than Annie had ever heard him. "I'll see that she gets the rest she needs."

He walked with Dr. Martell back out to the horses.

Annie could tell it was getting late; her stomach growled, and she wondered what she needed to do about supper for them. She was just trying to reach the closest chair to move herself into it when Isaac reentered.

"What are you doing?" he exclaimed. "The doctor just told you to stay in bed."

"He told me to rest, and if I'm sitting in a chair instead of standing, that's rest, isn't it?" she protested weakly. "If you can carry me over to the fireplace—"

"Absolutely not. No. Annie, please. It's going to be hard enough having you off your feet for that long. You can't risk making it worse."

"But you can't do all this on your own. I know I've been disappointing and making mistakes lately, but that doesn't mean you need to take over everything entirely."

"I can do enough. We're not in such dire straits that you need to be risking that ankle, though, so don't you let me catch you out of bed. Now, I'm going to go chop some more firewood, start something for supper, and I'll check if we have any whiskey like the doctor recommended for the pain."

"What about the game?" Annie asked, weakly.

"The what?"

"The deer and the pheasants that you wanted to get all taken care of before the end of the day. The smokehouse?"

Annie was having a difficult time hanging on to details; she had hit her head quite hard.

"Oh." His shoulders slumped, but only briefly before energy seemed to surge through him again. "Guess I better get to work then. Just stay there, wife. I'll handle everything."

And indeed, Isaac did seem unstoppable, bringing wood in for the fire almost immediately, and coming up with a meal he could make for supper without asking anything of Annie. He wasn't able to find any whiskey, like the doctor recommended for her pain, but promised her he would see to it the following day.

"If you can get through this one night, tomorrow will be better."

She nodded tiredly, amazed at how close she was to falling asleep even as every movement or twitch caused her pain.

"More good news, I guess," she said.

"What's that?"

"I won't be spending any more time trying to build the choir. I'll be home for supper every night."

"Oh, Annie." He came to squat by her side of the bed. "I'm sorry. I shouldn't have complained. Now I know it could have been much worse."

She smiled. "We'll get through this."

"We will," he agreed. "And faster if you rest."

She fell asleep early that night, barely able to finish supper, despite all her worries over what they were going to do. Mercifully, the dull thrum of pain that coursed through her was no match for the sheer exhaustion from her day.

CHAPTER TWENTY-ONE

"Are you sure you'll be all right on your own?" Isaac asked her, with a worried expression. "It should only be a few hours. I won't be gone all day, but there's always the possibility that something will hold me up."

After falling from a slippery log, banging her head, and spraining her ankle, Annie had woken early that morning with a gasp of pain from the bruise on the back of her skull. Her gasp had woken Isaac, and though he insisted it was fine and he had intended to wake early anyway, she still felt bad. But once he had made them both breakfast—slightly burnt jonnycakes—he told her he had an errand to run. He would go into town to find her one of the methods the doctor had recommended to manage her pain, and would she be all right alone for a little bit.

Annie smiled bravely. "I have everything I need." She gestured around her: a bucket of drinking water and an empty cup, a chamber pot, an extra blanket for when the fire started to die down. Isaac had brought everything within her reach. "I'll stay off my feet as much as I can. Just . . . hurry home, please."

Isaac knelt by the side of the bed and took her hand, kissing each knuckle. "My poor, brave girl. I'm so sorry. I'll be back as soon as I can."

When Isaac had gone and Annie was alone again, she burst into tears.

The pain was so much, but, more than that, she hated feeling so helpless. How would she ever last through weeks and weeks of this?

Before he left, Isaac had brought Annie's knitting over to sit within her reach, but she couldn't bring herself to make any effort at all. As the fire slowly died down, she let herself rest, dozing in and out of sleep for much of the morning. When midday came around, she was surprised at how hungry she suddenly felt. Even while spending all morning in bed, her body had still been working hard to heal her numerous bruises and abrasions, and Annie was craving something hot and hearty.

But, relegated to the bed as she was, there were only a couple slices of cold bacon and a biscuit she had made a couple days before within reach. Tired and hungry, Annie broke down crying again. Everything seemed to be a mess, and she didn't see any way out of it. Gnawing on the cold biscuit, she wished she had taken Rebecca up on her offer to come visit this week. Then, at least, someone would be here to put another log on the fire, and maybe even make some fresh biscuits.

After eating what little food she had, Annie tried half-heartedly to focus on her knitting again. Her arms were still sore from the jarring she had gotten when she fell, and she couldn't maintain the strength in her wrists long enough to make much progress. Promising herself that she would keep trying, keep working at keeping her strength up, she set aside her knitting and lay back in bed.

This was going to be a very long few weeks, she realized.

If she thought she was lonely before when she had chores to distract her, Annie had no idea how she was going to manage filling her time when all she could do was stay in bed. If only she had someone to talk to, even if there was nothing else to do. If only the pain didn't consume her thoughts and she could at least maybe plan songs for her choir to sing one day.

She looked at the logs that made up the roof of her small home. Isaac had promised her that this small cabin was just the start. As more skilled carpenters and tools made their way to the Oregon Territory, more folks would build what he called real houses: two-story homes that felt more like what they'd had in the east. At the moment, though, Annie was just grateful they had a shelter at all. Days were getting shorter, snow was bound to fall any day, but she and her husband had this cozy, dry space in which to safely winter.

She worried over the poor women—like her sisters—who didn't have a man like Isaac to look after them. The coming winter would be harsher than many of the emigrants had ever endured, and all without the benefit of months of preparation.

She hoped once again that her ankle wouldn't take too long to heal.

With nothing else to do, Annie closed her eyes, allowing her body to fade into the restless sleep of the injured.

She was woken a few hours later when Isaac returned. Though it was clear he had been trying to be quiet, in his rush to get to the work he'd left undone he had tripped up on the leg of the table, stumbling several feet. The resulting thud against the cabin wall had pulled Annie out of her nap.

"You're home," she said weakly.

"You're awake. How do you feel?"

"I don't know . . . cloudy? I've slept a lot. My body still aches. But better, I think. It's hard to know when I haven't gotten out of bed."

"And nor will you as long as I'm around." He was putting another log on the fire, which had died down in his absence. "I've got to chop some more firewood and collect water, and then I'll make supper. How does that sound?"

"Really? Thank you. So much. You know it's all right if we just have cold biscuits again, or . . ." Her voice trailed off. She didn't exactly expect her husband to cook, but a hot meal was all she wanted at that moment.

"No, I'll . . ." He looked around the kitchen area distractedly. "I'll figure something out. You just rest."

"I hate to even ask," she called to him before he went outside again, "but did you get any whiskey like the doctor recommended? Or laudanum might be better."

Isaac groaned. "No. I got caught up talking to Mills about the families still out at the campsite. I'm sorry. I can get it tomorrow, if you'll be okay until then?"

Annie nodded bravely, though even that small movement hurt.

He beamed at her gratefully. "I don't know when Daniel is making another trip to Fort Vancouver, so I may need to ask folks, make a couple tries to find something, since the doctor didn't have any. I'll take care of it though."

"Thank you."

He nodded and darted out.

There was nothing Annie could do but watch and wait. Certainly she wouldn't be sleeping at all while he was home and banging around the house, and her mind was too unfocused to be able to knit. Isaac seemed to be so busy with all the tasks on his mind that she didn't even want to interrupt him with questions about his day. So she quietly watched as her husband tried to take on everything Annie usually did, along with his own responsibilities.

After chopping more firewood, getting the fire going, and deciding what he was going to cook for supper, Isaac seemed harried and exhausted. Annie stayed quiet, not wanting to distract or worry him, though she did wonder how he was faring.

True, he had lived on his own after his first wife had died, but that was in Dempsey, with neighbors and friends who were likely happy to feed him. Isaac could cook some things, Annie knew, but she still didn't have high hopes.

"All right, here we are," he said finally, crossing the room to where she sat in bed.

Annie had lost track of time and events—in all his running around, she had no idea what he had prepared for their supper. When he handed her a bowl of rice and beans with some bacon pieces on top, she sniffed appreciatively.

"This is too much. How did you have time to do all this?" she asked in wonder.

Looking quite proud of himself, he pulled up the other chair to her side of the bed so they could eat together.

"Well, I haven't sat down since I got home," he said with a laugh. "But don't praise me too much before you try it. I don't pretend to know everything."

She took a mouthful, bit down—and felt like she might have broken a tooth.

"Um, Isaac?" she said around a mouthful of beans.

He looked at her expectantly.

After spitting the beans back out into the bowl, Annie said, "Did you soak these first?"

His mouth fell open and his brow furrowed. "No. Was I supposed to?"

"Well . . ." She pushed the beans around, attempting to cut one in half with her utensil. "They take longer to cook if you don't. So these aren't really done yet."

He took a bite himself, chewing hard before swallowing. "Ugh. I can't believe it. I'm sorry."

"The rice is good though," she said encouragingly, before taking another, more hesitant bite. "And the bacon adds such flavor."

"I'll put the beans back over the fire." He stood and picked up both their plates, moving to return the beans to the pot with the rest. "I'm really sorry."

"Isaac, it's okay. I understand. There's a lot to remember, and you're doing it all by yourself."

"I'm still sorry."

She quietly waited while he took care of their supper, trying to ignore the hunger in her belly. If the situation had been reversed, would Isaac have been as uncomplaining to not have supper ready? But that was a fight she didn't want to start. She had already seen his reaction when on the other side. All Annie wanted in that moment was food and rest, and there was nothing she could do to get either.

CHAPTER TWENTY-TWO

Though Annie had not said anything beyond pointing out that the beans were not cooked all the way through, Isaac seemed self-conscious and defensive the rest of the night. After a few futile attempts to make conversation, to soothe his self-respect, Annie finally lapsed into silence while he worked; her body was still in too much pain for her to be able to offer him any more. The beans finished cooking, and Isaac warmed up the rice and bacon so they could eat it all together. It was so late by the time she finished eating that Isaac had barely had the chance to take her dish before she found herself drifting off to sleep.

She woke the next morning surprised by how rested she felt. For the first time in days, Annie thought she could focus on her knitting, maybe even talk Isaac into letting her get out of bed.

"Good morning," her husband called from where he hovered over the fire.

Annie sniffed—fresh coffee, almost ready.

"I'm surprised you slept so soundly," he continued, "especially with as much noise as I was probably making last night. The rice was stuck to the pan, and the utensils slipped right out of my hands when I was washing them."

"I must have been tired. I still feel tired, to be honest, but better."

"How are your injuries?" He poured a cup full of coffee for her and brought it to where she was sitting up in bed.

"Better, I think. I'm stiff all over, but the bruises seem to be less severe. I must be healing with as little of everything else that I'm doing, don't you think? Just lying in bed has got to help. Thank you so much." Annie accepted the steaming mug and held it up to her face, taking a deep breath of the bitter scent. "I'm really sorry I can't do more."

"Oh, well," he said, leaning against the edge of the table. "We'll get through this. Everyone's got trials to go through, and maybe this is ours. It's a lot, but it's not insurmountable."

Annie nodded, sipping her coffee. "Whose home are you working on today?"

He ran a hand through his hair. "I don't think I'm going. They'll have to get along without me. I'm just . . . completely overwhelmed. Yesterday was far more difficult than I'd expected. I need to be here, taking care of things, I suppose, if you're going to be off your feet so long."

Annie felt his words like a sting. Though she didn't think her husband was trying to make her feel guilty for the injury, there was an undeniable tone of accusation in his words.

She nodded, putting on a smile. "Well, then, I'm glad to get to spend time with you."

He offered her a thin smile in return before standing again, and headed to the tub of hot water where the breakfast dishes were waiting. Annie watched as her husband set to work again, doing one of the things she would have done if she could be on her feet. While there were certainly some tasks that could wait until she was healed—her knitting, for example, or baking fresh bread—it was true that many of the household chores needed to be done. The dishes wouldn't wait; the laundry could only wait so long. Someone would have to walk the half mile a couple times each day to collect water, and soon the floor would be so filthy it could no longer be ignored.

Annie was lost in thought, calculating exactly how much work would be waiting for her when she was able to stand again, when she noticed Isaac had finished washing and drying the plates and other dishes they had eaten from, and was now moving to the bigger pans. As he lifted the skillet where he had made bacon, Annie gasped.

"Wait!" she called out, with more sharpness than she intended. "Don't—Isaac—"

"What?" He looked alarmed, frozen in place to stop doing whatever his wife was worried about.

"Don't put that in the soapy water."

"But it's dirty."

"You don't— We don't wash the cast iron. The dutch oven, or that pan."

"What do you mean, not wash it?" He frowned, looking from her to the pan in his hand and back again. "That can't be clean. Have you never washed it?"

"No, it's just . . . I think the word my sister used is 'seasoned.' I wipe it down, sometimes add oil or other fat when I need to, but there's no need to scrub it or use soap at all."

He stayed quiet, looking from her to the pan again.

"You didn't scrub it, did you?" she asked softly. "If you did, it's okay. We can probably fix it."

Isaac shook his head, setting the pan down on their table.

"Are you all right?" she asked, hesitant. "Isaac?"

He looked up at her with an expression of frustration. "Man wasn't created to do all these things."

"All what things?"

He gestured, a splash of soapy water flying across the small space and sizzling on the fire. "This. The dishes. The cooking.

Everything in this home that needs attention or cleaning. I just can't— Men are built differently, and I just don't know how I can take care of all this in here while also taking care of our land, and construction, and everything else."

"Isaac, it's not forever—"

"It's not?" he returned bitingly, raising his voice. "You sure about that? Because it seems like you continued to make mistake after mistake, expecting me to fix everything for you until you finally just made yourself useless altogether."

Annie's mouth fell open in shock. "Excuse me?"

"I can't believe you just fell into the dirt rather than be able to climb into a horse's saddle. I never would have thought you could be so helpless."

"I— Isaac!"

Annie was at a loss for words. His anger was making him cruel, pointed, putting voice to all the fears she had kept hidden away for weeks. She knew she owed him so much, but the idea that he saw her as this burden broke her heart.

"No, it's fine," he said dismissively. "Don't worry about me. It's not like having help with my household was the whole reason I advertised for a wife in the first place, why I helped her and her entire family come west to Oregon, is it?"

Tears fell down Annie's cheeks. She didn't know how to talk to him when he was like this. His anger and sarcasm went far beyond any of the bossiness she had endured from her sister. Annie had never been so yelled at before.

"I'm sorry," she said desperately. "Maybe if you brought the tub over here to me, I could do the dishes from where I'm sitting in bed? I could help."

He looked at her, blinked several times as though pulling himself out of a fog, and slumped back against the table, shaking his head.

He sighed. "No, that's not . . . I'm sorry."

She watched silently, unsure how to respond.

"That was unfair of me," he continued. "I'm not trying to make you feel badly, you understand. But I am overwhelmed. Men are meant to have a helpmate, and at the moment I don't have one, and yet I still have an entire household to take care of."

"I can imagine that must be very trying," Annie responded in a small voice. "I don't know what to say."

"There's nothing to say. I'll figure it out."

"I'll help however I can."

He turned back to the dishes, carefully wiping his wet, soapy hands on a towel before wiping down the inside of the skillet. Annie opened her mouth, but she closed it again when she realized she truly did not know what to say. It was true that taking care of everything for a family was far more work than one person could do easily, but it was also true that Annie had been given strict instructions to stay off her feet.

Though she hated to be in the position to tell Isaac he was doing any part of it wrong, nevertheless Annie was grateful she had caught him before one of their pans had been ruined. With as angry as he had been over the spoiled butter, she had no doubt that her not telling him about the pan in time would receive the same reaction and she would be blamed.

Isaac banged around in their small kitchen area, cleaning, putting things away. Annie tried to put from her mind all the other things that needed to be done—sweeping the floor, baking extra bread for the following day, boiling water to drink, among so many other things. If Isaac needed her help or advice, he knew he could ask, and she didn't want to imply he was incapable in the meantime.

CHAPTER TWENTY-THREE

"Wife?" Isaac called out before he had even opened the door. "Are you in bed? I have a surprise for you!"

Annie pulled herself into a sitting position in bed, pushing the quilt down to pool around her waist. Another day had passed in which Isaac had left her alone to rest her ankle. He had stayed home one day, but couldn't stay more than that. While there was still plenty to do around the house, he also had plenty to do outside on their homestead, and so she had assured him she would be fine on her own. It was another day in which she had a stale biscuit, slept a lot, and wished she could even just get up to stretch. Her joints ached, and as much as she had lamented her own cooking skills, Isaac's were even worse.

But this was all just a trial they had to get through. Temporary. There was nothing for it but to take one day at a time. Or that's what she told herself, anyway, during the hours she lay alone wishing for a friend or a miracle cure.

All in all, Annie was tired, hungry, and a bit melancholy. If this was how just a few days of healing were spent, she didn't know how she would get through another couple weeks. She could not imagine what surprise Isaac could possibly have brought her that would make any difference. What she needed most was rest, but with so much to do she didn't see how she would get it.

But that thought flew from her mind when she saw what entered her home with her husband.

Josie, Margaret, and Lawrence all filed into the Wheelers' cabin just behind Isaac, all three beaming at her.

"What? Why— What are you doing here?"

"About that," Isaac cut in, before any of the Hudsons could respond. "I've been thinking this over for several days now, and meant to talk to you about it, but with everything that has happened, I just thought this was the best choice. Surprise!"

"What are you talking about?" Annie asked, bewildered.

The small house was full with the three additional people. Her sister, Josie, had already set to work putting a couple logs on the fire and coaxing it to flames. Annie saw her check the water level in the kettle, while Margaret whispered something to Lawrence that made him leave again.

"What is going on?"

"Your family is going to live with us," Isaac said simply. "For a little bit."

Annie burst into tears. "What?" She looked from her husband to her sisters and back. "Really?"

"Oh, honey, don't cry." Margaret removed her gloves and hurried to Annie's side. "This is good news, isn't it?"

"Yes, of course. I—I've missed you so much, and I didn't know how we were going to get through this, and I never dreamed in a million years . . ."

"Well, the truth is, it's a blessing for all of us," Josie said. She stayed near the fireplace, keeping an eye on the fire and assessing the supplies and needs of the kitchen.

"The weather is just getting too cold for anyone to comfortably live in a tent," Margaret explained. "And we're still at least a week away from our home being finished. Now, don't fret. We're not the only charity case. I think maybe half a dozen other families are doubling up for a bit, just in case the snow comes earlier than we expect."

"But when Isaac told us what had happened with your ankle, we had to come as soon as we could," Josie cut in. "It will be tight quarters, but at least you'll have the help you need so you can stay off your feet safely."

"Perfect timing for all of us," Isaac assured her.

"This is . . ." Annie began, sniffling. "This is too much. I can't believe it. Thank you so much."

"We should be thanking *you*," Margaret insisted. "You just sit back, and we'll take care of all of it."

Annie let out a grateful laugh, just as her tall nephew entered with his arms full of a wooden crate stacked tall with food. Isaac conferred with him about something Annie couldn't hear over Josie's cheerful chatter as she and Margaret took stock of the Wheelers' kitchen and larder, unpacking some of the items Lawrence had just brought in. Annie had not felt so taken care of since Louisa had been alive. Her oldest sister had always been happy to take charge, make sure things got done, and find even the smallest details to ensure the happiness of her loved ones.

Josie set a pot of water to boiling over the fireplace, sighing happily. "Oh, yes, I can get used to this. You may never get rid of us!"

Isaac had not even stopped to remove his hat and coat, but crossed the room to squat by Annie's side. He brushed the hair from her face, looked into her eyes, and cupped her cheek. "Are you happy, wife?"

"So happy. Thank you so much."

He kissed her, heedless of the other people in the house who would see. "Now, since you are in good hands," Isaac said, "I do actually have a lot that needs doing."

Annie laughed. "You are free to go, sir. Thank you. Very much."

"You don't have to keep thanking me. I'm happy we can do this."

"I have the laudanum," Josie said, patting her apron pocket. "She'll be fine."

"No whiskey?" Annie asked with a smile.

"I'll see if Ernie Schmidt has any to spare," Isaac said. "I think he was passing around a bottle the last time the Jameson boys had a dance. Then you ladies can get rip-roaring drunk next time I'm gone."

"Oh, heavens, don't let Mrs. Mills hear you say that," Margaret said.

"Thank you again, Hudsons." Isaac kissed the top of Annie's head once more before darting out the door again.

"Now." Margaret looked around the room at the Wheelers' scant space and furniture, while Josie started pulling out ingredients. "Where do we begin? Annie, love? Any requests?"

Annie felt tears sliding down her cheeks again, but more than anything she felt grateful and taken care of. Moments like this were precisely why she was so happy her family had chosen to travel west to the Oregon Territory with her. Though she likely could have made it on her own, it was so much better to not have to.

"I haven't had fresh bread in several days," she said. "Just a warm slice of sourdough would make my whole day."

"Sourdough?" Josie said with a nod. "I can do sourdough."

As Lawrence continued to bring the Hudsons' belongings into the house from the wagon stationed outside, Josie and Margaret set to putting the small home in order. It was truly astounding how much chaos had been wrought in just the few days Annie had been off her feet. She caught Margaret grimacing at the smell of one of the Wheelers' dishtowels that should have been scalded and washed days earlier. Though a week ago, Annie never would have guessed she had that much effect on their surroundings, now that she had been forced to stop, she could see what a difference her effort made.

Annie tucked this thought away for the next time she felt lonely, the next time she felt useless. Her best might not be perfect, but it was still something. And she hoped that Isaac would notice, too.

Over the course of the afternoon, Lawrence got all the family's things moved into the house and chopped some more firewood, setting them up for the cold week ahead. Josie baked not one but two fresh loaves of sourdough, and Annie gratefully ate three warm, buttered slices all on her own, heedless of the crumbs that were no doubt settling in the bed around her. The Hudsons had brought their own food stores with them—including butter—and Annie could not stop thanking them. And through all of this, Margaret busied herself with giving the entire cabin a good cleaning and conferring with Annie over sleeping arrangements.

"It will be tight," Margaret said, tucking one of the chairs farther under the table. "But not as tight as that wagon was for six months."

Annie chuckled, thinking about the cramped sleeping wagon where the four sisters had slept for six months. There had been two cots on each side, one above the other, with an aisle between them that could not have been more than ten inches wide, and Lawrence sleeping in a small tent outside. Through the heat and the rain and the cold, from Independence, Missouri, until they'd reached the Oregon Territory and she was married, she and her three sisters shared a space that at times felt little bigger than a coffin.

Yes, she thought, looking at her cozy home, her family settling in. This was better.

CHAPTER TWENTY-FOUR

A year had passed since the Hudson sisters had left their small town on the coast of Virginia to come west. The decision to leave the east had been difficult, and every step along the way had been a trial, even before Louisa had died. It was no stretch for Annie to conclude that she had never been as happy in all that time as she was now—even with her injury. Having to stay in bed and off her feet as much as possible was frustrating, yes, but with her family there to gladly help with whatever they could, Annie didn't feel quite so overwhelmed by this new life in which she had found herself.

It was crowded and loud at times, and the room often got stiflingly hot and smelly, but still Annie would not trade it. Part of what made this time with her family so special was the knowledge that it would not last forever. Margaret and Josie would have their own home soon, their own hearth to care for, and they would leave Annie to hers. All over Eden Valley, more cabins were being finished, as the community was under the threat of snow any day. Annie half expected Isaac or Lawrence to come home each afternoon and tell them it was time for the sisters to move. So, with that possibility ever-present, she cherished each moment, as tight, inconvenient, and unpleasant as it might be.

As Isaac intended he and Annie to make this structure their home for several years—rather than a temporary shelter just for this winter—he had invested in the largest logs he could manage, building a solid home that they could add on to over time. Even so, the cabin was only about twelve by fifteen feet, though that was still larger than some of the shelters other men were making. With the large stone fireplace taking up the bulk of one side wall, the remaining floor was a careful balance of simple, select furniture and open space in which to move around.

If Annie had not been relegated to the bed, navigating around their small house with all the people in it might have been more trouble. As it was, she stayed put, out of the way, watching as her sisters took care of everything she had been responsible for.

Finding room for the three extra people to sleep in the tiny home was the biggest challenge. During the day, Isaac and Lawrence were gone and the women were busy with their own tasks, but at night it felt as though the five were practically on top of each other. Margaret and Josie both squeezed into the bed with Annie, Margaret sleeping in the middle with her head between the feet of the other two women; Annie slept fitfully, always afraid of rolling off the edge of the bed or kicking her sister-in-law in her sleep. Isaac and Lawrence had narrow mats on the floor of the cabin, with the boy even having to sleep with his feet under the bed because there was no other convenient spot.

But still she was happy; still she was grateful. There were so many worse things that could have happened when she was injured, and sharing her bed with two sisters who she dearly loved was a small price to pay.

On the fourth day after her accident, Annie was listening to Josie explain what plants she looked for in the winter when dying homespun, excited that she had seen a black walnut tree not far from town. Though this was not a project either of them would have time for that year, Josie had started wishing aloud for a loom, when the door to the cabin opened unexpectedly.

"I'm home, wife," Isaac said as he entered. "Not for long, but I've brought you something."

Dr. Martell stepped through the doorway just behind him.

"The doctor is going to check on your ankle, and then I need to take him back to town to look in on Mrs. Waters."

"Oh, thank you," Annie said, trying to sit up in bed more elegantly. "I know it's a journey to get out here."

"I'm happy to. Especially as your husband told me you seemed to be feeling a lot better," the older man said, as Josie took his coat. "Best part of my job, don't you know—giving and receiving good news."

Annie nodded. "My bruises and scratches are well on their way to healing, I think, and my joints no longer feel stiff from the jarring fall. So that's all something. I haven't tried to put weight on the ankle yet, though."

He crossed the room and pulled a chair up to Annie's bedside, smiling kindly at her. "I must say, having your family here seems to have done you a world of good, too. Just these few days of rest are very helpful."

"I'm very lucky, Doctor," Annie said. "And very grateful."

"I imagine this would have been a much different experience on your own, hmm?"

He settled in to give her a full checkup, ensuring her pulse was not too erratic and her breathing not too labored. "I confess," he said, as he had her take deep, slow breaths, "when I was here a few days ago I tried not to show you the depth of my concern. You had quite the fall. But it seems as though all is in order—all except that ankle."

"Do you know how long I need to stay off of it still?"

"Well, let's see, now." He moved his chair to the foot of the bed, where Annie had poked her toe out from under the blankets.

"You keeping warm enough? Your husband seems to have done a wonderful job making this cabin tight as a drum."

Annie smiled at Isaac, who remained on the other side of the room by the fire, watching. "Yes, he's been wonderful. And with the extra people here, we've all been plenty warm, I think."

"Now, I'm going to slip your stocking and bandage off, if that is all right with you, Mrs. Wheeler. Yes? Wonderful, wonderful," the doctor murmured, as he carefully unwrapped the tight wool bandage that had been holding her ankle in place.

Though Dr. Martell handled her gingerly, Annie's ankle was still quite sore and swollen. Taking the pressure off brought the ache rushing back. She winced as the doctor gently pressed on the pink and purple, sensitive skin.

"How does it look?" Isaac asked.

Annie looked over at her husband in time to see Josie hand him a piece of buttered bread, though he barely acknowledged it in his concern for his wife.

"Will it still be weeks yet that she's off her feet?" he continued.

"Oh, no, maybe not that long." The doctor frowned, bringing his face closer to Annie's foot. "I don't think it's quite as bad as we feared. Maybe only another week more before you can try walking on it."

Annie let out a sigh of relief. "Oh, heavens, really?"

"Yes, my dear. Just don't take it too quickly. There needs to be far more resting still. Even if you think you can manage limping across the room, try not to."

The doctor smiled kindly at her, with a warmth and protectiveness that made Annie wish her own father had lived longer. Both of Annie's parents had died within a few weeks of each other when she was only ten years old. While her oldest sister had shielded her siblings from the fever that had taken their parents, and then immediately poured herself into her business to be able to support them, there was no real substitute for a father.

"I promise," Annie assured the doctor, feeling lighter with just that tiny sliver of hope. "I don't want to hurt myself worse and be laid up even longer."

Before he left, Margaret came in and peppered Dr. Martell with questions about Annie's limitations and goals, when they could get her on her feet again, and precisely how long she could try before needing to rest again. Annie stopped paying attention after the first two questions, confident that her sister-in-law would have it all in hand. This was part of why her family was there, after all—to help take care of her.

With a contented sigh, grateful for her prognosis, Annie leaned back against the headboard. Her husband and Dr. Martell said their goodbyes, leaving the women alone for the rest of the afternoon.

"Well, now," Josie said, sitting carefully on the edge of the bed by Annie. "How do you feel? Must be right thrilling to get that news, huh?"

"I don't know quite how to feel," Annie admitted. "I had resigned myself to weeks more of this, and to know that in only a few days I can at least try to stand . . ." She shook her head in wonder. "Seems almost too good to be true."

"*I* call it Providential," Margaret said, taking the chair where the doctor had sat.

All three sisters leaned forward, toward each other, closing their small, tight circle.

"Our home is bound to be finished very soon," Margaret continued, "and if you can be at least able to do some things by then, we won't have anything to worry about."

"You will find plenty to worry about," Josie teased. "But she is right." She turned serious, addressing Annie. "I know we talked about you learning how to better manage the household, cook more recipes like I do, so whatever is on that list that we can focus on while we're here, we should. Maybe soup broth to start? Or do you need me to show you how to patch a shirt?"

"Yes. Please. Thank you," Annie responded. "All of it. Whatever you think I need. I'm sure you know better than me. I'm so grateful to you. And, of course, I know that I can come ask you any time, but getting any kind of guidance while I have you is such a blessing. I certainly don't know what I would do without you two."

She leaned forward, grasping each sister's hand in her own.

"I would not be here without you two," she repeated. "I love you so much, and if there's any way I can ever repay you for all of this . . ."

"That's what family does," Margaret assured her, squeezing her hand.

"But I'm sure we can think of something," Josie added with a wink.

The remainder of the day was filled with Annie asking Josie all the questions she could think of to better be able to keep house, until finally her brain felt overtaxed. Time seemed to fly: the men returned, the family ate supper together, and all through it Annie felt as though her heart could burst from gratitude. When the cold December night fell, Annie cuddled down under the quilts, Margaret's stockinged feet up by her face, and drifted off to sleep as the fire across the room died down.

Her last thought before slipping into unconsciousness was one of simple contentedness.

CHAPTER TWENTY-FIVE

In spite of the optimism she felt the afternoon after the doctor had told her the injury was better than he'd thought, Annie's impatience soon flared up again. She was grateful that her family was nearby to help and support her, grateful that some of the burden had been lifted from Isaac, and she knew quite well how lucky she was; but in spite of all this, the frustration at her injury and limitations was only growing.

As she tried to stretch her back and shoulders from a sitting position, Annie groaned. Her neck felt stiff, her hips ached, and that was all aside from her actual injuries.

"I don't know how much longer I can stay cooped up in here," she said one morning, two days after the doctor had visited. "I've been off my feet for almost six days already. I'm going to get bed sores."

"You've been off your feet *only* six days," Margaret corrected her, from where she sat at the table, peeling potatoes. "And you know the doctor said it wouldn't be that much longer. If you can just stick it out another couple days, we can see how much of your weight you can hold. Maybe even walk across the room."

Annie groaned again. "But, if Josie is going to teach me how to make maple sugar candy, I need to get out of bed, don't I?" she asked hopefully. "Can't do that from bed, surely. Way too messy."

"Did I hear my name?" Josie asked as she entered the house. "Are you getting me in trouble, Annie?"

"Never."

"Good, because if you did, I wouldn't tell you my good news!" Josie's eyes flashed excitedly as she held up one of her hands in triumph, carefully cradling what she had brought in with her. "Two eggs. The first ones in a bit. I bet the girls will be stopping altogether for the winter soon. I'm rather surprised we got these, so we certainly need to treasure them. What should we do? I know I said maple sugar candy, but that was before we had eggs. Small cake? Breakfast? Annie, as our hostess—"

"And invalid," she interjected.

"As our hostess," Josie repeated, "I'd like to leave the choice to you. What would you like?"

"I can hardly think. I feel like my stomach is going to growl just at the thought. But, yes, please, a small cake sounds like exactly what we all need. Do we have enough sugar, though?"

"We have some sugar," Josie said. "And the maple sugar will help sweeten it a little bit more. I have a handful of dried apples left, which isn't *quite* enough, but we can make it work. It won't be anything like I could make back east, of course."

"It's better than anything *I* could do," Annie assured her.

"Maybe we can see if the Abbotts have any milk we can trade for," Margaret suggested, "and we can whip some cream to go on top of the cake. I can walk over to their homestead in a few minutes."

"Oh, stop," Annie said with a laugh. "You're going to make my stomach growl!"

By the afternoon, the smell of sweet, fresh-baked pastry filled the small space. It made the home feel even more homey, Annie thought. She had only been able to do the bare minimum until now, but somehow the prospect of having even a small apple cake on the table offered the same kind of comfort that Isaac had described looking forward to. Cake was not the same as a chandelier, but somehow it helped in a similar way. The sisters were eagerly looking forward to their treat, and Margaret filled the time by regaling Annie and Josie with stories about her childhood milking her neighbors' goats.

"There were only three of them, but I had to go over there every morning. And let me tell you, those goats were in no mood to make friends."

"How have we never heard this before?" Josie asked in wonder. "You married our brother almost twenty years ago!"

"Oh, it's not as though tales of goats come up in everyday conversation, do they? But Annie's fall reminded me somehow. Or, rather, her convalescence. When that billy goat knocked me headfirst into the stable wall, I thought I was going to be laid up for days."

Lawrence arrived home just as his mother was describing her graceless fall, but she clammed up as soon as she saw her son.

"What?" he asked, looking from his aunts to his mother and back again. "What did I walk into?"

"Nothing, my love. Welcome home." Margaret rose from her seat to offer it to Lawrence. She reached for and squeezed his hand as he passed her. "I was just telling your aunts about how I have never done anything clumsy or ill-advised in my entire life, and I am sure you will follow suit."

"Oh, so we're just making up stories, then? I've got one about the man in the moon."

His mother and aunts all burst into laughter. As an only child, Lawrence had long ago developed the skills to hold his own in adult conversations, and Annie marveled to see how well he was growing into a responsible young man.

When Isaac returned home soon afterward, the laughter and delight must have been heard all the way from outside. He opened the door, and had not even hung up his coat before saying, "What are you all doing, having so much fun without me?"

"Nothing," Margaret said hurriedly. "Never!"

"Can we get goats?" Annie asked, sending the other women off into laughter all over again.

Isaac looked confused, but waited to be let in on the joke.

"Oh, it's just something Margaret was telling us," Annie explained hurriedly. "Neighbor goats and accidents, and"—she shrugged—"it sounds fun."

"It was *not* fun," Margaret said with a laugh.

"Goats?" Isaac repeated as he hung up his coat and pulled off his gloves. "So it sounds as though you all have had an entertaining day, at least."

"Come, sit," Margaret said, patting the empty spot at the table across from Lawrence. "We've just been here talking. You men must have had a long day. Tell us all about it."

Isaac made himself comfortable at the table, pulling off his shoes and leaning back. He thanked Josie when she brought him a cup of coffee. Margaret had given up her own seat for her son, letting the men who had been constructing homes all day have the most comfortable seats; she moved to help Josie with the last steps for supper as they relaxed.

"Did you finish the Valentines' house today?" she asked.

"All but the front door, but Joe can hang that in the morning once they are all moved in. I tell you," Isaac said, "it's been getting mighty cold out. It's a relief to me that we're so close to finishing these houses."

He took a small sip of his coffee and grimaced slightly.

"Oh, this is— Can you bring me sugar for this?" he asked Josie.

"Oh, no, I'm sorry. This cake used the last of the sugar we had."

"You what?"

A stark silence fell.

Annie flushed. Even from where she sat in bed, she recognized the coldness in Isaac's voice; it felt almost like a hunter giving his game a head start to run, to save themselves.

"It's my fault," she said, cutting in. "It's just sugar, so I didn't think—"

Annie got to her feet, intending to put her body between Isaac and Josie, but her ankle twinged, and she couldn't take more than a step before she had collapsed under the pain.

Isaac turned to face her, but didn't make any motion to help Annie to her feet again. Instead he took a step toward her, looming over her in his anger.

"You didn't think. You used all the sugar, without even a thought to how I like to take my coffee or how we'll get any more? I am gone all day, building entire houses out of the goodness of my heart, and when I come home I can't even get one of the small comforts that I have worked hard for."

"It's not like that . . ." Josie began. "We thought with the eggs—"

Isaac whirled on her, the words dying uncertainly in her throat.

"It's my fault," Annie said again, as she pulled herself back up onto the edge of the bed. "I wasn't clear with Josie. I should have made sure we saved some."

"You didn't save a single grain? Do you think sugar just grows on trees? Oh, how about I go down to our sugar well and pull up another bucket of sugar so we can just have cake every day, huh?"

Annie felt numb as her husband's sarcasm washed over her. Every other time he had gotten angry with her, she had been able to take it, knowing she had done wrong and he was justified in his upset. Now, though, she saw it all through her sisters' eyes, his meanness and unreasonable reaction.

She was so embarrassed. But how could she stop him? How could she even defend herself when he wasn't listening?

"Who knows when we will have a chance to get more?" Isaac

continued. He had stood up by now, pacing angrily in the corner of the room, while the rest of the family watched him warily. "You want me to go all the way to the fort, is that it? Twenty-some miles in winter? I know, I'll just risk my life so you can have a cake, brought to you while you loll about in bed, huh?"

"Isaac—"

He tossed his coffee cup into the fire, the steam from the undrunk coffee creating a brief cloud and the tin cup clattering against the stone at the back of the fireplace.

Josie gasped.

Annie felt her face flush. Though Isaac had gotten angry with her in the past, she had hoped that he would at least be able to keep his temper while her family was here.

And she would never have expected he be angry enough to throw something.

He whirled around, his fury cold and barely restrained.

"Isaac . . ." Annie said softly, her tone pleading.

His eyes flashed as he looked around the room at the four faces watching him fearfully. With a huff, Isaac stalked toward the door, seized his coat, and left, walking off into the night without another word.

As soon as the door shut behind him, Annie burst into tears, too embarrassed and ashamed to look up when she felt Margaret and Josie come sit on the bed next to her.

CHAPTER TWENTY-SIX

Isaac was gone the rest of the night. Annie worried and fretted over his safety, while her sisters reminded her there was nothing to be done and tried to gently comfort her. Annie tossed and turned all night, only sleeping soundly once she heard the front door open and her husband enter.

The following morning was tense; Isaac seemed to be overly conciliatory and polite to his in-laws before he left for the day, but not once did he apologize for his behavior or even refer to it at all. He accepted his slice of the small cake without comment, tucking it away and disappearing out the front door with Lawrence.

Throughout the day, Annie vacillated between apologizing again for her husband's behavior and ignoring the incident completely. Her mind was in turmoil, and she was grateful for all the other topics Josie and Margaret talked about instead of forcing Annie to face anything she wasn't ready for.

That afternoon, Annie cajoled Margaret into letting her get on her feet. Though it took what seemed like an excessively long time, she was able to cross the room with only minimal support, leaning on the back of a chair or the table every few steps.

"You do seem to be doing better. We'll have to have the doctor come take a look again," Margaret said, assessing Annie's limp. "I know what he said, but I still worry."

"He said I could try after a few days."

"I know. You're right. And I suppose I'm inclined to believe if you are able to walk already, maybe the bruising just makes your ankle *look* worse than it really is."

"Let's hope so. I don't know how I could manage staying in bed any longer. Even if I wasn't also afraid you all would be leaving any day."

"We won't leave if you need us more," Josie said. "We would never do that to you."

"Oh, I know. But, also, I don't want to be holding you back. Once your home is done, you should go settle in. I can be fine here by myself again. Or just me and Isaac. Which is why I need to get used to being on my feet more."

"Annie," Margaret began gently. "Speaking of Isaac, what he did last night . . . losing his temper and throwing something. Has that happened a lot?"

"No. No, not at all. Or . . . not really. He gets upset, like anyone would, of course. There are so many things he needs to worry about, and I mess things up a lot, which must make things harder for him—"

"But . . ." She looked apologetic, as though reluctant to even say the words. "The throwing things. That must be scary for you, isn't it?"

Margaret's voice was low and gentle, as one would speak to an agitated animal. Annie recognized how difficult broaching the subject must be, but she just couldn't bring herself to be completely honest about how upsetting his anger could be.

"He doesn't throw things—he hasn't, I mean—and he didn't really— Well, he didn't throw it at any of us. Did you hear about that family back in Norfolk? The one whose father all but threw his children down the stairs? I can't even imagine how people can be like that."

"We're talking about *you*, Annie. And your husband. Don't forget I have a young son." Margaret smiled kindly. "I know all the tricks for trying to change the subject. You won't distract me."

"Annie." Josie came to sit at the foot of the bed. "We love you and we love Isaac, but if you need help, you have to tell us. We can get you out of here."

"No. It's not like that, I don't think. Not really. He gets angry, but, you know, we've lived without any men in our home for years now. All of us. Maybe this is just what it's like to be married."

"Annie—"

"I am certainly not blameless," she hurried on, cutting off Margaret's words. "The times I have seen him the angriest were all because I messed up. That's my fault. Did I tell you I spoiled an entire batch of butter? A pound or two of it. He had worked hard, trading the labor of building a stable for the milk for it, and then it all went to waste because I wasn't paying close enough attention."

"That's not a reason to throw things."

"He didn't throw things, not that time. He was just angry. Which you would be, too, wouldn't you? I was so wasteful."

Josie and Margaret looked at each other.

"And then another time," Annie went on, "I accidentally ripped one of his shirts while I was washing it. And, you know, we can't just easily replace it. And it wasn't fixable without being completely obvious. I know he must be embarrassed having to go to church with that clear indication of my poor skills. Of course he would be angry."

"But, Annie, you just said it was an accident," Josie said. "Does he think you're not allowed to make mistakes?"

"No. I mean, yes—of course I am allowed to make mistakes,"

she responded, though there wasn't any conviction behind her words. "And his anger didn't really last too terribly long. He raised his voice, but only for a little while. I'm sure most husbands in this town would be just as angry."

"You keep saying things like that," Margaret said. "Justifying being yelled at by saying that other husbands do the same. But, Annie . . ." She shook her head. "That's just not true. Your brother was not like that at all. Ever. I don't think your father was either, the little I knew of him. There are ways that men can express their anger without raising their voices."

"Without throwing cups into the fireplace," Josie added.

"And we just worry that if this is happening now . . . what if it gets worse?"

Annie blinked at them in confusion. It had not occurred to her that she should be this worried; she had been more embarrassed than anything. But now, seeing her sisters' faces, hearing them ask if she needed help getting out of this situation, the true grim reality of the situation sank in.

"I don't think it's like that," she said, unsure. "He's so kind. He's generous, and he always apologizes afterward. He has done so much for me. For all of us."

Margaret pursed her lips. "That may be, but I want you to come straight to us if any of this gets worse. Please. We're smart and capable women, and we will figure something out."

Annie nodded, though in her heart she could not imagine ever getting to that point.

"Goodness, I wish Louisa was here," Josie said. "She would know what to do."

"But you remember how Louisa was," Margaret added. "She would be yelling at Isaac right back. Maybe not angry, so much as domineering."

"Yes, and remember how long it took me to be able to stand up to her?" Annie said. "Twenty-five years or so? How am I supposed to do that with Isaac?"

"That just means you've already proven you can do it," Margaret said, putting her arm around Annie.

"It's different."

"I understand, dear," Margaret said. "Men are different. Even if you are certain that he would never hurt you, the sheer dominance coming from a man that much larger than you brings its own fears. I remember, when your brother was alive, I always made sure to bring up delicate topics when we were both sitting, on the same level, neither with more power than the other. And you remember—your brother was possibly the most gentle man I have ever met. Anger is worrisome, no matter who it is coming from."

"Just be careful, please," Josie added. "We can't lose you, too."

Annie nodded, but didn't say anything more. Her only hope at that moment was to just do whatever she could to not upset Isaac again. Maybe that would be enough.

Soon after Margaret and Josie came to Annie with their concerns, Lawrence returned home, forestalling any further conversation. The small cabin was filled with the scent of rosemary as Josie put the finishing touches on their supper. Margaret asked her son about his day, awkwardly avoiding the very topic that was on everyone's minds still. Soon, they heard the sounds of Rocky and Isaac in the yard outside, and Josie nudged Lawrence into setting the table.

The door burst open, letting in a cold draft, as Isaac returned.

"I have good news!" Isaac hung his hat and coat on the pegs near the front door and turned back to the family with an expression full of expectation. "Well, good and bad."

"Bad news first," Margaret said, wringing her hands in front of her.

"The bad news"—he looked somber—"is that you will not be here for the holidays when Annie and me get our piano."

"Huh?" Lawrence asked.

"You mean . . . ?" Josie added, excitement dawning on her face.

Isaac nodded vigorously. "The good news is that your house was completed today. Zeke Emerson took care of the final bit of clay to seal up the gaps, and it is ready for you to move in tomorrow."

"Oh! Thank heavens," Margaret said, collapsing into a chair. "I thought this day may never come. Not that I'm not happy to be here with you all, of course."

Annie laughed, the tension of the previous twenty-four hours released. "You don't have to lie to us, Margaret. It's been a test of patience for all of us."

"Can we go *now?*" Lawrence asked.

His mother shook her head. "It's too dark. Too much trouble. But we can go first thing tomorrow morning."

"What about me? What if *I* just go? I'll sleep on the floor, I don't care."

"Lawrence Hudson, you will freeze and be unable to sleep, and then you'll be absolutely no good to us tomorrow. I'm sorry, son. It's just one more night here."

Lawrence nodded gamely. Annie wondered if she would ever see him ruffled. He seemed to be growing into the kind of even-tempered young man his father would have been proud of.

"Supper is ready," Josie announced.

While she served up quail and potatoes to each member of the family, Lawrence kept trying to cajole his mother into letting him sleep in the empty cabin, though more to make her laugh than any real attempt to change her mind. Annie chuckled along with everyone else when he swore that someone was needed there to protect their home from wild hogs.

"No, really!" he insisted. "Did you know there are wild hogs all over the southern states? Billy Whitson told me the Spanish brought them over, and they've just about taken over South Carolina in parts."

"And, what?" Isaac said, taking his seat at the table. "You think they followed a wagon train all the way to Oregon and no one has seen one yet?"

"You never know." Lawrence widened his eyes dramatically. "You wouldn't want our home to be the first one taken over by such things, would you?"

"Oh, darling boy," Margaret said with a laugh. "You know whatever wild hogs are around are going to go straight for Jameson's General Store."

"All that food," Josie agreed knowingly. "I hope the hogs brought enough coin."

"What? No—"

The adults all laughed—Annie most of all—at the mock dismay on Lawrence's face when he realized he had been outmaneuvered in his reasoning.

While her sisters and nephew chattered animatedly about their moving the following day, all Annie could think about was how lucky she had been that they were there with her at all, and how much she would miss them when they were gone. This last week or so with her family back was precisely what she needed and far more than she could have hoped for. Though she would forever be grateful to have had this time, Annie would miss them terribly when they moved the following day.

CHAPTER TWENTY-SEVEN

When Annie awoke the next morning, it was to the early sounds of the rest of her family preparing for their day, all of them getting ready to leave. The door opened and closed as Lawrence took some of their belongings out to their wagon. Bacon sizzled on the hot skillet as Josie made breakfast; Annie breathed it in appreciatively.

"What time is it?" she asked, sitting up in bed. "You should have woken me. There must be so much to do. How long have you been awake?"

"Almost an hour. It's moving day!" Margaret said, eyes lit up. "I don't know how you slept through all this." She shook out one of the blankets Lawrence had been using as a mat on the floor; dust flew up in a cloud before settling again as she folded the quilt. "We've got to collect all our things, hitch up the oxen for the last time, and set off to our new house."

"I'm coming with you." Annie put her feet on the floor and reached for the nearby chair to hold her weight.

"You can come," Margaret said, bringing the chair over to

within reach, "but you're not carrying anything. I will not be the reason your ankle doesn't heal."

"Better hurry up and get ready," Josie said. "I think we're almost packed."

"And not a moment too soon," Lawrence said as he entered. Isaac was right behind him, his arms full of firewood. "It's starting to snow!"

Josie gasped. "No!"

"It's not much." Isaac placed a log on the fire, a brief thread of steam curling up. "Might not even stick. But it's only going to get colder from here."

"Oh, I hope it doesn't stick," Josie said, as she pulled cooked bacon out of the pan to serve for breakfast. "I can't imagine having to drive the wagons through snow."

"You'll have help," Isaac assured her, stacking the rest of the firewood neatly near the stone hearth. "I'll be there, and I think the mayor planned on sending at least one other man to help, too. No one in Eden Valley is going to let you ladies move all of this on your own."

"I am certainly not prepared to be snowed in all winter," Josie added, shaking her head. "Not yet at least."

"It snowed in Virginia," Margaret protested.

"Not like this. Not where we lived. We usually only got snow a handful of times in January and February. Nothing like northern snow without even the benefit of a growing season to prepare for it."

"I wonder if it will snow for Christmas," Lawrence said wistfully. He held a wooden crate full of the Hudsons' bed things as his mother stacked folded quilts atop it.

"When it snowed in Virginia," Josie added, "we had had months of plenty of food and time to store more for the winter. Not to mention the easy access to the general store, butcher, even shipyards if we needed it. A foot of snow here will be a much different prospect than a foot of snow there."

"I wish I could help," Annie said. "This ankle is just never going to be done causing us trouble."

"Could be worse, could be worse," Margaret reminded her. "The snow could have arrived yesterday, and we could all be snowed in here together instead of setting off for our own home."

"Stop saying 'snowed in'!" Josie protested. "It's not going to stick."

"Do you all want to wait out this snow, or go now and risk it?" Isaac asked.

"Risk it," replied all the Hudsons in unison.

Josie laughed. "Thank you, Isaac, but the sooner we can get settled in the better for the rest of the winter."

"I agree completely. Come on. Let's get these last things packed away and then head over."

Annie felt helpless, watching as her family bustled around cleaning, packing, and carrying everything out to the wagon. She could only get herself ready to leave, taking her time to pull her boot on up over her sore ankle. The swelling had gone down, but she knew better than to try to help with the packing. Her limp was pronounced, and she would only be slowing them down. Instead, Annie brushed and pinned up her hair, tied a clean apron over her dress, and slowly made her way across the room to where coffee was waiting for her.

"What will I do when you're gone?" she asked Josie, as she hugged her from behind. "Make my own breakfast? That seems absurd."

Her sister laughed, then broke away to carry a plate with bacon and biscuit to the table, as Annie carefully followed close behind.

"It's a tragedy, I know. But rest assured, Annie—if the effort kills you, we'll be sure to put up an elaborate headstone."

"Oh, thank you so much."

Josie laughed again, and Annie settled in to eat.

Though she was making light of it, trying to be as buoyant

and cheerful as possible for her family's new home, her worry was genuine. It had taken a lot of effort for Annie to even cross the room with her injury, and Isaac could not stay home to tend to her. She told herself there were plenty of other folks dealing with plenty of more difficult trials, and she would be just fine.

More even than her dread at being left alone, however, Annie knew missing her family would be the harder part.

Not long after Annie had finished eating, everything had been loaded into the Hudsons' wagon, the team of oxen was hitched up, and their three chickens were tucked away safely in the small cages that had carried them all the way across the continent. After limping outside, Annie was helped up onto the wagon bench by her husband, and the family was on their way.

She had not yet visited the site where the Hudsons' homestead would be, so as Lawrence led the team and wagon, she tried to memorize each turn and tree between her home and that of her sisters. The snow continued to fall, but lightly, as though offering a blessing on the family's move, rather than a hindrance. Tiny flakes landed on Annie's coat sleeves.

"Smell that?" Josie asked, sniffing the cold air.

They had traveled only about thirty minutes; Annie realized that once her ankle had healed, it would be an easy walk to visit her family. At Josie's words, she looked on ahead and noticed a plume of smoke curling up out of the chimney that rose above their roof.

"I wonder who did that," she said.

Lawrence led the oxen the remaining fifty feet to the small yard that surrounded the empty cabin. Before he had even stopped the team, the front door burst open and Mrs. George Mills greeted them, arms wide as though ready to hug the whole family at once.

"Welcome home, Hudsons!" she called to them.

Behind her poured her husband and daughter out into the

yard. The mayor went immediately to Lawrence, to help with the team, while Abby hurried to help Josie with the chickens.

Though the Hudsons had driven two covered wagons across the plains to Oregon, over the previous couple months settling in, they had sold one of the teams of oxen and one of the wagons. In a series of barters and trades, Margaret had maneuvered to swap the animals and wagon for the bare-minimum sticks of furniture for their new home, as well as tucking away a few coins for the future. Not long after they arrived at the cabin, John Pierce showed up with the table and chairs he had built for them.

Annie stayed where she was in the wagon seat while everyone else got right to work. The snow had stopped, so she could simply settle in and wait, staying out of the way and breathing in the fresh, crisp air as she looked around.

The structure was roughly the same size as Annie's own home, but without the stable and smokehouse that Isaac had built for the Wheelers. The Hudsons were blessed to have chickens, oxen, a couple goats and a horse, but that also meant they had a lot of work ahead of them. The open area where the house had been built was smaller than Annie's own yard, but the creek where they would draw their water until the well was dug was closer than Annie had to walk. Mrs. Mills—in her capacity as the mayor's wife—had come ahead and started a fire, and the home was warm and cozy to welcome them. Once Mr. Pierce had brought the furniture in, he lent a hand in unloading the remaining wagon.

From the wagon seat, Annie watched as the rest of the Hudsons and the Millses hustled around to get everything unpacked. Three of the four Hatchleys showed up soon after they'd arrived, adding their own hands to the labor, and every-thing was unpacked and out of the snow in no time at all.

"We'll be your closest neighbors," Mrs. Hatchley was saying, when Annie finally climbed down from the wagon and limped toward the house. "And I'll send Josiah over later once it has finished snowing to help lay in a stock of firewood for you all."

Her husband chimed in, "We should really get up a roof of some kind for the animals, too. Before too much snow falls. And a chicken coop certainly." He frowned, looking out through the front door. "Maybe young Lawrence here would like help with that in the next couple days."

"That is so kind," Margaret said. "I surely don't know what we would do without all you folks."

Mr. Pierce had noticed Annie limping in and offered her one of the three chairs that he had built. "Go ahead, then, Mrs. Wheeler. You need this more than the rest of us, I should think."

It transpired that in addition to helping the Hudsons unpack, Mrs. Hatchley had also brought a loaf of brown bread with a sprinkling of raisins baked throughout.

"It's better fresh and warm, of course," she said as she sliced up pieces on the Hudsons' new table. "But I knew we would be hungry. Better this than to put any onus on Miss Hudson to be hostess before she has even unpacked her water bucket."

"I assure you, I will return the favor," Josie said, accepting her slice of bread with a warm smile.

CHAPTER TWENTY-EIGHT

"I wanted to ask you something," Annie said the next morning as she limped around their small cabin preparing breakfast. "Yesterday, when we were at Josie and Margaret's home, the Hatchleys were talking about the Jamesons having a holiday dance tomorrow night. Christmas is soon, and I'm feeling festive. I think we should go!"

Annie and Isaac had stayed at the Hudsons' new home most of the previous day until just before sunset. Between Isaac, Josiah Hatchley, and Lawrence, they had managed to cobble together a good enough shelter for the animals, and the Wheelers hadn't left until it was complete. Annie made no complaints, happy to sit in her sisters' home with her injured foot up while they unpacked. Having her family living with her for a little while she healed had been such a gift, and Annie stretched it out as long as she could.

"A dance?" Isaac said with a frown. "You can barely stand. I'm not sure that's a good idea."

"Oh, please, let me go," Annie pleaded. "The ankle isn't much still bothering me, and this is likely to be the last gathering of all the folks for weeks, if not months. I couldn't stand it if I missed out on seeing everyone before we all hunker down for the winter."

Isaac shook his head. "I know you can limp around the house now, but being on your feet for hours is quite another thing."

"I won't dance. I promise. I'm not that foolish. And if we take the wagon, we can bring a chair so I can sit on the outside circle. Please, Isaac."

The incident with his anger just a few days earlier had not been forgotten, but Annie had decided that she would treat it as an anomaly. It was possible such a thing would never happen again, and as long as it did not, she would ignore that it had happened in the first place. In spite of this resolution, however, asking him for something she was not sure he would give was scary, and Annie found herself more anxious about his response than she felt was warranted.

He looked at her for only a short moment before smiling. "All right, then. But we're taking a chair, and you are staying put in that chair, and I don't want to even see you tap your foot to the music."

"That's fair." Annie clapped in delight. "Oh, thank you! I can't tell you how good this will be for me. I had been so sad thinking about my sisters gone and being on my own again in this small cabin without even laundry to distract me."

Isaac laughed. "And we both know how much you love laundry."

Looking forward to the dance made the next couple days pass slowly, somehow making Annie's limitations and the quiet when she was alone even more excruciating. When Isaac returned home that second afternoon, supper was ready, and Annie hovered—as much as she could with her limp—ensuring that Isaac had everything he needed and there was no reason for them to be delayed setting off for town. Finally, he hitched up the wagon, stuck one of their chairs in the back, and helped Annie up into the wagon seat so they could be off.

The narrow road into town—to the clearing where the Jamesons had held a gathering just a few weeks prior—was dark, and it took longer than Annie expected. She spent the entire ride chattering away inanely, more talkative than usual in her excitement.

"Christmases in Virginia were always big to-dos," she explained to Isaac. "Louisa acted grumpy about it, called it frivolous, but she was the most festive of all of us. If we weren't invited to at least one party, Louisa insisted we host one. One year she even took off two whole days from work to help Josie bake."

"That doesn't sound like the Louisa you've told me about."

"No. It was special. Every year she found a way to make Christmas special. Especially those first few years after our parents died. One year, she even somehow—I still don't know how she managed this, and now I can never ask her . . ." Annie sighed before continuing. "One year, I think I was fourteen, Louisa managed to hire a carriage to take us to the shore for Christmas day. Can you imagine? She packed food, and Tom and Margaret came with baby Lawrence, and we spent hours in the sunshine and sand."

"That doesn't sound very Christmassy."

"No, I suppose not. But it was special. And it let us spend the whole day together."

"The beach is a mite far for us to go to this year," he said, teasing.

"Goodness, if Louisa were here I can't even imagine how she would be making the most celebratory holiday out of the scantiest of resources. She was magical—my sister could do anything. I miss her so much."

Annie could feel Isaac watching her as she spoke, reminiscing about her sister, but he didn't offer any comment. In his silence, she continued to tell him stories from her childhood, of

Christmas past, all the while hoping they would make similarly special memories on Christmases in the future.

They heard the music before they saw anyone. There was a bend in the path, and they came upon a small area where other animals and wagons had been corralled. Annie could hardly contain her excitement, seeing the dozens of folks who had come out, even bundled up against the cold. No sooner had her feet touched the ground than her husband had swept her up in his arms and begun walking toward the crowd gathered.

"I can walk," she said, squirming a little. "Isaac, you don't need to carry me!"

"Absolutely not. I will not have anyone saying that I made you stay on your feet any moment longer than necessary. Hey there, Stephens!"

Rebecca's younger brother, Jasper, looked up at the sound of his name. He had been laughing with a couple other young men, but came when Isaac beckoned.

"Grab that chair in the back of my wagon, would you?" Isaac asked. "And follow me."

Charming, good-natured Jasper seemed happy to help, though Annie was a bit embarrassed by the spectacle. Everyone, it seemed, turned to look as her husband carried her through the crowd to where several couples were gathering on the edge of the dance circle.

"Go ahead and set that there." Isaac indicated a place near the campfire with a nod of his head, and Jasper obliged.

"Is your sister here?" Annie asked him, after Isaac had carefully set her down again.

Jasper looked around, then pointed to a cluster of women gathered on the other side of the dance circle. "Think she was hoping to see you, actually, Mrs. Wheeler. I'll make sure she knows you're here."

"Oh, thank you, Jasper. You've been so helpful."

"Happy to, ma'am." He tipped his hat to her before striding off toward his sister.

"Ma'am?" Annie repeated with a slight chuckle. "I suppose I'll get that all the time now that I'm married, won't I?"

"That you will, wife." Isaac stood behind her chair, his hands resting on her shoulders while he took in the gathering. "More people here than I would have expected, given the cold."

"Maybe everyone's like me and just needed to see some company before we're all snowed in for the winter."

"Snowed in," he repeated, laughing. "Oregon is nothing like Vermont or the Minnesota Territory. We will all be fine, and winter will be over as soon as it's started."

Annie sat forward, keeping one knee crossed over the other so her injured ankle had as little weight on it as possible. Her hands were clasped in her lap, but her eyes never left the whirl of the dancers. The lively music was all around her; the joyful couples were all around her. This was exactly where she wanted to be, soaking up all of this cheer and joy before she had to return to her home and spend the days quietly on her own.

The song ended and a lull followed, the silence quickly filled with laughter and chatter from the couples.

Mr. Jameson, raising both of his hands in the air, stepped into the middle of the quartet of musicians and called for the attention of their guests.

"Evening, all! I know we're all eager to get on with the fun, but if I could have your ears for just a moment?"

The crowd quieted down, turning toward the older man. There had been a pair of young women standing in front of Annie's chair, but they moved aside when they realized she could not see.

"Seems like most folks who were going to come are here." Mr. Jameson looked around at the gathered crowed. "My sons and I are so gratified. This is a cold December night, and to see so many—two? three dozen?—all here to dance and be merry, is just one more sign from the Lord above that this new community is precisely where he wants us to be. We want this to be the start of your holiday celebrations, all of us gathered together with the love and intention of the season."

"And the dancing!" someone called from the back of the crowd, followed by general laughter. Annie recognized it as Jasper's voice, though she couldn't see him from where she sat.

Mr. Jameson grinned. "All right, no need to say any more. I'll let you all get back to it. Thank you again for coming!"

With a flourish, he waved his hat in an arc, stepping back to allow the attention back on his son and the other musicians. Without hesitation, they launched into another lively waltz, and in moments a dozen couples were whirling around the dirt circle set aside for dancing.

Rebecca would soon come talk to her; Isaac would soon find one of his own friends, or maybe dance with one of the wallflowers. But all Annie truly wanted was to be there, in the center of it all, whether she was dancing or talking or not. All too soon she would be isolated at home again, nursing her injury and trying to keep from putting too much strain on her ankle. While she was here, now, she let the music and the jubilation wash over her, grateful for the opportunity and the celebration of the holiday.

CHAPTER TWENTY-NINE

On the way home from the dance later that night, Annie's pleasant humming was interrupted by a gentle question from Isaac.

"Wife, I know you've been having a hard time spending days on your own. Are you at all afraid about how it will be to be stuck inside over the winter? I'm worried you might fall into melancholy. Especially after how much you pleaded to be able to start the church choir."

"Oh." Annie looked at him appreciatively and slipped a hand into his coat pocket. "I've been thinking about it too. I guess I'm not sure."

"What are you going to do about it?"

"I don't know," she responded in a quiet voice. "You'll be home more, and that will help. But I don't know what options we have. Maybe I'll just have to keep looking forward to spring . . . or maybe, if the snow isn't too bad, I can visit my sisters."

"I'm sorry we chose a homestead so far away from everything."

"You couldn't have known. And there are still men who

haven't picked a claim yet. Maybe we'll have some closer neighbors next year."

He didn't respond. He didn't even look at her. He kept his eyes on the dark road ahead of them, careful to not let Rocky step wrong. Without the crowd and the campfire around her, Annie felt the cold of the December night sinking into her bones. She scooted a little closer to Isaac, but still he didn't say anything. They both fell into silence, and Annie worried that she hadn't been clear enough. The last thing she wanted was to hurt him.

"Isaac," she started hesitatingly. "I'm really very happy. I am."

He cleared his throat, but didn't interrupt.

"I don't want you to worry about that at all," she continued. "Even with the injury and living far from other folks, there's plenty for me to be grateful for. I don't know what I would have done without my sisters this last week or so. And you did that. You invited them and brought them to me. You figured out how I could attend the dance tonight. And . . . I just don't want you to think that I'm not grateful or that I'm unhappy."

"I know."

"Please don't be mad."

She couldn't read his expression in the dark, but when he didn't respond, Annie nudged his shoulder with her own.

"I don't know what I would do without you," she said softly. "I don't know what I would have done if you hadn't brought me out here and given me this life. I'm so excited to make it exactly what we want it to be. With you. Every day."

He cleared his throat again, and Annie wondered if she had prompted tears from her husband. But she didn't press it any further; their silence the rest of the way home was companionable, and Annie was at least assured he didn't seem angry.

Home alone again the following day, Annie did her best to stay off her feet while still tending to what the house needed. Isaac had gathered water before he left that morning, as well as brought in firewood, so she could stay in the small home, walking only a few feet at a time. Her ankle felt better every day, and with only herself and Isaac to take care of, she was able to rest it more often than not. Though she was lonely, with the days getting shorter Annie looked forward to her husband being home earlier.

Everything, she thought, was working out.

And when Isaac did finally return for the evening, she'd had the time and skills to have a tastier supper than she had managed before Josie had come to stay.

"A letter came for me today," Isaac said as soon as he was through the door, right at sunset. "Wife, you'll never guess."

"A letter? Did Daniel go to the fort?"

"No, it came special by messenger." He hung up his coat and hat with one hand, patting his shirt to find the letter with the other. Turning to Annie, Isaac's face was all lit up with excitement. "Our piano is ready. It's here."

"What? Here? Really? Now? Goodness! What does that mean?"

"It means I need to take our wagon and a few days to retrieve it." He shook his head. "The ship landed in Seattle a couple weeks ago, and the piano got as far as Fort Vancouver, but it's waiting for me."

"Fort Vancouver!"

"It's going to be a trying journey in this weather, but there's nothing for it. It could be worse, I suppose. I could have had to go all the way to Seattle. Fort Vancouver isn't so far in comparison."

"Isaac, no. Do you really think you should go? What if it snows more, and you get stuck out there, or something happens to me again while you're away?"

"Annie, I have to go. If I don't go now, before the worst of winter hits, our piano is going to sit . . . maybe in a shed, maybe not even that, over months of cold and rain. I can't risk it."

"But you can, Isaac. I understand it's a lot of money, but—"

"No, you don't. You *don't* understand."

He slammed a fist down on the table. Annie flinched, realizing that maybe she could have been more considerate. Her husband had come to her excited about what he was providing and all she'd offered in return was worry.

"You have no idea what I have been through to get where I am today. To have the kind of capital that I can even consider buying a piano, let alone having it shipped all the way here for you. We have neighbors who are still sleeping on the floor, without beds or furniture of their own, and you are getting a piano. You think I can just leave it to sit for months? I would have thought you would be more grateful."

Annie was stricken.

"I'm sorry," she said softly. "I don't mean to sound ungrateful. I didn't mean . . . Isaac, please. I've tried so hard to show you how much I support you, and I don't mean to question you, but . . ."

What had she gotten herself into, she thought. How had the conversation gone so wrong so quickly?

"You're right. It's just that . . . I'm worried about you going. And being gone. My ankle is still healing, and you're talking about leaving me alone here for how long?"

He hung his head, his shoulders slumping, defeated.

"I'm worried about you not coming back," she finished. "It's so dangerous to go by yourself at all, let alone to go when we could have snow any day and when you are trying to drive a heavily loaded wagon. It's such a risk, Isaac, and I just want—"

"I *know*," he exclaimed. "I know you just want me to stay home here with you all day because you can't bear to be alone! And I can't take care of you all the time. You need to be more self-sufficient, Annie. This is the territories, for goodness' sake, not your precious town back east."

Annie shrank back. His anger was palpable.

"I'm sorry," she whispered again.

He paused, seeing her shrink back into herself. As she watched, his breathing seemed to slow; his face lost some of its redness. Whatever had made him stop before yelling at her again was enough to leech away some of the anger. Finally, he turned away from her, walked to the far side of the room, and turned around again.

"I thought I could avoid telling you this, but it seems like I should be honest with you."

Annie's heart pounded. What was he about to reveal?

He sighed. "Truth be told, Gertie always told me I had a temper. I just thought it was because she could be so aggravating. Always so exacting and demanding. She was a perfectionist and expected me to be the same way. I was sure things would be different with you."

Annie's eyes widened. Through all their fights, all the misunderstandings and all the times she had taken responsibility and apologized for making him angry, he had known this truth about himself, yet he'd neglected to at the very least mention it to her?

"Why didn't you tell me? You could have at least— Any number of conversations we have had when you were not angry, and you didn't even warn me that this was something you were even a little bit worried about?"

"I am not beholden to you. I told you everything you need to know, and you were eager enough to accept my proposal."

Annie was so surprised at his insinuation that an involuntary laugh escaped her lips. "Excuse me?"

"But things are not different with you, are they? Maybe it is different in some ways—Gertie never spoiled perfectly good butter—but you still drive me to anger more and more."

"Isaac, please . . . if we could just talk calmly—"

"A man needs to have some outlet for his anger. I can't be expected to simply turn the other cheek over and over again. Not when every day there's some trying failure that I then have to fix."

There were at least a dozen things Annie could say in response to that, but she was far too afraid to make the argument worse. To make his anger worse. Especially as, with every day that passed, he seemed more and more entitled to blow up at her.

"This isn't a discussion," he said. "I'm going to get the piano —*your* piano—and if you are so ungrateful as to want me to stay home, you don't have to touch it when I do return. I'll sell it to the church or someone else, if it's so much trouble for you."

The sarcasm in his tone cut her deeply; her breath was shaking as she tried to stay calm. "I never meant—"

"But if you are determined to vex me, then I have no choice but to simply leave instead."

"Isaac!"

He shrugged, as though to say he didn't care at all what she might think. Annie watched in dismay, realizing that he was packing to leave for the fort that instant, despite the lateness of the hour and the heatedness of their argument.

"No, wait. Please, stay and talk to me about this. You don't need to leave now, do you? It's almost dark. It's too cold. I promise not to fight you anymore, but at least stay until the morning. Please."

Her voice cracked, and she was ashamed of her own desperation, but at the same time she did love this man, loved him so much, and she wanted him to stay safe.

"Isaac?"

"Yes, fine. You're right." He sat on the edge of the bed.

She hesitated before blurting out, "I'm sorry."

"I'm sorry, too. I wish things could be different."

CHAPTER THIRTY

The rest of the night was stilted and near-silent, both Annie and Isaac cautious around the other but neither reigniting the fight. It was awkward and difficult, but at least Isaac was there with her. At least he hadn't disappeared into the cold night again.

When Annie woke the next morning, she had been dragged out of a dream that left her breathless with worry. She rubbed her eyes as the sounds of the room around her indicated what had woken her up. Pulling herself to sitting, she saw that Isaac was already up for the day, fully dressed, alternating between taking sips of his coffee and stuffing things into his satchel. He seemed either uncaring or oblivious to how loud he was being and how it might affect the other person in the house.

"Isaac? Is everything all right?"

He glanced at her, but said nothing. Instead, he crossed to the larder and pulled out the last of their beef jerky and dried apples, stuffing that inside the satchel as well.

"Are you leaving right now? Already?"

"Yes, I am. I told you that." He looked up at her again, his expression both defiant and sad, before turning his focus again to checking the contents of his bag.

"Isaac? I thought we could talk about it more. Please don't go just yet. I'm so worried."

"There's nothing more to talk about. I told you what is happening, and that is that."

She wavered over whether to say anything else. If he truly was leaving to go to Fort Vancouver, he would be gone for days, and she didn't want another fight to be the last thing they said to each other. There was too much between them for her to risk making it worse. Better for her to simply acquiesce and keep her mouth shut, she supposed, since that seemed to be what he wanted from her.

When—if—he came back, there would be a chance to address their disagreements then.

"Can I help you, at least?"

Annie put her feet on the cold floor and leaned forward for the nearby chair. She would still need to rest her weight as much as she could—the ankle was still sore—but she could walk some.

"No." He drained the last of his coffee and put the dirty cup on the table for Annie to wash.

She paused, debating with herself as to whether saying anything more would be pushing him too far.

"Are you still angry? Please don't leave without talking to me."

That stopped him. With a sigh, he put down his satchel and gave Annie his full attention.

"I'm not angry," he said, "but I'm not going to discuss this anymore with you. Going to collect our—*your*—piano is something that needs to be done sooner rather than later, and you're not going to change my mind about this."

"All right," she said meekly. "Thank you for doing this, then. I suppose. I just wish—"

"I know, Annie." He sighed again. "I know what you wish, but we can't do that. I'm sorry. I wish it didn't make me so angry. I don't mean to snap at you."

She nodded, wanting to believe him.

"I really hope that you have a peaceful few days on your own," he said, clearly attempting to sound gentle. He crossed the room and, sitting on the edge of the bed next to her, put his arm around her waist. "And when I get back, with your piano, we'll start fresh, all right? I don't like being angry any more than you like making me angry."

He smiled at her, and though Annie tried to smile back, she was hurt by his implying that it was her fault he couldn't control his temper. She opened her mouth to retort but closed it again, knowing it would only make things worse.

"I'm worried you won't come back," she said instead, repeating the same argument she'd tried to make the previous evening.

That, evidently, was the wrong thing to say. Isaac withdrew his arm and stood.

"I know," he answered coldly. "I heard you. You've been very clear about that. More than once. Now I need you to hear me. I am going. Everything will be fine, but I need you to not hold this against me or pile your worries on to me."

"I don't mean to. I'm sorry. It seems like you've been angrier more often," she said. "I'm sorry if I am vexing."

"Yes, well, maybe this is another reason why it's good for me to go. We can each have time to think about how difficult things have been over the last few weeks and what we can do to change that."

Annie could not help but feel that, in Isaac's mind, she was the one who needed to change. She was the one, after all, who had ruined the butter and his shirt. She had not had nearly the anger toward him as he'd had toward her, so maybe he was right. It was not as though she had a choice. He was leaving her alone, and all she had were her thoughts and chores to occupy her while he was gone.

"Please be careful," she said. "That's all I'm asking."

He seemed to soften at this but did not return to her side. Instead, he picked up his satchel and canteen, and placed his hat on his head. "I will be. I promise. And I'm leaving you Pansy. I thought about taking both horses, to ease the load on the way back, but I don't want you to be completely stranded."

"Oh, thank you," she gasped out.

"And I'll be back here as soon as I can. You be careful here, too, and don't put too much stress on your ankle."

She nodded.

He offered her a small smile and left, closing the door gently behind him.

And then Annie was left alone for who knew how long.

The logs crackled in the fireplace; the scent of fresh coffee lingered in the air. The slight chill that had wafted in when Isaac opened the door reached Annie now, and she pulled the quilt tighter around her.

She forced herself to take a long, slow breath.

After all the stress and trouble of her hurting her ankle and being incapacitated, her husband had left her by herself the moment she was well enough to shuffle across the room.

After all the sorrow and melancholy of being lonely during the days, her husband had left her by herself for several days at a stretch, without even the reprieve of him coming home to sleep.

Annie looked around her house, at the firewood and water Isaac had collected before he left, at the food stores that should be plenty for her by herself. At her knitting, still unfinished, as she had been unable to focus. At the bed where she would sleep alone for a few nights or more.

How was she to put in these days completely alone, especially distracted and worrying about Isaac?

Maybe she should pack up and leave, go stay with her sisters.

Rather than be alone for days, out here on the edge of town, she could be with people who loved her, safe and warm and taken care of. It was far too easy to imagine herself tucked into bed by Margaret, fed by Josie, Lawrence chopping firewood so she could stay off her ankle. Such an idea was incredibly tempting.

Annie got to her feet, testing her weight on her ankle.

The rest of the bumps, bruises, and stiffness she'd felt in the immediate aftermath of her fall had healed by now, but the ankle remained fragile. While leaning hard on the back of the chair, Annie slowly let more and more of her weight be held by the injured leg.

A sharp pain radiated up through her leg.

With a sigh, Annie leaned again on the chair, taking the weight off her injury. Gritting her teeth, she slowly limped across the room to where the rest of the coffee waited for her—near but not in the fire, enough to stay hot, but not enough to burn. Isaac had taken care of her as best he could before he left; she knew, despite all her objections, he really did believe that going all the way to Fort Vancouver in this weather was his only option.

It had even seemed, at times, like he had tried to hold his temper that morning before he left.

Isaac was doing his best; Annie had to as well.

And, she had to admit, that meant not running off to be rescued by her sisters. What would Louisa think if she were here, after all she had done to get Annie to this point? After all they had given up in Virginia so Annie could marry this man in Oregon?

No, she would stay where she was, caring for her home, just as Isaac always wished of her. It was the very least she could do. He would be home soon, she told herself, and they would be happy and cozy with their new piano, and she could figure out how to fix things after that.

For now, all Annie could do was settle in for a few days by herself. Rest her ankle. Keep things clean. And practice being all right while alone, seeing as that might be how the rest of her life could be.

She wasn't looking forward to it, but as long as Isaac came home safely, Annie told herself, she could manage the next handful of days.

CHAPTER THIRTY-ONE

With cold fingers, Annie dragged her chair closer to the fire. She was almost done knitting this scarf, and only wished she had been able to finish it before Isaac left. It was so cold outside—far colder than she had been prepared for, and she worried it was colder than he had prepared for as well. Although Isaac had lived in the Oregon Territory for over a year and presumably was ready for the absolute bone-chilling winter, Annie still regretted that she couldn't have done more, that she couldn't have been a better wife, taking care of her hard-working husband.

But, nonetheless, he had left early that morning, guiding Rocky to pull their empty wagon as he traveled north to Fort Vancouver to meet the merchant who had procured their piano from the east coast. Although Daniel Mills and Benjamin Findley often made the trip to the fort and back in one long day, this trip would be different; with the uncertain weather and the weight of the instrument, Isaac told her not to expect him for nearly a week.

A week was far longer than Annie thought she could manage alone, but she would endure as many days as she must—as long as he did come back. That was her biggest fear: that between the hazards of the journey and his unhappiness with her, the risk of Isaac not returning at all was too high.

The people of Eden Valley were expecting more snow all the time. The light dusting they had gotten a few days earlier was not enough to halt travel, though the Hudsons had rightly hurried to get themselves all moved in before the weather got worse. There had been no snow when Isaac had left a few hours earlier, but Annie had no illusions that it would stay that way.

Annie bundled her coat up around her, pulling the collar tighter around her neck in hopes to keep in more of the warmth. While she knitted, thinking over plans for the spring, she had thoughtlessly let the fire die down. She hadn't even noticed how cold the room was getting until her fingertips suddenly felt numb. When her joints began to sting from the cold, Annie pulled on her coat and gloves—even while inside—and tossed the last two logs on the fire. She held her breath as she poked at the embers to get a spark.

Annie settled in to warm up again before she ventured outside for more firewood. It was still early afternoon, still the warmest part of the day, and she would have plenty of light as long as she went out soon. But it was cozy by her fire, cozy as she let the knit scarf grow longer and drape over her lap. While her fingers slowly wove the yarn, her mind went to worrying over all the things that could go wrong on Isaac's trip north for the piano. Weather, and injury, and Indians, and the wagon getting stuck, and so much more. All the hazards she had endured on the Oregon Trail, amplified by the brutality of winter weather.

She looked again at the log walls on either side of her fireplace. The gaps between the logs had been filled in tightly with clay, and the corners of the home were fit together as snugly as could be managed. She was as warm as the place could be made, but it wouldn't stay that way for long. Just as she knew what could go wrong with Isaac's journey, she also could imagine a dozen different things that could go wrong with her staying here by herself—including running out of wood for the fire. With a sigh, Annie returned the skein of yarn, her needles, and the scarf still in progress to the basket set aside for that purpose.

While she was still warm all the way through, Annie would need to go outside to chop more firewood. Isaac had brought in all that was already split, but it wasn't enough to last the several days she needed to be prepared to wait.

Her gloves had been tucked into the pocket of her coat, and she pulled them on now, just before opening her front door. Isaac's axe leaned against the wall just inside the door, and she picked it up carefully as she passed.

Stepping out into the winter afternoon, Annie smiled. This wasn't so bad. The tip of her nose got cold immediately, but she could spend an hour or so chopping wood, warm herself up again with the exertion, and bring what she needed indoors for overnight, all long before it got too cold.

She breathed out a long, slow breath, watching the fog of air curl out of her mouth like smoke. She nodded resolutely: When Isaac returned home, he would be so proud of her. Impressed that she had figured out how to do this thing on her own, without his help, without making a mistake. Though her confidence was like a garment she had pulled on and might be ripped away at any moment, Annie got to work.

She limped down the step and across the small yard to where several trees had been felled. The axe was a bit heavy for her, and it had been years since Annie had split wood, but, she told herself for the hundredth time, if she did not do it now she would likely freeze.

In the first weeks of her arrival in Eden Valley, even as the men were building her house, Isaac and the others had felled several dozen trees that had previously covered the Wheelers' homestead. Many of the bigger trees had been cut down and fit together to make the house itself, but several of the thinner trees had been set aside for other uses. Isaac had cut one down every day or so since, chopping it into more manageable sizes, pieces that would easily fit in their fireplace.

Even now, one of the trees had been cut down into half a dozen smaller logs, but each of those needed to be split before it could be used. After that, it would need to dry at least some before Annie could burn it in the fireplace.

With her gloved hands and her careful limp, Annie awkwardly grasped one of the logs and moved it into position, up on one end, to be split. She gripped the axe with both hands, testing the weight of it, pushing her fear and uncertainty from her brain.

Just like visions of Isaac stuck in the snow somewhere had taken over her mind, now Annie could not help but imagine her axe slipping, her being injured and cold out here alone.

Her hands shook as she lifted the axe, though whether that was from fear or from the cold or even the weight of the blade, she didn't know.

"You can split wood," she told herself, her voice sounding loud against the quiet of the nearby woods. "You have to do this."

Her survival could no longer be dependent on those around her. Though she often found herself supporting her loved ones, helping with someone else's plans, there was no one around now. She was all she had at the moment. But her sister Louisa had always been the perfect example of a capable woman; Annie pictured herself as strong as Louisa and tried again.

Annie took a couple deep, calming breaths, reminding herself that this was silly. She had split wood before, even if it had been years earlier. This was something other people do every day. There was no reason for her to hesitate; furthermore, if she waited too long it would only get colder.

Adjusting her grip on the axe's handle, Annie steeled herself, lifted the tool, and swung down as hard and as fast as she could.

Her aim was off. Annie succeeded only in getting the blade stuck on the rightmost edge of the log. And because of her ankle injury, she had to pry the axe out of the wood with just the strength of her arms and while standing off balance.

For the first time, Annie was grateful no one lived nearer to her: no one could see her failing out here in the cold afternoon. She laughed out loud at that, at the absurdity of it all, then groaned, stepped back, and tried again.

Over and over, Annie swung the axe that was just a little too heavy for her, standing on an ankle that was not quite healed all the way, trying to make progress in the cold that was only sinking deeper into her with every moment outside away from the hungry fire. It was undeniably difficult, but she was managing. Not merely managing: by the fourth attempt, Annie realized she was proving to herself what she was truly capable of. All the things she had let Louisa or Isaac or even Lawrence do for her, coddling her a bit, guiding her as they needed, she now needed to do for herself. And she could.

Her husband and her family would always be there to support and protect her, but that didn't mean she had to remain fearful and helpless.

And if splitting logs was where she had to start, it was just as good a place as any.

After several more attempts—so many she lost count—Annie finally successfully split the log in two even pieces. She gasped out her delight when she saw her accomplishment, gave herself a moment to celebrate, and then set up another log on end to do it again. Soon, Annie settled into a rhythm, and she continued to split logs as long as she was warm enough to manage it.

The stack next to her grew slowly, but she felt so much satisfaction in knowing that she had done this thing. She had conquered yet another of the many skills she would need to develop in her new life on the Oregon frontier.

It wasn't until she stopped to move the newly cut firewood to the stack in the house that Annie noticed the small droplets on her gloves. Thinking nothing of it, she looked closer, rubbing one of them to see what it might be.

When she felt a similar cold drop onto the back of her neck, Annie looked up, into the sky, into the pine trees that surrounded her home.

It was beautiful.

Though it was just starting, the soft white of snowfall was clear, stark against the dark green of the pine tops. The gray skies above promised more, and Annie held out a hand to try to catch a couple snowflakes before she had to go back inside. Small, delicate flakes landed in her palm, the ice crystals visible against the dark of her glove if she looked carefully.

But even in the short moments in which she watched, the snow fell harder, thicker, faster. Annie got snowflakes in her eyelashes as she looked up at the sky, and she realized she didn't have long before everything would be coated.

Hurrying as fast as she could with the limp, Annie made several trips from the wood pile to her front door and back again. First with the axe, leaning it against the wall inside the door, and then with arms full of wood for the fireplace. She all but threw them to the floor inside her cabin in her haste to get all the logs indoors to dry before they were covered with snow.

Finally, all the logs she had split were under the roof, but even in that short period of time the snow had begun to stick to the ground, the roof, the treetops. The temperature felt as though it had dropped precipitously, and the dark gray clouds had quickly blotted out the sun. Annie hastened to get indoors, in the warmth, settling in for the rest of the afternoon.

CHAPTER THIRTY-TWO

Before Annie closed the door behind her, she checked her stack of firewood. It seemed to her she had enough for at least a day and a half, maybe more if she was careful. Glancing back out into the growing dark, however, Annie realized she didn't have much choice at the moment. The snow was falling too fast, the light fading too quickly. Even if she was a master at chopping firewood rapidly, it wouldn't be safe in these conditions. She was lucky she went out when she did.

She closed the front door tightly, fastening the latch Isaac had installed for an occasion just like this. The wood she had split was scattered all over the floor just inside the door. In her haste to get it all inside, Annie had not stopped to stack it neatly and so did that now, limping slowly, taking her time, and organizing her firewood in a pile near to the fireplace. As she worked, just on the other side of the door snow continued to fall.

Outside, the wind picked up; Annie heard the rustling of the trees as the storm grew. Not for the first time she wished for a window, even just for a small glimpse at what was happening on the other side of her wall, though merely from the sounds of the snowfall she could easily guess that this was far more than had fallen a few days earlier. Maybe even enough to keep her stranded here, snowed in.

And Isaac . . .

She said a quick prayer for his safety. Hopefully he had reached the fort by now and could sleep with a roof over his head.

The crack of a branch outside startled her, and Annie resolutely turned her attention back to settling into her warm home for the night.

Though she was still a bit exhilarated from the accomplishment of chopping down all this wood herself for the first time, Annie wondered if she had truly made the right choice. Maybe she should have gone to her sisters when she had very first thought about it that morning. Maybe being alone with all this snow was foolish rather than brave.

But it was too late now.

Here she was, snowed in for who knew how long, not only dealing with the loneliness and danger of being by herself in such a storm, but also living with the stress and fear of her husband's safety in the same storm.

She would just have to settle in for the night and hope for the best. It was still early enough in the winter that maybe the snowfall wouldn't be too bad just yet. Melted by morning, perhaps. For not the first time, Annie wished another neighbor lived nearby—anyone close enough to whom she could walk through the storm, someone she could ask for help or even just companionship.

She spent the rest of the afternoon and evening trying desperately to find something that could occupy her thoughts. Without any company to distract her, it was far too easy for her to be consumed by thoughts of things she could not control. And so, she arranged the logs near the fireplace to dry. She washed the dishes. She knit. She read her Bible. She even opened her front door quickly to peek out, but it was too dark for her to see much beyond the snow piling up around her step.

Finally, Annie ate a cold supper and crawled into bed. She didn't bother looking at what time it was, already exhausted from the day. Maybe in sleep she could escape thoughts of her fear and loneliness.

When Annie woke the next morning, she was shivering. The room was almost completely dark, lit only by the embers in the fireplace on the other side of the room. She had overslept, and the fire had died down far enough that the chill was beginning to seep through the walls.

She climbed out of bed, but grabbed the topmost quilt from it and wrapped it around her to keep warm. The corners of the quilt dragged across the floor as Annie made her limping way to the fireplace and carefully placed several more logs on the fire. She blew gently, coaxing the embers into lighting the new fuel, while she remained huddled with the quilt wrapped around her.

That done, she limped to the front door, opening it just a crack to assess the storm. The bright light told her it was well after sunrise and that the storm had indeed passed as she'd hoped. Before passing, however, what looked like five or six inches of snow had fallen, blown up in drifts against the house and the tree trunks nearby.

Grateful it wasn't still snowing, Annie closed the door again. Hopefully, she thought, the fire would start to warm her home soon.

Was Isaac warm enough?

It was unsurprising that her mind went immediately to her husband and his safety. This snowfall was precisely what she had been afraid of when he had insisted on leaving to travel all the way to Fort Vancouver. It was possible he had reached the fort before the snow got too bad the night before, but that was the best she could hope for, though truthfully it seemed unlikely. And even if he was safe and dry at the fort, the snow meant that he wouldn't be leaving to come home anytime soon.

But there was nothing she could do about any of that.

And she had plenty to worry about on her own.

One of the few nice things about all this snow, Annie realized, was that she didn't have to go all the way to the creek to collect their water. She could just step outside, fill a bucket with snow, and bring it indoors near the fire until it melted into liquid.

Small flurries of snow struck throughout the day, keeping Annie inside near the fire. She told herself that if the storm didn't clear up by the following day, she would need to chop more firewood regardless of the weather. She kept her coat on in the house much of the day, trying to use as little of the fuel as possible, but this late in December meant constant cold.

Annie knew, too, that her horse must be cold. The stable Isaac had built was only two walls and a roof so far. He kept promising to put up more walls before it got too cold, but that hadn't happened before he left for the fort. And now, with the snow blowing every which way, with the temperature dropping below freezing at night, the horse was somewhat sheltered but not so much that Annie could ignore her. Even if the bucket of water she had left for Pansy had not frozen over—which it certainly had —the horse needed something slightly warmer to drink. Animals were resilient but not invincible.

Annie gathered a pot full of snow from the drift outside her front door and put it over the fire. It didn't take long for the snow to melt to liquid and then heat up to just before boiling. As steam wafted up out of the pot, Annie pulled it off the fire and poured the warmed water back into a bucket. Next, Annie pulled on all her warmest clothes, collected an extra quilt that Lawrence had slept with, carefully lifted the bucket of warm water, and ventured out into the snow.

The moment she stepped outside, the warm bucket of water emitted a cloud of steam, unceasing. The storm had stopped sometime in the night, leaving several inches of snow behind. The storm had passed and the sky was clear; by early afternoon the sun had already started to melt icy patches here and there.

Annie's ankle was no better than it had been the day before, so with her limp, the risk of ice, and the burden of carrying a bucket of hot water, she had to traverse the distance slowly.

The temporary stable was—fortunately—only about forty feet away from the front door of their home. Building a new, larger, and more permanent structure for their animals would be one of Isaac's first projects in the spring, but for this first winter they were making do.

Annie carefully put one foot in front of the other. After what had happened when she accompanied Isaac hunting, she couldn't risk falling and hurting an ankle again, especially now, on her own and out in the elements. So step by slow step, she crossed the yard, around the side of her house to where Pansy stood under the meager shelter. With each step, she sank several inches into the untouched snow, but Annie kept going.

"Hey, girl," she soothed. "I'm so sorry. I brought you this."

Pansy nuzzled Annie's ear; it almost seemed as though the horse was trying to warm herself with Annie's own body heat. Although she knew logically that the horse was likely fine, was nowhere near as cold as Annie herself was, guilt still gripped her.

"I know. It's no fun to be out here all by yourself, huh?"

Annie threw the quilt over Pansy's back, rubbing the horse's shoulders roughly to help her get warm and dry.

"Is that all right? Okay, then. Now, where did I put your water bucket?"

They didn't yet have any kind of trough for the animals, but the day before Annie had left a bucket of water on the ground just inside the opening for Pansy. She looked around, trying to remember where she had left it, and finally spotted a glimpse of wood through a small snowdrift. Brushing the snow away from the pile, Annie uncovered the half-full, frozen-over bucket of water. She tried first to break the top of the ice in the water bucket with her gloved hand, but it was too thick. The cold easily penetrated her gloves, and she felt the numbing of her fingers.

Even in the middle of the day with the sun directly overhead, the cold crept under her collar, found the narrow strip of her wrist. She couldn't feel her cheeks, and she knew the tip of her nose must be bright red already.

She shuffled over to where she had left the bucket of hot water, noticing immediately that the steam had slowed considerably. Hurrying to Pansy's supply, Annie slowly poured the warm water over the ice, melting the latter and filling the bucket with now-drinkable water.

"I hope that works. I'll try to check on you again in a few hours, if it doesn't snow more." She pet Pansy's neck, talking to her calmly and cheerfully. "Glad you're here, girl. Glad I'm not completely alone."

She leaned her face against the horse's neck and breathed in her earthy, familiar scent. Tears sprang to her eyes; Annie felt overwhelmed and sad, all alone in the snow. But at least she had Pansy—at least she had some means of travel, some company.

Only a few more days of this, she reminded herself.

She gave Pansy a goodbye kiss before heading back into the warm interior of her home.

CHAPTER THIRTY-THREE

That evening, Annie again spent hours trying to distract herself from her thoughts. Her hands stayed busy, but her mind wandered. She felt as though she had avoided obsessing over thoughts of disaster for short stretches of the day, and she clung to those small successes desperately. She wanted to get through this; she wanted to do her best. She didn't want to run from her own life, escaping into a situation that could not be sustained. With these thoughts in mind, Annie again crawled into bed early, eager for the release of sleep.

And, again, another day dawned in which Annie was cold and alone.

She went through the motions of making herself coffee, adding more logs to the fire, and getting dressed for her day, but at the same time she wondered what the point of it all was. If only she could just sleep the several more days until Isaac was home. Even if they fought again, at least she would have a reason to get out of bed.

As she sat at her table, hands wrapped around her coffee cup, Annie wondered how she would spend the day. She would need to chop more firewood, whenever she thought the day was at its warmest outside, and she should check on Pansy again. But otherwise, Annie remained utterly consumed by her fearful thoughts of what Isaac might be going through and when he might return. And what their conversation might look like when he did.

"Annie Wheeler!"

Annie almost spit out her mouthful of coffee in surprise. Hearing her name from the mouth of another human just outside her front door was jarringly unexpected, but still incredibly welcome. Though it hadn't snowed in the last day, she had not realized that the roads were passable yet. She limped to the door as quickly as she could and threw it open to the cold morning, eager to greet her unexpected visitor.

No, she realized. Visitors. More than one.

A broad grin spread across her face when she saw who was outside her home. Rebecca Tenney and her brother, Jasper Stephens, both rode astride one horse that carefully picked its way through the still deep snow that lay as far as Annie could see.

"What are you doing here?" Annie exclaimed. "I don't understand!"

"I was going to come earlier, but the pesky snow started falling and then I was stuck," Rebecca called to her from atop the horse. "But as soon as I could I cajoled Jasper into bringing me out here. No one would let me come by myself, which is just as well, because the trail all the way out here is just about disappeared."

Annie continued to gape open-mouthed as Jasper dismounted and helped his sister down.

"How's your ankle doing? I imagine Isaac's grateful for all this snow so he doesn't have to be the one to keep going to collect all your water."

"Oh, um, actually . . . Isaac isn't here."

"What do you mean?" Rebecca asked with a frown.

Annie's mind whirled. With everything she had been through over the previous couple days—the fighting with Isaac, his news from the fort, his leaving her alone—she had forgotten that none of her friends or family knew what had happened. She didn't even know where to start.

"Come inside where it's warm and dry, at least. I'll tell you all about it."

Annie led them into her small cabin, immediately limping to the fireplace to put another log on and then setting up her kettle in the fire.

"Is tea all right? The coffee isn't hot any longer."

"Annie, where is Isaac?"

"I don't know precisely this moment, but . . ." She sighed. "I know how this is going to sound, and I need to tell you right off the bat that I tried to keep him from leaving."

"What?" Rebecca turned to her brother. "Jasper, you don't want to be in here for all the gossip."

"Oh, I don't know about that." He leaned against the wall lazily, crossing his arms across his chest and looking for all the world as though he planned to stay awhile. "You women seem to have far more interesting conversations than the men do. Learned that at a young age, having you as an older sister. So, Annie, where'd Isaac run off to?"

"Out," Rebecca said. "Firewood or water. See to the horses."

"I'll freeze!"

"Not if you keep moving." She glanced at the few sticks of firewood by the wall. "Really, though, she could use more firewood, please. Be a good neighbor?"

"Fine," he said, moving to the door. "But you fill me in on all the gossip on our way home."

Annie laughed. "I don't know what news you think I have, since I've been snowed in alone for days."

Jasper shrugged and grinned at her. "You never know."

"Thank you!" she called after him, as he put on his hat and headed outdoors.

Rebecca watched her brother leave and then turned to Annie with an exaggeratedly shocked expression. "All alone for *days*, Mrs. Wheeler? Where is your husband?"

She took a deep breath. "Well, um, good news, actually, I suppose. He got a letter to tell him that the piano he had ordered for me last year was waiting for him at Fort Vancouver, so he took the wagon and left for there."

Rebecca looked skeptical. "All the way there in the snow?"

"He left the morning before the storm." She shook her head despairingly. "But I was so afraid of something like that happening, of his getting stuck, or sick, or I don't know what, and we fought about it before he left. And I have no way of knowing if he even made it to the fort, let alone if he's on his way back yet. I'm so afraid, and so . . . helpless."

"Oh, honey." Rebecca leaned forward and took Annie's hands in hers. "I can't even imagine. I'm so sorry."

"I don't know what to do. The fight we had was . . . it wasn't even the worst fight we've had, but I'm worried he won't come back."

"I'm sure it's fine," Rebecca said. "Married folks fight all the time. He went off to fetch your piano, don't forget. It's quite the gesture from someone who you worry cares nothing for you."

"No, you misunderstand. It's not that I think he cares nothing." Annie searched for the right words, the right description for this delicate balance of passion and withdrawal. "He loves me. I think. He *must* love me. But he gets so angry . . . and one time he threw a cup into the fireplace and—"

Annie stopped herself when she saw the expression of horror and shock on her friend's face.

"Annie," Rebecca said in a hushed tone. "Are you all right? All joking aside, please tell me everything."

Annie hesitated; she was already so embarrassed that her

sisters had witnessed Isaac's explosion, and opening that wound to show another friend would be difficult.

"Do you want me to stay with you?"

The word *yes* almost escaped her lips. For a brief moment, Annie felt as though that would solve all her problems. Not only would Rebecca's company and that of her brother keep her from getting too lonely and share the load of chopping firewood, cooking, and cleaning for the household; in addition to all of that, having a friend around would distract her from the fear that consumed her.

But she had already promised herself she would do her best; she had agreed with Isaac that this time alone should be used to think over things. How could leaning on her friend like a crutch accomplish that?

"No, I think I need to do this," she said, surprising herself at the words coming out of her mouth. "I can't explain it, but something inside me tells me that if I do not learn how to manage, how to do these few days by myself, I will never be able to. And then . . . then, in that case, I don't know what might happen with Isaac." She rested her head in her hands. "I don't know if I'm making any sense at all."

"Some." Rebecca smiled understandingly. "Maybe this is a kind of courage."

"That's it, exactly! And, goodness, it's embarrassing, isn't it? To admit that I need to dig deep to find the courage just to be by myself?"

"Not at all. Someone else would need to find the courage to willingly go to a party with a dozen strangers, or perhaps travel west on the Oregon Trail, for example. We all have our struggles. The key is to just worry about the things that we can control and acknowledge what we can't. If you had seen me in the weeks following my Andrew's death, you would not think your own struggles all that different."

Annie nodded. "And my struggle just happens to be learning how to be my own person, I suppose."

"That, and responding to your husband's anger," Rebecca said softly. "What are you going to do about that?"

Annie shook her head. "I don't know what I can do. It's not as though I am deliberately trying to frustrate him. I will make mistakes again, and I can't even guess at his reaction."

"Well . . . again, focus on what you can control. Maybe the pastor has advice? I don't know. You might not be able to stop Isaac from losing his temper, but you can keep from yelling at him in return, or from staying in the house if he gets violent. You can come to me, or your sisters. You are already focusing on doing the things to take care of yourself, and this is part of that."

"I know." Annie sighed. "You're right. It's just . . . it's scary."

"I believe in you." Rebecca leaned back in her chair, giving Annie an appraising glance. "Do you want me to come back and check on you tomorrow?"

"No, no. Thank you, but I'll be all right. I've already got this far, haven't I?"

"True, but I just don't want to think about you wallowing. Remember how hard it was for you to be out here by yourself all day even before Isaac left."

"It's different now. Or, I want it to be. I don't know how to describe or explain it. It's like I pushed through the hardest part so everything else is easy. Easier, at least. I can see the ending somehow."

"Aren't you afraid your worry is going to keep you from doing anything else? If Isaac doesn't return for a few more days . . ."

"No, you're right. If I can just focus on the things I can control, I can get through it. Isaac will be home soon. Or . . . he won't, I suppose. But either way, the only thing that I can do anything about is myself. And I can do that."

"Promise me."

Annie nodded. "I promise. Really."

Rebecca looked at her skeptically.

Laughing, Annie grasped Rebecca's hand. "I *promise*."

Jasper knocked briefly before letting himself in. "Sorry, but clouds are coming in and I think we should get back in case there's another snowfall." He brought an armful of logs to the stack near the fireplace and set them down neatly. "We'll have to come back for more gossip."

Rebecca groaned reluctantly and stood. "This was far too short of a visit. And I'm still worried about you."

"I know." Annie stood too. "But please believe that I at least know what I need to be doing. Actually being able to do it is a different thing, but I suppose it's a start."

CHAPTER THIRTY-FOUR

Annie woke the next morning, alone again, to a cold and dark house. The fire had again died down in the night, and Isaac had again not arrived home. Though her stomach growled at her, Annie could not bring herself to get out of bed just yet; it was too cold, too sad, too scary and stressful to start her day. Instead, she pulled the blankets up over her head, closed her eyes, and tried to forget that the world existed.

Her conversation with Rebecca the day before had lifted her spirits, but even just spending the afternoon alone again had dashed them. It took all her willpower—and even a little berating herself—to push back the blankets and get out of bed. She limped across her home, adding a log to the fire and putting the coffee on, before going to her front door.

When she pulled it open, she could see that no new snow had fallen overnight. The snow that covered the ground was beginning to melt, and there was not yet another cloud in the sky. Maybe the worst of it was over and Isaac could be on his way home.

But even that one small crumb of hope threatened to over-take her thinking for hours.

With a deep, sad sigh, Annie closed the door again and let her eyes adjust to the dim light within.

What did she have to do that day but wait?

Annie sank down into one of her chairs and leaned forward, closing her eyes and resting her forehead on the tabletop. If only she could crawl back into bed, pull the blankets up over her head, and shut out the world until Isaac returned. All she could see ahead of her was another day of distraction, of worry, of feeling bad about the life in which she found herself. She struggled to remember why she had decided to come west to Oregon in the first place.

What would Louisa say to that?

She sat up abruptly, remembering the last time she had seen her sister—her sister who had sacrificed so much to get her here. Louisa had come down with Mountain Fever while they were traveling west on the Oregon Trail, and for days she tossed and turned in bed, weak and hallucinating, as her body struggled to fight off the illness. She ultimately lost that battle, and her grave remained in the mountains east of Oregon, too far for any of the Hudsons to ever visit.

Annie knew without a doubt that spending days in bed was anathema to Louisa's entire personality. If she knew that Annie had an entire home to herself, had a whole new life to build, and was instead wishing she could crawl back under the covers, she would be aghast. Louisa would be out there shoveling snow or building the stable or something to make progress.

Enough was enough, Annie told herself.

Louisa didn't sacrifice everything she had for Annie to fall apart like this. Rebecca was right: she couldn't just wait around for something to happen to her. Though Annie knew that no part of her marriage could be fixed in an instant, she had to at least try *something.* She couldn't just wait here for Isaac to come home and yell at her again.

If he was coming home at all.

Enough time had passed that he could have made it back to Eden Valley by now. If nothing had gone wrong.

What could have gone wrong?

She shook her head; she couldn't think about that now. There was nothing she could do to help Isaac from where she was, and she had promised herself and Rebecca that she would focus on the things she could control. Which started with pulling on her boots, her scarf, her heavy coat, and her gloves, and heading out into the wintery morning.

Her coffee finished brewing as she got dressed and pinned up her hair. She was too distracted to eat, too anxious to wait. Now that she had a plan and had taken the first step, Annie just had to keep going.

She was going to get out of the house. And she was going to seek out advice about her other problems. That was all she could manage, all she could control at the moment, but she could do that. Little by little. If she just looked forward to the next step, she could do this.

Her ankle was still sore. Though she had been walking on it the last few days, in order to mount Pansy, Annie would need to put all of her weight on that injured ankle, even for a brief moment. She hadn't ridden since her accident weeks earlier, but somehow risking injury again was less scary than standing up to her husband when he was angry. Saying a small prayer that the horse would not get spooked and that the pain would not be too excruciating, Annie maneuvered the horse near to the front step of her cabin. She needed that small assist to get up into the saddle. Though it was awkward and ungainly, Annie managed to get herself up into the saddle, stick a foot into each stirrup, and gently guide the horse down the path into town.

Though the snowstorm had dropped several inches a few days

earlier, fortunately no additional snow had fallen since Rebecca and Jasper had visited the day before. The trail from her own homestead into town was narrow and rugged, and snow now covered it, but Annie was able to find her way into Eden Valley by following Rebecca and Jasper's tracks from the day before. She pulled up her scarf to cover her nose and nudged Pansy forward.

The few miles into town were quiet and serene, the blanket of snow covering the landscape as far as she could see. The sight of smoke curling up from chimneys warmed her heart. Knowing that there were people nearby—even if she couldn't see them—was almost all she needed after so long being alone.

After a couple miles, she rode past the site where the wagon company had all been camping for the previous couple months. It looked abandoned. Though all the families now lived in more sturdy, wooden shelters, some of the covered wagons had been left behind. The snow drifts had piled up around them, white against the dirty canvas, and without any humans around, the deserted site seemed sad.

Annie kept riding past it, farther into the center of Eden Valley.

Directing Pansy over the small bridge, Annie had her eyes on the low church building and the parsonage just behind it. When she arrived, the church itself was closed up and cold, as expected, but a fine plume of smoke emitted from the chimney above the parsonage. The pastor or his wife were home, or both, and Annie hoped they would have some advice for her.

At this point, she was willing to take anything.

After dismounting and ground-tying Pansy near the house, Annie took a deep breath, approached, and knocked on the door to the parsonage. It opened a short moment later.

A flicker of confusion crossed the pastor's face when he saw who stood at his front door, but he immediately stepped back to invite her in. "Mrs. Wheeler, what are you doing here? Is everything all right? Come in out of the cold."

His wife hurried forward to take her coat, and together the Montgomerys led Annie deeper into their small home. The pastor pulled out a chair from their table and bade her to sit, while Mrs. Montgomery bustled over to her fire to put the kettle on. In those few short minutes, Annie explained what had happened—the letter, the fight, the days alone worrying—and that she needed advice.

"I guess I can't help thinking this is all my fault."

"How so?" the pastor asked, frowning.

Mrs. Montgomery placed hot cups of tea in front of Annie and the pastor, before busying herself again on the far side of the house.

Annie picked up her drink and wrapped her fingers around the hot mug. The steam and scent of chamomile wafted up into her face, comforting her in a way that coffee never did.

"I made him angry. I pushed him away, didn't I? Rebecca Tenney came to visit yesterday, and she told me that his anger is his own choice, but I still feel as though if I had been better prepared, a better homemaker, more secure in being left alone, he wouldn't have such cause to be angry."

Pastor Montgomery sipped his own tea as he listened. He set his mug down gently and leaned forward across the table. "Mrs. Wheeler, do you believe you did your best?"

"The butter and the shirt. The other mistakes you say set off your husband's temper. Were you willfully negligent or lazy? Was it your sloth or pride that drove those things to happen?"

"Well, that seems like all we can ask for, doesn't it? To do your best with what you have at that moment. And I believe your friend, Mrs. Tenney, is right."

The pastor nodded. "This anger, this temper you speak of. It sounds as though this might be something he has been struggling with a while. I apologize, I don't know the man well, but from what you tell me, this was a problem before he met you. And while, yes, of course you would prefer to not make mistakes that create waste or hardship, none of that is a reason for your husband to yell at you, let alone slam or throw things. You understand that, don't you?"

"I think so. I'm beginning to. My sisters said much the same thing when they witnessed his temper."

Pastor Montgomery sipped his tea again, watching her with a compassionate expression. Just as Annie knew she should only worry about the things she could actually control, she also knew many of them were things no one else could help her with. If nothing else, this confirmation from her pastor had shown her that she had no choices left.

"Can I pray with you?" he said finally.

Annie nodded. "Do you think it will help?"

Pastor Montgomery looked thoughtful for a moment, as though considering his words. "I think that God knows what is best for us, all the time. And I think that if someone is willing to open themselves to God's perfect plan then everything can fall into place. In this case, I think the fact that you came here, you asked for help and insight, indicates a way of thinking that allows for healing and progress. Not everyone in a position like yours would be so brave, or so willing to be vulnerable. That alone will help matters with Mr. Wheeler, even if he might not be quite as willing to work on the problem as you are."

"I understand."

Annie felt a wave of emotion—heartbreak, hope, vulnerability—as she bowed her head to pray with the pastor. If he was right, if taking this step was a sign that things could change, Annie would hold tightly to that hope with both hands.

CHAPTER THIRTY-FIVE

Annie returned home tired but determined. She had finally accepted what she could change and what she could not, encouraged by the pastor's belief in what she could do. All that was left now was to learn again how to live with her husband, equipped with this new knowledge. When he finally returned home, she at least had a plan.

As more time passed and Isaac still did not appear, however, Annie's dread grew, and it became harder for her to remember the resolution with which she had come home. Surely he should be back by now, shouldn't he? The longer he was gone, the easier it was for Annie to convince herself that he was not coming back at all, whether because an accident had befallen him or because he was angry with her. It had been five days already—more than enough time for him to reach the fort and come home, provided nothing had stopped him.

Soon, it was two days before Christmas and Annie was still alone in her small home. Though her ankle had mostly healed by this time, the fear of being by herself at the edge of town, in the blank starkness of winter, made her unusually aware of all the other things that could go wrong for her without her husband home. She could fall and hurt herself again while gathering water; she could slip and injure herself while chopping wood.

But if Isaac never returned, she would still be at the same risk. So Annie approached every moment with that possibility in mind. If her husband was not going to be present, she could at least live her life in a way that would make her sister proud.

Annie sat at her small table knitting when she heard the sound of a wagon approaching just outside her door. When she had been outside earlier that day, the sky was clear and the bright sun promised to melt at least some of the snow that had stuck from the storm. The wagon sounded halting, heavy, as though the driver were being overly cautious with every bump and rut in the road.

Annie stood. She didn't want to get her hopes up. Maybe it was Rebecca again. Or maybe her sisters had somehow acquired a wagon.

She held her breath.

The door swung open and Isaac stepped inside, stamping his feet at the edge of the door to knock off whatever snow had stuck to his boot. He removed his hat, holding it in front of his chest.

Her body seemed to thrum with anticipation. Annie watched but said nothing, suddenly remembering his anger and his expression in the hours before he had left her alone so many days earlier.

Isaac avoided her eyes as he closed the door, leaving on his coat, gloves, and scarf. Annie felt her entire body freeze up in her fear. She couldn't take her eyes off him, vigilant and ready for however he would greet her.

When he finally met her eyes, it was clear in that brief moment that all the anger that had spurred him on before had melted away. He seemed just as relieved to be home as she was to have him there.

"Wife," he said.

She tried to smile but was simply too overwhelmed.

"I'm back."

She nodded.

"I've brought your piano."

She grinned suddenly. "I . . . Thank you."

He nodded, seeming to understand why she was not saying much. "I'm going to go into town to see if I can get a couple men to come help get the piano out of the wagon and into the house."

"Now?"

"When I'm done unloading everything else. I filled the wagon with other supplies and food, since I had gone all the way there anyway."

"Would you like help?"

"How's your ankle?"

"Still a little sore, but better," she acknowledged. "Mostly healed."

His expression softened. "Go ahead and sit. You'll be no good to anyone if you hurt yourself worse. I won't be long."

Before she could respond, he was out the door again, back to the wagon, and she sat, stunned. So many questions crowded in her mind—wondering why he had been so long, wondering how he had filled her days. But when he reentered, his arms full of canvas sacks, all she could think was to be grateful he was there.

"I'm so glad you're back," she said, as he carried the sacks inside.

"I brought home more sugar, too," he said. "With enough to share with your sisters when we see them."

"Oh, goodness," she said with a self-conscious laugh. "Thank you. That's really . . . very thoughtful."

He nodded and continued making trips out to the wagon and back into the house. Annie felt helpless, useless, just watching him. But he had told her to stay seated, and defying him as the first thing she did when he finally came home seemed the wrong way to start.

Worry about the things she could control—that's what both Rebecca and the pastor had advised her. At this moment, that meant resting her ankle. Not harassing Isaac with questions the moment he walked in the door. Calming herself and just being thankful he was home.

She could do that.

She was doing that.

Maybe this was the first glimpse of what their life could be like, as she figured out how to be a better homemaker and a wife.

After several trips bringing food and supplies in, Isaac finally took a break, sitting at the table across from her and pulling off his gloves.

"Do you want to tell me about your trip?" she ventured. "Did you get caught in the snow?"

He nodded, leaning back in his chair as he removed his gloves. "It was just one thing after another. We were still miles away from the fort when the storm hit, and couldn't very well stop. Finally got to shelter late that night, then ended up staying at the fort for a few days. I helped the soldiers there shore up some of their structures, making repairs in exchange for some of this food." He gestured to the sacks and crates behind him. "And for help getting the piano into the wagon. That was a trial too. And then, when we finally left, the snow had so torn up the road that we barely made seven or eight miles each day." Isaac shook his head. "Glad I don't have to do that ever again."

Annie nodded as he spoke, but she didn't know what to say. It seemed as though he was ignoring the fight, ignoring the things they had said to each other. Did she want to be the one to start it up again?

"How's the piano?" she finally asked. "Did you play it?"

"Oh, I hit a few of the keys, making sure it was still in one piece before I carted it all the way out here. But, you know, I'm no musician. You'll have to see what kind of shape it's in. The cold can't have been good for it, but I tied it down firmly and covered it all with oilskin, so it should have stayed dry."

"That's good. That's perfect. Thank you."

"In fact . . ." Isaac stood again, as though to indicate the conversation was over. "I am going to go now before it gets too late. I think I'm going to need at least two more men to get that thing out of the wagon and into the house. Best to get it out of the cold as soon as we can."

"Oh—yes, of course." Annie stumbled over her words.

Through all her time alone, she imagined so many different versions of her conversation with Isaac, but none of them involved his disregarding the past completely.

"I'll start supper soon," she continued. "It should be ready whenever the wagon is fully unloaded."

Isaac nodded. He was already back at the door, pulling on his warm weather attire that he had just taken off. "Might have to go all the way to the Hatchleys or Waterses for enough men. But I'll be back here as soon as I can."

A low ache radiated through Annie as she remembered the last time he had left. He had told her the exact same thing. *I'll be back here as soon as I can.* This was different, she knew, but the pain remained.

"Isaac?"

He looked up at her.

"Thank you," she said.

He smiled, nodded, and was out the door without another word.

Annie slumped back in her chair. Maybe this was just the way it would be from now on, tiptoeing around each other, without the easy friendship they'd had before—but also without his anger. And without Annie herself having to confront him.

It somehow didn't feel like a fulfilling marriage, but perhaps it was the best she could hope for.

CHAPTER THIRTY-SIX

"Will you play something for me, wife?" Isaac asked, nodding to the piano from where he sat at their table. "Now that everything is settled?"

He had been home less than twenty-four hours, and their interactions had been stilted and awkward, as though neither wanted to upset the other too much. It had taken four men and quite a bit of effort to get the piano into the house and against the wall opposite the front door. Annie did her best to stay out of the way and offer the men food for their trouble—it was important that she be the model housewife as much as she could now that Isaac was home—but no sooner had the neighbors left than she and Isaac lapsed back into uncomfortable silence around each other.

Even sleeping next to him that night had not brought back any of their camaraderie.

But she was trying; both of them were. Trying to connect to each other again, after the struggles of the last week and the fights that came before that. Which was undoubtedly why he was now prompting her to play the piano this first full day home.

It was Christmas Eve; she hoped the holiday hymns she had grown up playing would come back to her easily.

But first, her duties as the homemaker: she checked the level of heat under the pot of soup she was making—simmering broth like Josie had taught her—and replaced the lid. It was just starting to smell tasty, and should be ready by the end of the day as she had planned. When she turned back to Isaac, her smile was broad.

"I'd love to. I have some time before I have to get to sweeping, I suppose."

As she crossed the room to the piano, Isaac said, "You know, Gertie would always sing while she cleaned." He chuckled at the memory. "Didn't have nearly the voice you do, though. Got to be that I tried to be out of the house if she started in on the songs."

"Gertie," Annie said. She put her fingers on the keys but didn't play yet.

"I suppose, now that we've got the piano, you'll be playing that more than cleaning while you sing, huh? Oh, well. My loss."

"You think I'm a better singer than Gertie?"

He nodded and chuckled again. "Probably because you're not distracted with cleaning, right? She was always busy, kept our place neat."

Annie looked down at her hands and took a deep breath. She pulled them into her lap, her fingers twisting together. Her feelings of being rejected, of being discarded, were bubbling up, and she couldn't stop them. Instead, maybe this was her chance. Maybe this was the moment she finally stopped waiting for things around her to change and actually took the opportunity to change them herself.

With another deep breath, Annie turned around on the piano bench to face her husband.

"Actually . . . I wanted to talk to you about that," she began hesitatingly. "I haven't said anything before now, but that is something that has really bothered me. For weeks, in fact."

He frowned. "Weeks? But then why haven't—"

"Please. Let me finish. Please. This is hard enough."

He gestured, without speaking, for her to continue.

"There have been quite a few times— Wait, let me start over." She let out a sigh and took a deep breath. "I'm sorry. This is hard. I know you aren't trying to hurt me with this, but there have been a number of times—so many I've lost count—when you compared me unfavorably to your late wife."

"To Gertie? But—"

"Isaac, please. Let me finish."

He closed his mouth again, but Annie could see the way the muscle in his jaw twitched. Though he was holding his temper successfully thus far, Annie couldn't be sure when he might explode.

"Um . . ." She looked down at her hands, her fingers woven together, and then back up at him. "So, right, I would just ask that you . . . Of course, I understand if there are reasons or occasions when it makes sense to mention her. I know she was your wife for several years. But it really feels like the only time I hear Gertie's name is when you want to tell me something she did better than I do."

"I just said you're a better singer than her."

"While also making a point to say that she made more of an effort to clean than I do." Annie tried to hide her frustration. "Isaac, I'm doing my best, but I am not the same person as the one you used to be married to."

"Oh, you mean like how Gertie always cooked potatoes all the way through before serving them to me?"

Annie took a sharp intake of breath. "Isaac. I don't want to have the same fight again. I've said I am sorry so many times. What good do you think it is doing to bring it up again?"

"I cannot even believe we are having this conversation." He rose from where he sat at the table and paced angrily back and forth in front of the fireplace. "What are we even doing? I thought, after the days we spent apart, I could come home and we would be past this."

"So did I."

He stopped in his pacing to look at her in disbelief.

"Stop, please," she said desperately. "Please don't throw anything again. Can we just talk about it calmly? Please." She stood, taking a few steps forward to meet him, to close the gap between them, to somehow maintain a connection.

He looked stricken. "I'm not going to throw anything," he said sullenly, "but listen to what you're saying. Disagreeing with me when it's very clear what I'm saying is right."

"Disagreeing with you is the last thing I want to do," she insisted. "It's not as though conflict is any fun for me, let alone all the mistakes I seem to be making and how it affects both of us. I wanted that butter just as much as you did, and I was maybe more upset about its spoiling than you were. But, Isaac, I can't . . ." She shook her head. "I'm not saying this right, I'm sure."

When she again looked at him to see how he was taking it, Annie took a step back. The fury in his eyes made him seem like a different person. Not her husband. Not someone who loved her and had made the trek and put in the expense to get her a piano.

He looked like a person who could lose control of himself and throw something heavier, destroy a part of their home if he wanted to. Annie had never seen him so angry.

"Please don't yell," she said again, her voice shaking. "Please . . ."

Annie's hands shook; her breathing and heart rate quickened. She backed up another step, and another, until she felt the edge of their bed against the backs of her legs.

"I'm sorry."

She turned away from him and crawled onto their bed, putting her back against the far wall and pulling her knees up. Annie tried to make herself as small as possible; she rested her forehead on her knees and wrapped her arms around herself. With her eyes closed, Annie focused on calming her breathing. On slowing her heart.

This was nothing like the domineering control that she had endured under her sister. Isaac's anger was beyond what Annie had ever endured. How had she found herself married to a man like this?

The tears fell faster now as Annie realized that this might be what the rest of her life was like. She tried holding her breath, to muffle her sobs, afraid that her crying would just make him more angry.

But Isaac didn't push it further. He stayed quiet. Waiting.

She didn't dare look up at him, not until she had gotten herself back under control. After all those days by herself, all that time she thought she had everything under control, all it took was one fight with Isaac for her to see that nothing had been resolved.

When Annie finally lifted her head, Isaac was sitting in his chair, one elbow on the table, watching her. Though the fury had left, the expression on his face was both hurt and regretful, and Annie wondered how quickly he would get angry at her again.

"Are you afraid of me?" he asked carefully.

She nodded, tears in her eyes. "A little? Yes. I'm sorry. I'm not used to being yelled at like this. Even when my father was alive, he never yelled, never lost his temper. This is all . . . I'm sorry, I don't know how to handle your anger."

He nodded somberly, but didn't answer.

"I spent much of the time you were gone trying to figure out what I had done wrong. What I could change about myself so you wouldn't be so angry all the time. But what I came to realize is . . . well, that's not something I can control."

"You don't think it's your fault you make me angry? You bear no responsibility?"

"Isaac," she said, sitting up straight. This was her chance to tell him the truth, tell him how she felt. She put as much authority and steel into her voice as she could, not wanting to give him any weakness with which to attack her. "I don't know how your pa was like when you were growing up, or what you were raised to think is normal and acceptable, but I cannot abide you talking to me like that. It really hurts me."

He looked at her from across the room, but betrayed no reaction.

"I am not perfect," she continued. "You can't expect that of me. I just ask that you try to manage your temper. Please . . . Your anger is making our home a hostile place. I don't want to live like this."

He stared at her, took a deep breath, and looked down again, as though thinking.

"Isaac? I'm sorry if that hurts you—"

"No. You're right." He looked up at her and cleared his throat. "I need to—" He stood and crossed to the door. "I need to go out. I'll be back for supper, though."

"It's Christmas Eve," she said. "Where are you going? I thought—I thought we could at least have a couple days as a family. Just the two of us. You've been gone so long, and I've been alone, and we need to talk about this and—"

"I'm sorry," he said, and to Annie's surprise he seemed to mean it. "I am. I won't be gone all day, but there are things I need to take care of."

She watched as Isaac pulled on his coat and gloves, readying to leave. Once he had opened the door, he paused, looking back at her.

"I hope with me gone for a few hours you can feel more at home, maybe. Calmer."

"Wait, I—"

But he was gone. Annie was still all but curled into a ball on their bed, and her husband had just walked out the door, leaving her alone all over again.

CHAPTER THIRTY-SEVEN

Even though he had been home less than twenty-four hours, Isaac had still found a reason to leave Annie alone once more. He had promised to be home for supper, which was a vow she clung to. She tried to object, she tried to plead, reminding him how long he had been gone already, but he was adamant. He left without even hearing her, it seemed like. Though he had been unyielding in his decision to go into town, Annie still felt an apology of sorts in his demeanor, as though he did not want to hurt her, even if this was what needed to be done.

After he was gone—after Annie had been left alone again— the house felt even more empty than it had before. Having Isaac home felt right; it felt like the way her life should be, even as they were awkward together. And now there was this hole where he was meant to be.

And she had no idea where he had gone.

She moved to the edge of the bed, sitting for a moment to gather herself. The last twenty minutes had been the most stressful of her life since when she had to watch her oldest sister die and was unable to do anything about it. Enduring Isaac's anger was difficult enough, but actually being honest with him, letting him see how it was affecting her, was almost as scary. She had had no idea how he would respond to her tears and her panic, which had only made that panic more acute.

Annie took a long, slow breath. Her heart rate had returned to normal.

Worry about what she could control—that was what she kept coming back to. And being honest with Isaac about how she was feeling was the one thing that she could control in such a difficult situation.

She wasn't sure she could have done anything differently.

Standing, Annie looked over her home, cozy and clean. And now with a piano against the front wall, crowding the doorway and taking up far more space than they had to spare, but she wouldn't want it to be any different.

She crossed the room to the instrument and ran her hand across the top of it. This piano was not only a symbol of Isaac's love and commitment to her and to their marriage, but it was a veritable piece of her heart. She had been without music for so long, the joy that she felt upon having it again felt as though it belonged to someone else.

Annie pulled out the piano bench, marveling at the carved detail on the wooden legs. She had long ago assumed it would be decades, if that, before she had such fine things as she had left behind in Virginia. She sat, lifted the lid protecting the keys, and played a C major chord. Bright and cheerful.

E major, with a seventh. Hopeful somehow.

Even just sitting at the instrument, so much of her training and practice came rushing back. Her fingers itched to be playing something, and half a dozen Christmas songs floated through her head.

Annie wondered idly how she was going to be able to tune the piano. It was not in great shape after the journey and the cold, but it was playable.

E minor, into C, and suddenly she was playing "God Rest Ye Merry Gentlemen."

As her fingers played over the keys, Annie felt a peace fall over her. As always when she was immersed in music, the real world and all its accompanying concerns melted away and seemed so much less important than they had just moments earlier.

She could sit here and play for hours; she wished she could.

It was Christmas Eve. Between her injured ankle and Isaac being gone, the month had flown by and she could hardly realize the holiday was already here. The next morning, the pastor would be holding a Christmas service, and Annie wondered if she and Isaac would even go. Could they put aside their fight for church?

Though she wasn't sure precisely when Isaac would return, Annie thought she probably had enough time to make them some kind of special holiday feast. Isaac had brought back sugar, root vegetables, eggs, and other goods from Fort Vancouver; surely a holiday would be the ideal time to use them. The soup currently simmering would be good, but she could do better.

She wanted this to be a home that Isaac was excited to return to.

No matter what happened with Isaac, no matter what revelation or rejection he might come home with, Annie knew they would get through it. She meant her wedding vows when she had said them, and she was committed to figuring out a way through this, focusing on the things that she could control when she could.

As the afternoon progressed, Annie got to work making her husband a holiday feast. Frying up potatoes, baking a small cake, even boiling greens—the few that were still available this late in the season. The scent of rosemary and pepper filled her small house as the soup cooked; she was operating simply on Isaac's promise that he would be home for supper. If he wasn't, this was far too much food for her to eat by herself.

But as the sun set, she heard Rocky approaching in the yard outside. Isaac had come home, just as he said he would.

Annie threw open their front door to find Isaac on the step. "Where have you been?"

He glanced at her, brushing snowflakes out of his hair and stamping more snow from his boots. She stepped back to give him room to come in. Looking him over, Annie satisfied herself that he didn't seem hurt.

"You're all right?" she asked.

"I went into town today to ask the pastor to pray with me."

Annie was startled. "But—is everything all right?" She hesitated to press; he must have a reason he hadn't told her anything more, and she didn't want to make him angry. She returned to her chair, waiting for whatever her husband wanted to share with her.

"Everything is all right. I, um . . ." He sat at the table across from her.

Somehow, though they had sat in these very places dozens, if not hundreds, of times, she felt closer to him now than she ever had before. Somehow the space between them had shrunk. Maybe it was her new commitment to staying vulnerable and present with him, or maybe it was a change in Isaac. Whatever it was scared Annie a little in its intensity, but still she wanted more.

"Is there anything I can do to help?"

Isaac shook his head, looking down at the table. "This is something I need to manage on my own."

"Can you tell me what . . . what it is you think you need to do on your own?"

Finally, Isaac looked up at her. He reached across the table for her hands and clasped them desperately, like a man trying to keep from drowning.

"I love you," he began.

"I love you," she responded gently.

"And I am so sorry."

She waited, knowing there was more to it. Without even knowing what he was apologizing for, she could hear the sincerity in his tone.

"I went to the pastor today," he continued, still looking at her, "to pray about how much trouble I have keeping my temper. And how it has affected you. And to ask his advice about how to stop."

"How to stop losing your temper?"

He nodded. "I didn't see it before, and I'm so sorry. But your panic and your fear this morning—" His voice cracked and he cleared his throat. "You're right. That is what I grew up with. My father ran hot and cold all the time. I didn't realize it wasn't the way everyone lives, but you helped me see that. And helped me remember what it was like to be on the receiving end of such a temper when I was young. I don't want to be the reason you feel that way. Ever. I'm so sorry."

"What did the pastor say?"

He smiled. "He told me you had been there a couple days ago. And I could guess what you talked about. He told me just noticing there's a problem and wanting to do something is a good first step. But I think I'm going to go back again in a few days. I don't know what the next step is."

Annie paused. She was grateful he had sought help, but would it be enough? While she knew that if she had to she could move in with her sisters, Annie was not quite ready to give up. Isaac's actions had at least shown her he was not oblivious to the problems, that he was willing to take action to fix things.

She sighed, tentatively hopeful that perhaps this was a turning point for them.

"Thank you . . . Can I help you at all?"

"You already are," Isaac said. "You're talking to me about it. And you're being honest about how it makes you feel. Beyond that has to be me. It's my problem, my flaw. Nothing will get better if I put all the weight on you to not do a single thing that might make me mad. I . . . I believe in your best intentions, if you will believe in mine. Even when I fail."

"Thank you," she said again softly.

"There is, though . . ." he began, hesitating. "I don't want you to think you've done anything wrong. Please believe that."

Annie nodded. "I'll try, but . . ."

"But what?"

"It's . . . it's not important. But I will try."

They held each other's gaze for a long moment, before Isaac took a deep breath. "This is actually what I wanted to ask of you. When you keep things from me, even when you're doing it so you don't burden me or upset me, I think it does more harm than good, to be honest. So the thing I wanted to ask of you is just that you talk to me more, I suppose. Maybe that's silly."

"It doesn't seem silly. But I'm not sure what I have to say is going to be that interesting to you."

"Oh, but it is, wife. It is. I don't want to feel like you are afraid of me or think you have to hide anything from me. And part of my struggle is . . . if there are things that might make me angry and I don't learn about them until much later, there's every chance that the delay will just make me even more angry. You see?"

"I . . . I think so."

"But, really, the point of all of this," he said, squeezing her hands still clasped in his, "is that I regret so much how much of my anger and temper you have seen, and I am taking steps to rectify that. You do not deserve such anger, ever, but especially from the man who has vowed to love you and protect you for the rest of your life. So, if you'll try to forgive me, I promise to do my best going forward."

She nodded eagerly, almost afraid at how happy she was. There was so much more they would go through together, enduring hardships and joys, trials and celebrations. All she wanted for the rest of her life was this man by her side, to feel safe with him, to be able to give herself to him without worry.

His promise to her now was exactly what she needed, precisely the foundation for beginning this new year together.

CHAPTER THIRTY-EIGHT

Annie woke with the dawn on Christmas morning, comforted by the even breathing of Isaac in bed beside her. She had gone so long without him home with her that, before rising from bed, she took a moment to listen, appreciating his warm presence there in the house with her. With her eyes still closed, she felt the weight of the blankets on top of her, the chill of the room where the fire had died down, the smell of their bodies in the closed space.

This was exactly the life she had hoped for when she accepted Isaac's proposal in the mail more than a year earlier. They had been through some difficult moments, but in each they had learned more about the other and come through the other side.

She rolled onto her side, closer to Isaac, and pressed her nose against his shoulder. It didn't wake him, and she took a long, deep breath, just inhaling the scent of him. She dropped a light kiss on his shoulder, then rolled over again and pushed back the quilt. Sitting on the edge of the bed for a moment, she smiled to herself, thinking about how much had changed in just the couple of months since they arrived in the Oregon Territory.

Her ankle was now entirely healed—a near miracle, given

what the doctor had prepared her for. In her stockings, Annie crossed the room quietly to the front door of her small house and cracked it open. The sun was just starting to rise in the east, and only the faintest warm light peeked over the mountains. Snow lay in patches all around, melted completely in spots where the sun hit directly but still piled under the shade of the trees. The crisp chill of the December morning was invigorating.

Annie closed the door again and set about to starting their coffee. She tried to be quiet, but she soon heard Isaac stirring on the other side of the room. When she looked up, he was sitting in bed watching her.

"Merry Christmas," Isaac said, rubbing the sleep from his eyes.

"Merry Christmas! Coffee is almost ready."

"Thank you."

She turned her attention back to their breakfast while Isaac got dressed on the other side of the room. The sound of his footsteps crossing the room made her happy in the simplicity of the moment, the comfort of having him home again. She was surprised, however, to hear him come right up behind her. Wrapping his arms around her, Isaac hugged her gently.

"How are you this morning, wife?" he murmured into her ear.

"Good."

"Just good?"

"I'm just . . . I'm grateful," she said, letting herself sink into his arms. "Grateful, yet cautious. I know there's still much to do, but this feels like the right foundation to be building on. I can't tell you how much I appreciate your willingness to hear me. Thank you."

"I appreciate your patience and understanding."

She leaned back into him, feeling her husband's protection all around her. "I know learning to live with each other has been difficult, but there isn't anyone I'd rather do it with. So . . . thank you."

"Well, I'm glad you want to do it all with me. Because there's so much more to do," he assured her. He turned her around so they faced each other, but kept her in his arms. "As soon as the frost lets up, we'll dig our well. I'll help you plant a kitchen garden, and we'll see about getting a plow. If not this spring, then next."

"And maybe a dairy cow and some chickens?"

He nodded. "And, sometime down the line, pigs. Goats if you still want them, though maybe I should talk to Margaret first."

"And children?" she asked tentatively.

He gazed into her eyes, pulling her closer. "And children," he repeated with a soft smile. "We'll have a calm, welcoming home just for them."

"Isaac Wheeler," she said, her voice low, "you are the best thing that has ever happened to me. In spite of everything, you're still exactly what I want."

Instead of responding with words, he brought a hand up to her cheek, touching her gently. Annie found herself leaning into his hand, wanting to soak up all of him. With two fingers, he tilted up her face to his before kissing her deeply. Tears sprang to Annie's eyes. After such a difficult several weeks, she never thought she would ever again feel this peace, this safety, and yet here was Isaac offering her everything she needed.

When he pulled away he looked at her curiously. "You're crying."

She laughed self-consciously, wiping away the tears with the back of her hand. "I'm just happy. It's silly, I know."

"Well, I may have brought home something that will help dry those tears."

Laughing again, Annie watched him cross the room to his satchel bag that he had stashed in the corner by the piano when he had returned home from the fort. "What are you talking about?"

"I brought you something," he said simply.

Squatting to paw through his bag, Isaac didn't have to look very long before he found the small surprise that he had squirreled away.

"What is it?" she asked.

"Our Christmas gift."

Standing again, Isaac came back to their small table, gesturing for Annie to sit across from him. She couldn't tell what he was carrying; he was making an effort to hide it until some proper reveal.

"So, this came on the same ship that brought our piano," he explained, setting a small tin on the table between them.

The label was crowded and detailed, and at a glance Annie could only recognize one word: *Chocolate*.

"What is this?"

"It's a chocolate powder. We can mix it with milk, maybe, or water. Might be good with some sugar, too, perhaps, and we can have a little Christmas festive drink. Is it . . ." He was watching her expression carefully. "Is it okay?"

She grinned at him. "You know, for my birthday last year, Louisa went out of her way to get us all chocolate to share too. This is perfect! I didn't even know I wanted it, but *you* knew. It's perfect. Maybe we can have it with lunch after church? If you still want to go to the Christmas service."

"Of course I do. And after church," he continued, "we'll come back here, and you can play piano, and maybe I'll figure out how to bake those cinnamon rolls I keep thinking about."

Annie laughed. "I can probably help with that too."

"We'll see. Maybe I'll try, and you can rescue me if I fail. I'd like us to be a team, wife. I expected more of you than you could give, and you have been unwilling to ask me for what you needed, and we fell apart. Let's not keep going down that path, huh?"

Annie nodded. "Thank you."

"You're welcome. Thank you for standing by me."

"You're welcome," she said softly.

The Christmas church service was later in the morning than it would be on Sundays, so the Wheelers had a leisurely breakfast, complete with their mugs of hot chocolate to help make their sacred day even more special. Annie's limp was almost imperceptible, and as she walked around her home, getting ready to leave, she thought about just how different that injury could have been if she hadn't had Isaac, if she hadn't had her sisters for a few days. Even with all the hours alone that Annie had spent over the last month, she knew now that help would always be there for the asking.

And as Isaac drove their wagon into town to the church, all around her Annie saw homes and neighbors and clear evidence that no matter what, she was part of a community, all willing to come together to help.

The church service for Christmas was full, with the handful of finished pews holding all they could and dozens more folks simply standing in the back of the room. The Sullivan–Mills wagon company had come so far, endured so much, that the pure joy of having a church home for the holidays was evident in each person's face as they listened to Pastor Montgomery preaching about their savior born on this day.

"And now," the pastor announced, "before I close in prayer, we have a special gift from a few members of the congregation. It is my understanding that the idea of a church choir was brought to us by Mrs. Wheeler, though in the last few weeks she has been unable to see it through. Nevertheless, the men and women who were able have practiced on their own and would like to offer you all the gift of a Christmas hymn."

Annie's eyebrows rose in surprise, and she looked around, identifying half a dozen of her friends and neighbors standing and gathering at the front of the church. Rebecca Tenney seemed to be their leader—just as Annie should have suspected.

"Did you know about this?" she whispered to Isaac.

He shook his head.

The eyes of the other five were on Rebecca as she nodded to cue their a capella song.

"O come, all ye faithful . . ." the six pure voices intoned.

Tears sprung to Annie's eyes.

"Joyful and triumphant . . ."

As she watched, the six faces of the small choir seemed lit from within with an inner glow. Though they had not had long to practice, and though they were small in number and crowded a bit in the corner of the church, the sincere worship and generosity of their Christmas gift to the congregation was heartfelt.

Annie cherished every moment as the notes washed over her, while still looking forward to the day when she could be part of such a demonstration herself. This was precisely how she had hoped her first Christmas in Oregon would be, though numerous moments along the way it had seemed completely out of reach.

"Are you happy, wife?" Isaac asked softly.

She nodded, unable to speak from the emotion that filled her.

"Merry Christmas," he whispered in her ear.

"Merry Christmas . . . with many more to come," she responded, before kissing his cheek and resting her head on his shoulder, listening to the soothing sounds of the blessed hymn.

———

THE END

Download your free book — *HANNAH'S HOPE* — at ATButler.com/Hannah

When Hannah Sullivan's family decides to head west to the Oregon Territory, she's exhilarated. The small town where she grew up was fine when that's all she had to choose from, but as soon as the horizons and opportunities open up, Hannah finds a whole new world, just built for someone as competent, kind and warm as she is.

Sign up for A.T. Butler's mailing list today and receive Hannah's Hope for free! Dive into a story

where romance blossoms against all odds, and be the first to hear about new releases, exclusive content, and special offers. Don't miss this chance to fall in love with Hannah and Benjamin's story.

ATButler.com/Hannah

AUTHOR'S NOTE

Thank you so much for reading *Christmas in Oregon*. At the time of this author's note, the book has been out for almost two years, and this spin-off series is being more well-received than I could have dreamed.

If you read Annie's first book, *Frontier Sisters*, in my Courage on the Oregon Trail series, you know that she is conflict avoidant and struggles to ask for what she really wants. Though that book ends just before they settle in the Oregon Territory, I knew that I would want to continue Annie's story as she figures out how to live with this virtual stranger.

A couple notes about little events in this story:

If you are on my email list, you might remember the first couple autumns that I lived in my central Pennsylvania house, when I suddenly had more walnuts to deal with than I knew to prepare for. I hadn't a clue what I was getting into. Over the several days that I dedicated to cleaning them up out of my yard, I ended up dying my gloves dark brown from all the walnuts. They were, in fact, a common source of dye in the 19th century, and it's so exciting to me that I get to try it out myself at home if I want to.

Another fun little detail was the moving of the piano. My family recently adopted a piano from Facebook Marketplace and the getting it from one house to another was such an ordeal. My brother-in-law threw out his back doing it. We deliberately rolled it into our house on a dolly instead of on the instruments wheels so it wouldn't scratch the wood floor. While in this book we brushed over some of the more inconvenient parts of moving a piano to the virtual wilderness, I know it could not have been easy. Not impossible, of course, but definitely not common.

When writing historical fiction, there's a delicate balance of fact versus fiction. I tend to think that if something *could have* happened, it probably did even if we don't have definite historic record of it.

One last personal note: There are some reviews on this book that express disappointment that Annie's reaction to Isaac is unrealistic. I am genuinely so thrilled for those readers if they have not found themselves in a similar situation. I can assure you, though, both in my own life and that of friends, there are some people who just ... hang on. Try again. Hope against hope that the other person is actually changing for real. It's just as difficult of a choice to make as leaving would be. I hope you never find yourself there.

And I am looking forward to giving Annie another book in the future.

Thank you for reading this series, this book, and for getting this far. A review on your favorite retailer, or getting this book into the hands of a friend would be so appreciated.

— A.T. Butler
September 2024

FREE PRINTABLE OREGON TRAIL MAP

Sign-up to download a FREE custom printable map of the Sullivan-Mills wagon company's journey on the Oregon Trail.

You'll also get news of future releases, updates for promotions and discounts, as well as occasional other exclusive goodies, created just for my subscribers.

https://atbutler.com/ot-free

NEXT BOOK IN THE SERIES

The next book in OREGON AT LAST series is available

Grab _Snowbound Promises_ here!
(on Kindle and Kindle Unlimited)

Is this really the home she has dreamt of?

.   .   .

The Oregon Territory, January 1851: Nora Cole didn't realize it
would be this hard. She thought had found a balance of communi-
cation with Jasper Stephens when she gave him permission to
court her. But the constant work and harsh winter of this new
country has put obstacles between them she's not sure they can
overcome.

*For all the stories of how these brave pioneers got to Oregon, look for the
book series Courage on the Oregon Trail by A.T. Butler.*

Grab *Snowbound Promises* here!
(on Kindle and Kindle Unlimited)

ALSO BY A.T. BUTLER

Courage On The Oregon Trail Series:

Westward Courage

Faithful Trail

Frontier Sisters

Unyielding Heart

Wild Promise

Fierce Dreams

Seeking Home

Trouble and Grace

Oregon At Last Series:

Journey's End

Christmas in Oregon

Snowbound Promises

The Pastor's Baby

Frontier Fortune

Reluctant Spring

Summer of Promise

Juniper Falls Series:

The Juniper Hotel

Building the Dream

Snowflakes and Sugar Cookies

Jacob Payne, Bounty Hunter Series:

Trouble By Any Name

Danger in the Canyon

Justice for Jasper

Blood on the Mountain

Outlaw Country

Death By Grit

Desert Rage

Arizona Legend

Fool's Demise

Silent Night

Bountiful Justice Series:

Loyalty's Price

Riding for Justice

Trail of Redemption

Other Western Novels by A.T. Butler:

Hawke's Revenge

Short Stories from Juniper Falls

ABOUT THE AUTHOR

I grew up in the southwest—California Missions, snakes and constant threat of drought weaving the backdrop of my childhood.

But it wasn't until I moved to Texas a few years ago that the magic and mythology of the American West began to seep into my soul.

I'd love to write about western adventures, strong women and noble men for a long time.

If you enjoyed this book, a review on your favorite retailer would be greatly appreciated.

- A

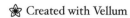

Milton Keynes UK
Ingram Content Group UK Ltd.
UKHW041654151024
449742UK00005B/51